CHRISTMAS STARS OF ZANZIBAR

written and illustrated by
judy bond

Charleston, SC
www.PalmettoPublishing.com

Christmas Stars of Zanzibar

Copyright © 2021 by Judy Bond

All rights reserved.

No portion of this book may be reproduced, stored in a retrieval system, or transmitted in any form by any means–electronic, mechanical, photocopy, recording, or other–except for brief quotations in printed reviews, without prior permission of the author.

First Edition

Paperback ISBN: 978-1-63837-923-2

CHRISTMAS STARS OF ZANZIBAR

*This book is dedicated to the
real Bursala*

*When I look, and I find
I still love you...
I still love you.
—Queen*

*Without you, Bursala, there would
not be a book.*

I hope to arrive to my death,
Late,
in Love,
and a little bit drunk.
—Atticus

This one goes out to my critters:
Otis, Morrison, Jerry, Shakespeare, Mercury, Larry-David, Lincoln, Juno, Harley, Venus, Tiger, Hazel, Sadie, Alfie, Mazzie, Aiko, Moon Bear, Clarence, Smudgestick, Frankie, Patches, Tweety, Shelly, Budgy, Jamal, PJ, Freddie, Jason, Damien, Sweetie, and Snickers...

And all the fur babies we have loved and have lost. For all the animals who have roamed the Earth, you humble us.

For Ann Wilson, Donny Osmond and Freddie Mercury xx

TABLE OF CONTENTS

PART ONE · 1
  1   The Water Globe · 2
  2   And They Spoke in the Swahili Tongue · · · · · · · · · · · · · 13
  3   An African Blessing · 26
  4   The Sign · 31
  5   Eden's Amulet · 35
  6   Christmas Stars of Zanzibar · 40
  7   New York (Present Day) · 45
  8   Feast of the Python · 49
  9   The Dance · 61
 10 Bale's Secret · 65
 11 The First Noel · 72
 12 Jita's Revenge · 79
 13 Bursala · 83
 14 Miracles · 86
 15 The Royal Enclosure · 90
 16 The Threat · 100
 17 Bursala's Rhapsody · 103
 18 The Weddings · 109
 19 The Awakening · 117

20	The Leopard Sleeps	123
21	Magic Potion	128
22	The Manhunt	133
23	The Escape	138
24	The Chase	148
25	Blood Brothers	153
26	Sleep in Heavenly Peace	158
27	Sleep in Heavenly Peace Sleep in Heavenly Peace	162
28	Taking Leave of the Dead	165

Part Two ... 175

29	New York (Present Day)	176
30	Zanzibar, Cry of the Living	197
31	The Dream	204
32	The Gazelle	213
33	Onward and Forward	218
34	Butterfly	225
35	Bursala's Return	233
36	The Forbidden Fruit	244
37	The Passageway	252
38	New York (Present Day)	254
39	Basque, Spain— The Crusade Years	258
40	Zanzibar (Past)	261

Epilogue ... 264

The Characters ... 267

About The Author ... 281

Part One

THE WATER GLOBE

The house was strangely sullen and still, the way a house usually is in the early stretches of the morning. Eden placed her feet on the floor and wrapped her husband's flannel robe snugly around herself. She nuzzled her body into the aroma of his scent, pausing for a moment, watching as he slept. She fought back the impulse to touch his long, sandy-colored hair. This was her time, the unfolding of a winter's day that veiled her as the sun filtered through the lace curtains. Dancing swatches of light played upon her honey hair, enhancing its sheen, glistening like the petals of daffodils in the dead of November. She knew she could make productive use of this time while the rest of her family slept. Careful to remain quiet, she slipped on a pair of fuzzy slippers and made her way downstairs.

Eden Salina was thirty-two years old. Her long hair flowed freely around her shoulders, and she tied it back into a loose braid. Wisps of hair framed her soft face. She was small and slender, yet she possessed an inner strength like that of a willow. Her eyes were as blue and wide as a child's and wild and exotic as a tigress's. Her nose turned up slightly, and her lips were full and perfectly shaped like soft and supple rosebuds.

She looked much younger than her years, mainly because of her slight stature. When she smiled, her eyes took on flecks of yellow and danced across her face like half-moons. "Sunshine Eyes," her daddy had called her when she was just a child. The tiny creases around her mouth, which lifted when she smiled, bestowed upon her a look of sensuality, the kind one gets from tasting life's adventures just by simply living. Eden was truly a timeless angel fallen from grace. Her bohemian heart layered beneath her gypsy soul furnished her with an unrivaled bearing that was privately her own.

Since she was a child of six, she knew she was born for grand and spectacular things. A sudden tragedy robbed her of the innocence of youth, shattering her life, stopping her world from turning...the loss of her daddy. In her eyes, no one walked taller than he. His untimely death was a severe shock to the family and friends who knew and loved him—especially to the little girl who was that sunshine in his eyes. He had left her, abandoned her. She felt so alone in a world of coldness and darkness. Her daddy's departure was her bane.

Eden's mother, sisters, and brothers were left to continue to pick up the pieces of their broken lives. She could remember her mother driving to the ocean while her older siblings were in school. It was a dank and balmy afternoon, and Eden shivered with a chill that swept through her as she watched her mother standing by the water's edge. In her arms, she held a bouquet of wildflowers that she dropped in the thunderous rushes of the waves, one by one. Eden stood behind her mother, observing solemnly. In her small and tangled state of mind, she knew and understood her mother's grief, for she felt it too.

The icy winds blowing off the ocean's waves began to sting her cheeks. She turned around to block the prevailing force that seemed to breathe an untamed gloominess deep into her and walked away from where her mother stood. Something drew her to a small mound of sand. She knelt down and dug her diminutive, numb fingers into the coldness of the wet ground. Her pale braids blew across her face as she scooped and shoveled like an explorer ready to uncover a buried treasure. And like an explorer, she was compelled to unravel the mystery that lay beneath the loose particles of rock that whirled around her like a storm in the desert. She forgot all about the frigid, glacial winds that continued to whip against her face as her impulse for the buried treasure grew more intense. An object revealed itself hidden beneath the depths of the beach. Eden placed her hands into the hole and tugged on the article until it was released from the grip of the sand. To her sheer amazement, in her hand, she held the most splendid water globe she had ever seen.

Eden traced the wooden base of the water globe with her fingers. The words *"Sleep in Heavenly Peace"* were inscribed on a brass plate. Inside the glass was the Holy Infant, Jesus, surrounded by the Blessed Mother and Joseph. She shook it and watched in delight as little white flakes of snow whirled around the Holy Family and then settled silently to the bottom. Eden held the water globe up to her face and peered through, watching the mist roll off the harbor.

Through the haze, she spotted a figure. At first, it was a blur, but as the person came closer to her, he began to come clearly into view. He was an old man, much like her grandpa's age. He did not look like anyone she had ever seen before. He had dark features and foreign eyes. She continued to watch him through the glass and listened carefully to his words:

"Little dreamer in the sand, you are blessed. For on this day, your father has entered into the Kingdom of Heaven." He spoke with a reverent gentleness, and she was not afraid. "Sweet child, I was sent by your daddy. He has a message for you to hear. 'When the time is right, glass will shatter, and the water will spill, unlocking the key to your soul. When your soul is revealed, it will take you to the sun, where we shall meet again. Believe in my words and tuck them into the safest corner of your heart. The water will guide you. You will never be alone...I will always be a part of you.'"

Eden gazed out from behind the water globe and saw no one...nothing. She held it close to her heart and ran over to her mother to show her the prized possession. That was twenty-six years ago, almost to the day. Eden remembered it vividly as if it were yesterday.

She walked over to the stove, filled the teapot with water, and set it over the flame. The kitchen was such a mess. She began to load the dishwasher with the dishes that had served thirty people their Thanksgiving dinners the night before: her mother, her sisters and their husbands and children, her brothers and their wives and families, her husband's side of the family, and her own three children, Benjamin, Tara, and Nicholas. Later in the evening, her best friends, Annie and Dean came over with their kids.

Eden was a gracious host and loved the holidays, always insisting that they be held at her house. Everyone enjoyed coming over. Her husband, Frank, teased her by saying that one day he was going to install a revolving front door because of the large amounts of company that always seemed to filter in and out. Eden loved people. Friends and family were always welcome into the Salina home. When everyone was gone, according to tradition, Ben, Tara, and Nicholas would persuade their father to bring up the Christmas decorations from the basement.

Eden fixed herself a cup of tea and walked into the living room where Christmas boxes were stacked one on top of another. Later, the kids would wake, and together, they would decorate the house until it looked like a postcard from *Currier and Ives*. It was a truly magical time of year, and no one loved it more than Eden Salina.

She set her tea down on the cherry-wood roll-top desk and knelt beside a box marked "Fragile." Eden lifted the cover and scrupulously unwrapped the tissue paper that cushioned her cherished water globe. This was, above everything, her favorite Christmas keepsake. She held it in her hands, walked into the kitchen, and set it on the table. First, she shook it and watched with the same wonderment she had when she was a little girl. She tucked her hand under her chin and watched as the tiny flakes of snow swirled around the Holy Family. She then left the kitchen and was gone for only an instant when she heard a loud, stertorous crash. She ran back into the kitchen only to find her beloved water globe shattered upon the ceramic floor. Sweet Darling, her cat, sat upon the table wide-eyed with his paw in the air.

"Oh no!" She knelt on the cold floor and held the tiny resin figures in her hands. Shards of glass lay haphazardly across the floor in a puddle of water. Eden sighed and brushed a tear from her eye. She covered her face with her hands and began to cry into them. Someone was behind her. Startled, she looked up and called out, "Daddy?"

Frank crossed his arms over his chest and smiled. "Daddy? Baby, you haven't called me that in a long time!"

Christmas Stars of Zanzibar

The November rains turned into the snowfalls of December. Frank had outdone himself in decorating the outside. Fresh garland draped across and outlined the front of the house intertwined with hundreds of twinkling white lights. The hedges glistened and gleamed with color, and a spotlight shone on the wreath that hung on the front door. Candy canes, lollipops, and gingerbread men lined the walkway. Santa and his sled were nestled on top of the roof. The children cut out snowflakes from paper and hung them on the windows.

The inside of the house took on a nuance all its own. A mechanical Mr. and Mrs. Claus sat in the bay window of the living room. The fireplace was garnished in holly and stockings, and Christmas cards adorned the mantel. The tree was dressed up in all its splendor with brightly colored packages peeking out from beneath its branches. The house smelled like a mixture of honey-dipped struffoli, homemade ginger snaps, and freshly peeled orange rinds.

Ben, Tara, and Nicholas were sitting in front of the fire making a paper chain from green and red paper, while Sweet Darling batted the end with his paws. Sting's Christmas song "Gabriel's Message" played while Frank roasted marshmallows over the logs of the fire.

"Tara, don't be such a dork!" Ben retorted. "You're messing up. Look... Do it like this."

"Mom! Ben's calling me names again!" Tara whined and then gave her brother a shove.

Eden called out from the kitchen, "Tara, stop that sniveling, and tell it to your father. Frank, they're at it again!"

Frank turned toward his children and pulled a marshmallow off the stick. "Come on, guys. Cool it. Here, Nicky, this one's for you." Nicholas took the charred marshmallow with his chubby little hand and popped it into his mouth.

"You think you're so hot because you're in fourth grade!" Tara continued. "Shut up, fatso."

"Mom! Ben called me fat again!"

Eden walked into the living room and placed her hands on her slender hips. "Benny, you know your sister isn't fat. Say you're sorry." She looked at her son through narrowed eyes. "Now, Ben!"

"All right! All right! Sorry...fatso."

Tara stood to her feet and clenched her fists. "Oh, you make me so mad!"

Nicholas popped another marshmallow into his mouth and shook his finger at his older brother and sister. "Santa won't come if you guys are bad," he warned.

Frank patted his young son on the head. "Nicky's right. He's watching every move you make."

The doorbell rang, and Ben and Tara raced to answer it. "It's Annie and Dean. Tell them to come in," Eden called over her shoulder and went back into the kitchen.

"Hello, Salina's," Annie said in her usual cheerful way. "Where is she? Kitchen? Hey, girlfriend, I made us our favorite cheese dip." Annie set the bowl down on the table and stuck a tortilla chip into it. "Mmm, good. Just what I need to maintain my girlish figure."

Annie Jurgens was Eden's oldest and dearest friend. They had been friends since childhood. They loved each other like sisters, and they could bicker like sisters, too. Annie's dark-brown hair was long and bounced all over her head like the curls of a child. She was funny, always making Eden laugh. They could laugh for hours over absolutely nothing. The two families lived only two houses away from one another.

When Eden and Annie were children, they grew up together on the outskirts of New York City in Queens. They would sit out on their stoops and blow smoke rings around the moon with their cigarettes as they dreamed of what their lives would someday be. "I'm going to marry a really cute guy, and we'll have five kids whose names will all begin with C," Annie would announce proudly. She was true to her word, and her children—Christina, Cody, Cassandra, and the twins, Chad and Cassidy—filtered into Eden's kitchen, each holding a snack to be set down on the counter. Eden and Frank and Annie and Dean and all their children were as close as two families could be.

Annie poured herself a glass of wine and hopped up onto a stool. "So," she said in between sips, "what's new?"

"Nothing since I last saw you. Which was what...a couple of hours ago?" Eden replied, looking at her watch.

Annie smiled. "Cute, Salina. The kids brought over the game Scattegories. It's a lot of fun. Should keep them busy for about two minutes. Oh, I almost forgot, have you heard the latest on Samantha and Gregg?" Annie's eyes widened. "Trouble in paradise. She kicked him out. I never liked him. Did you ever notice the way he looks at me?" Annie shuddered and moved her face close to Eden's. "I think he's got a thing for me; you know what I mean?"

The men were in the living room. They both cracked open a beer, and Dean plopped himself on the couch. "So how about those Giants?"

Frank ran his fingers across his hair and lit up a cigar.

"Outside!" Eden and Annie chimed from the kitchen.

"Women," Frank muttered under his breath.

It was a typical night on Long Island for the Salinas and the Jurgens—a typical, chaotic, fun-filled suburban Saturday night.

Eden sat at her kitchen table and watched from her window as the snow began to fall. She needed to plan the menu for Christmas Eve dinner: antipasto, baked clams on the half shell, scallops in butter sauce, flounder and calamari followed by a tossed green salad and three trays of lasagna and two trays of eggplant parmesan, chestnuts, finocchio, fruit, pastries, coffee, wine, beer, and soda. She chewed on the end of her pen and thought for a moment. Frank loved rum ham. Would it be too much food? *Never too much food*, she thought. She withdrew her phone calculator and began to figure out the budget. Just then, the phone rang.

"Oh, hi, Annie. I'm just figuring out the menu." She twisted a strand of hair between her fingers. "I'm going Christmas shopping tonight. Want to come?"

"No can do, babe. Dean's working late. What do you want me to bring for Christmas Eve dinner?"

Eden thought for a moment and then gave her usual reply. "Just yourselves. Everything's under control. Can you believe it's really here? Christmas week, I mean?"

"Are you kidding? I still haven't finished my shopping!"

Eden laughed. "Last minute Annie! I just have a couple of things to get tonight, and then I'll be done. Well, if you change your mind about tonight, just give me a buzz." They hung up, and Eden went back to her list.

※

The snow was coming down heavily now. Shoppers were snappy, and the salespeople looked weary. Their faces held expressions that read, "Go away. I only make minimum wage." Impatient children were crying and fidgeting while their parents kept spending money they did not have. Tired hearts and exhausted souls surrounded her.

Eden, too, was caught up in the hustle and bustle of Christmas week. Who wasn't? Ferocious faces pushed her about as she pulled off a glove and held it between her teeth. She withdrew from her pocket a list of things she still had to buy. She glanced around at the horribly decorated store. *OK*, she thought, *I have to plow through this crowd somehow*. Taking a deep breath, she fought her way into the ring of madness.

Amid all the shoppers and overstocked shelves of merchandise, Eden spotted something that caught her eye. It was a water globe much like the one she had. She made her way through the sea of people and rode on their waves of anger. She inched her way over to the spot in which it sat. The words *"Peace on Earth"* were inscribed on the wooden base. Inside the glass was the Holy Family in gold. She turned it over and discovered that it played music. She wound the little key and held it to her ear. The store was so noisy she could not distinguish what song it was playing. It was simple in design but beautiful all the same. She shook it and held it up to her face.

A large woman behind her was reprimanding a small child, and her voice boomed into Eden's ear, causing her to almost drop it. She moved away from the woman and continued to stare into the glass. Through the snow and around the Blessed Family, she saw a figure like the vision she had at the beach when her father had passed away. At first, it was difficult to see him, but if she turned the water globe just right beneath the lights of the department store, she was sure she could get a closer view.

He came into focus as precisely as he had that day twenty-six years ago. He was an elderly Asian man. He was slight in build and wore an old dark suit. Around his neck hung a pelt of mink, and upon his head sat a tattered black fedora. In one hand, he held a cane, which he seemed to be leaning on, and in the other was a water globe exactly like the one she had found when she was six years old.

He slowly held the water globe up to his face and looked back at her. She could see this beautiful and radiant light all around him. Through the mobs of people, she continued to stare at the one who continued to stare back at her. This man was positively glowing, and no one else seemed to notice. She peered out from behind the glass and watched as he scurried out of sight.

Eden tried to squeeze through the crowd. When she got herself to a safe clearing, she had lost sight of him entirely. That was him! The man on the beach all those years ago. He was so old now, but he was pretty old back then. Eden began to look around frantically. The store seemed to spin all around her. Where could he have gone? Who was this most peculiar man, and why was he here...now...after all this time? Eden blinked and placed her two fingers to the temples of her forehead. Could she be dreaming or losing her mind? She stood there for a moment while the people around her pushed and shoved. She shouldered her way over to the counter and paid for the water globe. Her eyes scanned the store for the eccentric man, who was nowhere to be found. The shoppers continued to lunge closer to the register, and Eden suddenly felt as if she was being crushed. She grabbed hold of her shopping bag and made her way to the exit.

"God rest ye merry gentlemen; may nothing you dismay...Remember Christ the Savior was born on Christmas Day..." The music sounded distorted to her ears, and the faces around her were the most hostile, unfriendly faces she had ever seen.

Eden stepped outside. The snow had turned to sleet by then, and her body shivered as the temperature drastically changed from the store to the outside world. She pushed a strand of hair behind her ear and watched as the people ran to their cars with shopping bags held over their heads. "Oh, tidings of comfort and joy…comfort and joy…O tidings of comfort and joy…"

She leaned up against the store window and closed her eyes. Would she ever see that man again? Shadows crept up from behind her, and in a single instant, she was mugged. She was pushed hard and fell to the ground never knowing what had hit her. Her body lay lifeless in the glistening wet snow next to the shattered water globe.

And They Spoke in the Swahili Tongue

When she awoke, everything was murky. She instantly remembered being in the crowded store, and with a jerk, she sat up and placed her feet on the floor. The dull ache in her head caused her to feel nauseous. She held a hand to her head and let out a low moan of discomfort and pain. Where was she? Everything was dark. What had happened? Yes, she could remember. She was Christmas shopping, and she was attacked. Eden tried to stand but collapsed. Her head hurt. She was weak and tired. Her eyes had trouble focusing. She lay back down, feeling rather dazed.

A small light shone through a crack in what seemed to be a tent of some sort. She could hear strange sounds, the beating of a drum, or was it her heart? Eden did not know. "Where am I?" she said aloud. She heard a rustling sound and tried to sit. "Who is there?" she asked through the darkness. Her voice quivered and shook with fear. Her body felt cold, and her head ached. "Frank?" Her voice echoed in her ears. "Frank, is that you?" She tried to squint through the blindness but could see nothing at all.

She could hear movement, and in an instant, a fire was lit atop of a long pole. Eden cupped her hand over her eyes. The light hurt; everything hurt. She removed her hand and saw a face. It was the face of a woman, a very peculiar-looking woman. The woman's skin was as dark as the unfolding surroundings. Her hair was cropped close to her scalp, and her ears were adorned with heavy ornaments that stretched her earlobes down to the middle of her neck. An ivory ring pierced her chin, and around her neck, she wore tightly wrapped strands of beads that glistened and sparkled through the darkness. Her bare brown shoulders were exposed and diametrically opposed to the stark white swags of cotton that swathed her large-framed body. There was an element of fear in this woman's eyes.

CHRISTMAS STARS OF ZANZIBAR

"Am I in the hospital?" she finally asked. "Does my family know where I am? I'm fine, really. A little weak, but I'm OK. I would like to go home now." Eden reached for the woman's hand, and when she did, the woman pulled away. "I am all right, aren't I?" There was no response from this person.

The woman picked up a wooden ladle and held it to Eden's mouth. Eden took a small sip. It was warm and did not taste very good. The woman stared at Eden through knitted eyebrows and then turned her face away. She reached for the lighted pole and left Eden alone.

"Oh, dear God, where am I?" Eden began to cry. After a few moments, another person came in through the opening of the tent. Eden could feel herself shudder as she let out a gasp. She was looking directly into the face of the old Asian man! The one from the beach! The one from the store! The same face that had haunted her dreams at night since she was a very small child. The man who spoke to her and told her that her daddy had a message for her to hear.

"It is you! It is really you!" she quipped. Her eyes followed his every move.

The man placed an object to her face. It was a glass with a block of wood over it and another block beneath it. It was held together with old pieces of twine that were securely fastened around each end. In the glass, there was a fire. Eden realized that it was some sort of lantern. When she looked into the fire, she could see the Holy Family submerged in water—just like the water globe. She squinted through the brightness of the flames and blinked hard. When she reopened her eyes, all she could see was the luminous light within.

"I have gone mad," she whispered. She could see the glowing face of the man by the light of the fire. "Am I dead?" she asked. "Are you God?"

The old man spoke. "No, child, you are not dead. I am not your God. Tell me, child, what is your name?"

"Eden." Her tiny voice shook with fear. "My name is Eden Salina. Who... who are you?"

"I am called Yallowahii" (pronounced "Yallow Wa Hee").

"Sir, you must help me. Please tell me where I am."

Yallowahii silenced her question with his hand. "You have been hurt. You must rest."

"But—"

Again, he silenced her, this time with a look of severance. He disappeared, leaving Eden alone in the dark with her pain and confusion. She bit down on her bottom lip to keep it from trembling and began to cry. She was terrified. She did not dare move or make a sound. The liquid the woman had given her made her very drowsy, and although she tried to fight it, she fell fast into sleep.

Eden opened her eyes to brightness. The morning sun was gentle and felt warm upon her face. She discovered that the bed she was lying on was nothing more than two sacks of grain covered with a thin piece of material. It was no wonder her body ached. She could see clearly, now. The tent or hut she was in was stark, empty except for a wooden bowl and ladle that sat on the dusty floor. She looked above her head. The hut was erected out of acacia branches, wire, and rock. The flap of the hut was opened slightly, and a ray of sunshine fell perfectly over her still body. Her long hair was racked with sweat and clung feverishly to her neck. Beads of perspiration trickled down her face, yet somehow, she could not keep herself from shivering. Outside, she could hear the sounds of children. Ben, Tara, and Nicholas? She closed her eyes and prayed that the noises she heard were the familiar sounds of her home—the sound of a basketball pounding upon the kitchen floor, the ring of the telephone. "Mommy, it's for you," Tara's voice echoed deep inside of her. "Frank? Is that you? I can barely hear you. Benny, turn that music down!" Eden opened her eyes. The voices from outside did not match the ones from her world. How she longed for the sound of a basketball, cell phones, the awful rap music...the chaos of home.

The flap of the hut widened, letting in a larger stream of light. A small child peered in, and Eden tried to prop herself up on one elbow to get a closer look at him. The little boy's eyes were dark and round, so unlike the eyes of her own children. She beckoned the child with a wave of her hand. "Do you understand me?" she asked.

The little boy stared at her wide-eyed and quizzically.

"Could you please get me some water?" Eden placed her hands over her throat. She leaned her body over the side of the makeshift bed and picked up the wooden bowl and ladle. With shaky hands, she extended them toward the child. "Water?" she repeated. Eden cupped her hands to her mouth and mimicked a drinking gesture. Slowly and cautiously, the boy moved closer to her and then quickly snatched the objects from her hands. He turned on the heel of his bare foot and ran outside.

When he returned, the bowl was filled to the top with water. He squatted low and pushed it toward her on the floor. "Maji." He smiled.

Eden picked up the bowl and held the ladle to her lips. She was so thirsty. The water trickled down her chin and neck as she drank. When she finished, she wiped her mouth with the back of her hand and then placed it to her heart. "Thank you," she whispered. The small boy placed his brown hands over his own heart and copied her. Despite the foreign surroundings, Eden managed a smile.

The child moved closer to her. He was bewitched by hair the color of corn silk. He reached out his hand to touch it, equally amazed at its silky texture. He moved his face closer to hers and stared into the bluest eyes he had ever seen. He did not blink. He moved in as close as he dared and gazed into the face that was as unfamiliar to him as his was to her. He wanted to touch her. He started to and then retrieved his hand. Eden took his small hand in hers and allowed him to trace the fine features of her face. He was mesmerized by such a vision. Her skin was as soft as the dew on the petals of a flower. He tilted his brown face to one side and smiled.

"Dahni!" (pronouncing it "Da Hee Nee.") The child stood erect at the sound of the voice entering the hut.

The Asian man spoke to the child in a stern voice and in a foreign tongue. He pointed toward the direction of the opening. Dahni hung his head low and slowly walked outside.

"I have warned Dahni not to bother you." Yallowahii spoke in a severe tone that frightened Eden. "He is too curious for his young years and for his own good."

Eden spoke in a small voice. "He brought me some water…I asked him to." She tried to hold back the tears. She had never been so frightened. Through her tears, she watched Yallowahii. He was indeed the same man she had seen twenty-six years ago. He was dressed differently. He wore a long white tunic and the skin of an animal tied at his waist.

"Where am I? How did I get here?"

"I found you down at the water's edge. I was hunting for fish. You were hurt."

"How long have I been here?" Eden asked as she wiped her tear-stained cheeks.

"You have slept for three suns," Yallowahii explained. He clasped his hands together and took a deep breath. "You were sent to us by the Spirits."

Eden shook her head. "Do you not know who I am? Do you remember seeing me at the beach when I was a little girl? You told me that you had a message from my father. Then I saw you at the department store. And what about the water globe?"

Yallowahii placed his hand on her forehead. "You have the fever. You talk nonsense. My eyes have never seen you before."

Eden laid her head back down and took on a confused look. "You speak English. I can understand you. That woman and child, you called him Dahni, they cannot understand me. Why?"

Yallowahii sat on the floor. "I was sent by the Spirits a very long time ago. My people left China when I was a younger man. I was in a shipwreck with my family. That is when I lost my children and my wife. I thought I died with them. I went into a deep sleep, and when I awoke, I awoke here in this far-off and distant land. The Spirits spoke to me about a mission. I did not understand then. Now, they sent you here to me."

"So, it is true. I am dead! I am dead, and this must be Heaven…or this must be Hell."

"No." Yallowahii stood to his feet. "Tell me, child. Touch me. I am not dead. Those tears that you cry are the tears of the living. However, the words you speak are partially true for this place is both a Heaven…and a Hell."

Eden heaved a sigh. "Dahni and the woman, what language do they speak?"

"They speak in the Swahili tongue. Open your heart. Free your soul. You walk with the Spirits now. In time, you will come to understand and learn as I had to."

Eden shook her head. "I am afraid that I do not understand anything. I feel so lost."

"You were lost. Now you are found. You were dead. Now you are alive. You were sleeping. Now you are awake and aware. You will see more with your heart than you have ever seen with your eyes. I must warn you. Things will happen very quickly here. There is no time to squander like in your homeland. You will learn to love fast…You will learn to hate quickly. You will learn more in this after-state than you ever dreamed was possible."

Eden's blue eyes locked onto his.

"You must be hungry." He called out over his shoulder, "Una, Chakula Gani?" (Una, what is there to eat?)

"Iko mchuzi wa samaki chapati." (There is fish curry with Indian flat bread.)

Eden caught sight of the woman Yallowahii referred to as Una (pronounced "Ooo Nah"). She was the same woman who had tended to her when she first woke up. She wore a light-blue kaniki decorated in dazzling swatches of red and yellow. It was refreshing to see some color after the somber hues of the hut. Una returned with food and knelt down next to Eden. Yallowahii gave her instructions to feed her and informed her that he was to be back soon.

The food tasted strange. It did not remotely resemble anything Eden had ever seen or tasted before. She took small bites and sipped the water in between. Una was transfixed with Eden, so fair and strangely beautiful. Even Yallowahii, who was not actually born to the Clan, was of darkened features.

Eden was still uncertain of her whereabouts and was unclear on everything that had happened. Yallowahii said that she would come to understand. Between feeding Eden, Una shyly looked down at her hands, which were folded in her lap. She did not smile, for she feared Eden terribly.

Eden sensed this and spoke. "I hope I do not frighten you. I wish you could know how very afraid I am. Of course, I know that you cannot understand me."

Una did not respond.

Eden blew a strand of hair from her forehead and sighed. "Maji?" she asked, remembering that was the word Dahni had used for water. Obediently, Una unfolded her hands and held the ladle to the stranger's mouth. Una did not make any further eye contact with the unique visitor. She continued to feed Eden until she was finished and then backed out of the hut, afraid to turn her back on the one who was sent to her people by the Evil Spirits.

Yallowahii had explained that she had slept for three suns, which meant today was December 22. She sat up slowly and held the temples of her head. The food had given her a surge of steadiness, though she still felt somewhat faint and weak.

She looked down at her clothes, and her hair fell into her face. Jeans and a red Saint John's University sweatshirt. Her Doc Martin boots were placed in a corner. Eden took a clenched fist and began to pull her sweatshirt to and fro, away from her chest as if to fan herself. It was hot. Very carefully, she lifted one foot and pulled off her sock. The remnants of a pedicure reminded her of home.

"I have got to get word to my family and somehow let them know that I'm all right." Eden lifted her other foot and pulled off that sock. "Then I will get out of here." Frank would wire her some money. It was all going to be just fine. Eden placed her feet on the sooty floor and slowly stood. The hut spun around her like she had a bad hangover. The back of her head had been bandaged, and the long strands of blond hair were clumped together with dried and hardened blood. She walked slowly toward the sunlight, holding on to each side of the grassy thatched hut. When she looked, Eden could not believe what wondrous sight she beheld as she observed the outside world.

The predominant colors outside of the hut were heavy greens, rusts, and all shades of browns. Lush hills of earth were speckled with date palms and mimosa trees. Tiny bungalows and thatched huts made up the small village. The sun was high in the sky, casting its jealous rays above the tawny-colored dwellings. And the people! Eden blinked through the bright of the day and swallowed. Children ran around in their nakedness, their brown skin shimmering beneath the sun. The older ones wore goat skins slung over their shoulders. They ran freely, happily, and carelessly among herds of goats and sheep under the fluorescent skies. The adults were busy tending to chores. The younger women wore only a ring around their waists, which was made from lizard skin. The adolescent men wore a piece of bark cloth around their loins. The older ones wore tunics as white and as bright as the new day sun.

Eden hid behind the opening of the hut, carefully, as she did not want to be seen. She shook her head in disbelief. How could this be? This world that lay beyond the tent was primeval, uncivilized, early, and archaic. She peeked outside again. She could see the woman called Una balancing a bundle of sticks upon her head. Una caught sight of Eden and turned toward the children in fear.

"Nadani!" (Go inside!), she commanded. The children tried to catch a glimpse of the visitor they had heard so much talk of. They giggled over their shoulders and whispered into one another's ears. Reluctantly, they obeyed her command. The two women stood in silence, eyeing one another, like a scene from a western showdown. Eden broke the awkward silence.

"I need to wash," she stroked her arms and made the gesture of bathing. She became obsessed with the thought of a bath. What she wouldn't give to sink into a tub with a glass of wine and some Bruce Springsteen. Ahhh, and food, real food, like a Christmas ham with all the trimmings, roasted chestnuts, cold cider, and fried dough dipped in powdered sugar. And her family. The pang in her chest tightened. Her babies, her husband. Where was she? Her hair fell over her face as she looked down at her feet.

Una walked across to a tiny hut and returned with Yallowahii. Eden lifted her face to his. "I need to wash."

"You, dear child, still have the fever. I do not think that you are strong enough or well enough to travel down to the ocean. It is quite a walk."

Eden bit her bottom lip and spoke gallantly. "I can do it."

Yallowahii eyed the frail creature. He sensed a spirit of dauntlessness about her. "Come," he motioned. "I shall take you."

Yallowahii summoned Una to fetch a clean tunic and instructed her to follow. His aged body was sturdy as he became a crutch for Eden to lean upon as they descended down a hill toward the water. Together, they walked down a wide road in a grove lined with extraordinary mango, coconut, and banana trees. The heavy red clay beneath their feet was lush and earthy. The sun was torrid, a blazing fire hanging low in the sky. Every few steps, Eden felt the need to stop and rest for a spell. Yallowahii was patient with her as they continued their stroll. Eventually, the three arrived down by the sea along the shores of lofty rocks that were elevated high above the ocean's edge. Eden had never seen such beauty.

"It is the Indian Ocean. Together, we stand at the edge of the reflective sky." Yallowahii sat on a rock and extended his arms. "As far as your eyes can see, the sun rides upon the waves of jewels."

This, Eden had to agree, was the most spectacular view her eyes had ever witnessed.

Una sat a small distance away with her knees bent over and back to one side. She glanced over at the way Eden sat with her legs outstretched in front of her.

"Why does she look at me that way?" Eden wanted to know.

"A woman who sits with her legs in front or apart is looked down upon in the culture. It is simply unbecoming. The Swahili women are taught from childhood to sit in such a fashion. There is much you must learn about our ways, I am afraid." As he spoke, Yallowahii's eyes never left the splashing waves of the sea.

"If this is the Indian Ocean, that means that we are somewhere in... Africa?" Eden squinted through the brilliant rays of the sun and turned toward Yallowahii.

"You are in the land of Zanzibar," Yallowahii corrected. "You have traveled far and wide with the Spirits. They brought you to a world long ago and far away."

Eden hugged her knees into her chest despite what Yallowahii had just explained about the proper way for women to sit.

"Here I sit in a land you call Zanzibar with the sun upon my face in the dead of winter. I still do not understand how such a thing could be possible. I feel as if I am dreaming, and soon, I will wake up and be in my bed at home." She looked out into the ocean. "Am I? Dreaming, I mean."

"Dreams are for those who sleep," Yallowahii replied.

"Tell me, why is Una afraid of me?"

Una recognized the sound of her name coming from the foreign tongue of the stranger. It made her uncomfortable to know that the visitor was talking of her. She shifted her legs to the other side of her body and continued to stare down at her hands.

Yallowahii spoke slowly. "Four suns have come to pass since the tragic death of Una's young sister, Wanyenya," (pronounced "Juan Yen Yah.") "She hung herself on a tree in the garden. The Swahili people believe that if you burn the body, then cut down the tree, the ghost of the deceased will be destroyed and then laid to rest. Una could not bring herself to do such a thing."

"Then you found me."

"Yes. I found you here at this very spot. Una believes that you are the evil ghost of her dead sister. She believes that you are the Spirit responsible for Wanyenya's untimely death. She fears that you were sent by the Spirits to harm and take possession of her soul."

"How horrible!" Eden made a face and touched her hands to her mouth. "That is such a dreadful story. She must hate me. Couldn't you just tell her that I am not evil?"

"Una has seen much sadness in her lifetime. She must learn for herself who you really are. She must listen to what is in her heart, and the truth shall be revealed. This I believe." Yallowahii stood. "Una, kuoga." (Una, bathe her.)

Eden grabbed hold of Yallowahii's hand, frantically. "Wait! Please do not leave me alone with her!"

"It is the only way. You are too weak to bathe yourself, and I cannot do such a thing. Una will only obey my commands. She is frightened; she is not evil. I will be on the other side of the jetty. I will not be far off. If you should call for me, I will hear you."

Eden held on to a rock and hoisted herself up slowly, for she still felt dizzy. She pulled off her clothes and felt somewhat embarrassed standing in her naked state. She could see Yallowahii fishing with a spear on the other side of the rock. Una led her into the clear, hot water. She felt the layers of grit being rolled away with the tide. Una's tunic was wet from her waist down, yet she did not seem to mind. She began to scrub Eden's back. The warm wind caressed her, and she closed her eyes and enjoyed the warmth of the sun-drenched sea. She felt like she was part of a dream, a dream filled with peace and tranquility. Eden's anxieties and fears washed away with the rush of each invigorating wave.

Eden could not see! She could not breathe! She could not move! Swirls of bubbles encircled her as her lungs filled up with fluid. A pair of strong hands held her securely beneath the territorial waters. Una was trying to drown her. Eden tried to fight with what little strength was left in her weary body. Her arms and legs flailed about while her body wiggled like a fish dragged to shore. Una's hold remained incompressible. Eden could not fight her any longer.

Yallowahii ran into the sea with racy speed, splashing water behind him like a barracuda trying to escape a deadly trap. He dropped his spear and pulled her body onto a clearing on the bank. He breathed every ounce of his life into her lungs. "I release you to the power in my soul. You are the Spirit Walker. Awaken from your sleep, and prepare yourself for your life's fate and eternal destiny!"

An overabundant spill of water protruded from Eden's mouth. She rolled onto her side and began to cough and gasp for air. She looked up into the face of Yallowahii. His eyes looked back like dark sparkling onyx.

"She tried to drown me." Eden dropped her head back down to the wet sand. Yallowahii lifted her head and slipped her tunic over her. It was large and sacklike on her small frame. He glanced over his shoulder in the direction in which Una was running. Yallowahii turned toward the fragile figure he held in his arms. She did not move. She only spoke.

"You have saved my life for the second time. Assente," she said.

Yallowahii smiled down at her for the very first time. His thin and weathered face lifted with joy. "Assente," he repeated, which meant "thank you" in the Swahili tongue.

Eden picked her head up again. The foreign word that fell from her lips had surprised her. "How did I know how to thank you in your language?"

"Now it is your language. You spoke from your heart, child." He picked her up in his feeble arms and carried her back to the village. Yallowahii was stronger that day than he had been in a very long time. "Rest." He laid her down on the sacks of grain.

Eden reached for his hand. "You are my friend. Perhaps the only friend I have in this forsaken place. Will you stay with me tonight? Will you stay with me forever?"

Yallowahii touched his heart and said, "Siku Zote," which meant "always," and Eden somehow understood.

An African Blessing

Christmas Stars of Zanzibar

When she awoke, Yallowahii was still sitting beside her. "I had a dream. I was back home with my family. We were decorating the Christmas tree, and we were singing...we were happy...we were together..." Her voice trailed off as she looked around at the darkened hut. "But...I am still here," she added dully.

Eden frowned. "Why me? I was so happy with my life the way it was before. I do not like it here very much." She fell silent for a moment. "Yallowahii?"

"Yes, my child."

"I am speaking to you in Swahili, and you understand me. Am I?" Eden listened to the sound of her own voice. "I am!" she cried. "I have forgotten my own native tongue. I am listening to what I am saying, and it sounds so peculiar, yet I understand! Why do I not remember the words I knew before?"

Yallowahii was amazed by her innocence. He could remember a time, so very long ago, when the same thing had happened to him. "Down by the ocean, you thanked me from your heart. Now, you too have been blessed with the tongue. The Spirits have blessed you."

"I can hear your words, and they make great sense to me; however, I am afraid that nothing else does. Please, tell me, will I ever forget my family?"

"I can still remember my wife, my children." Yallowahii lit the lantern and sat back down beside her. "In the days of old, when I was a young man, perhaps the age that you are now..." He cleared his throat and continued, "My family and I moved from China to America. It was a move of great difficulty for me. I remember China. I still think of it as my true native homeland. It was eight days before Christmas, and the journey we traveled had been long and weary. The ship that carried us across the sea had capsized. Many people died. I thought I died with them. My body fell deeper and deeper into the water. I saw this light, this glorious, brilliant light. I felt it calling me, drawing me closer and closer. A part of me wanted to swim away from it so that I could continue my search for my family. I laid out on that sky of the ocean like an unsettled navigator. Someone was calling out to me. It sounded so distant, yet I heard it clearly. My desire to find my family was strong, yet this light embraced me and filled me with such grand radiance. My will to follow it was stronger than my desire to stay. When I awoke, I was here. Like you, the Spirits have led me to this great destination. I am an old man now. I will be ninety when the seventh full moon rises in the sky. I have lived my life. The Spirits have been most kind to me."

Eden felt a surge of compassion for her new found friend.

Yallowahii added, "Una has not yet returned. She disobeyed her Chieftain. Bale and Mazi are searching for her. They will find her, I am sure. Una is a good woman, though I do not blame you for thinking otherwise. She has been very distraught since the death of Wanyenya." Yallowahii clasped his hands together. "We must pray for her safe return. You must eat something to regain your strength." Yallowahii left the hut and returned with a bowl of mashed corn, spiced goat's meat, and saffron liquid. He sat before her and fed her. They heard voices carrying from outside the hut.

"It is Bale and Mazi," (pronounced "Ma Zee.") "I must go to them." Yallowahii excused himself and left Eden to finish her meal alone. She could hear them talking.

"Have you found Una?"

"No, Chieftain, we did not."

Yallowahii gazed up at the night sky. "The moon is full, and the light is plentiful. We must locate her and bring her back. I shall go with you. Bale, go to Dahni. Stay with him. Assure the child that Mazi and I will return safely with his mother."

Eden climbed out of her bed and peeked out of the opening to catch a glimpse. Bale and Mazi were both very tall, well over seven feet. They towered over Yallowahii, who was small, like herself. Both men were dressed in the same type of white tunics that Yallowahii wore. The tunics were immaculate, considering how dusty the ground coverings were. One of the men wore a white turban on his head, and his skin was of the deepest black. The other had more of a cocoa complexion. Eden kept herself hidden as best she could. Only her face peered out of the opening, and a long strand of yellow hair fell forward.

 Yallowahii and Mazi turned toward the plantain fields and walked over a hill until Eden could not see them any longer. She dared not move, in fear that the one Yallowahii referred to as Bale would notice her.

Bale folded his arms across his chest and paced back and forth. He knew he should go to Dahni. The poor child was worried about his mother. Bale was worried, too. Una was his only living sister now that Wanyenya was gone. Wanyenya had been married to Jita (pronounced "Jee Tah"), and together they could not produce a child. On the evening before she hung herself, she had found Jita at the hearth of another woman. Jita had threatened to kill his mate if she spoke the truth to the others of the Clan. The very next day, in a weakened state of mind, Wanyenya took her own young life. She was fifteen years of age.

 Bale looked over at the hut where Eden was hiding and tried to peek inside. Una had told him that she was sent by the evil Spirits and that she was the ghost of their dead sister. Bale did not believe such tales. He was curious to meet the one Yallowahii referred to as the Spirit Walker. Bale walked toward the hut, and Eden let out a frightened gasp. Was he going to hurt her, too? There was no place for her to run and hide. She stood, frozen, like a wounded animal caught by a hunter's headlights. Bale saw her. She was so tiny and almost translucent in the pink luminosity of twilight.

 "Do not be afraid. I will not harm you. I come to you in peace and harmony." He spoke to her with a kindness in his voice, but Eden was frightened just the same. "My name is Bale. I am Una's brother and the uncle of Dahni. I am deeply sorry for my sister's actions. She has gone mad, I am afraid. Please, woman, what is your name?"

Eden looked up at him. His face was broad, and his eyes were deeply set, though spaced widely apart. His nose was ample, and his teeth looked so white against his skin, which was so black. Everything about him was enormous. His hands, his mouth, his teeth, his voice. He instantly reminded Eden of a gentle giant, and automatically she trusted him.

"My name is Eden."

"Edi...Edi..." Bale tried to pronounce her name and had great difficulty in doing so. "Edi, I shall call you. It is my deepest honor to make your acquaintance. Should you not be in bed resting? Yallowahii would be upset if he saw that you were up and about like this. Come. I shall help you. Then I must leave to check on the boy." Bale walked slowly behind her and gently guided her with an immense hand resting on the small of her back. Bale had never seen anyone as captivating as Eden.

In his own tamed and tenderhearted fashion, he continued to speak to her. "Please, Edi, settle down and be still. You must rest. Yallowahii said you have traveled with the Spirits. They are good Spirits, I am certain." He helped her onto the sacks of grain. "I searched for my sister; I did not find her. While I was on my journey I looked up at the heavens. In the rain, I heard a song for me. I took it as a sign that Una is safe and well, though I know she must be frightened. She disobeyed the mighty Chieftain. He will have to be firm with her." Bale covered Eden with a thin piece of bark cloth. "I must go to Dahni now. Welcome to our land." Bale smiled, flashing a set of startling white teeth. "You are home now."

Home.

The Sign

Una tucked her legs to the side, sat back in the cave, and watched as the rain fell. So much had happened to her, and she needed to take this time away to collect her thoughts and to properly mourn for her sister. She gazed high up to the water-soaked heavens.

"Why, Mungu, why? What is it that you are trying to tell me? The cruel winds took my sister away. I miss her terribly. How shall I go on from day to day? I have dedicated my soul to you. Why then have you treated me unfairly? Why have you left me to suffer in sadness? No one knows the pain I feel. I am not this strong. We are all alone. Dahni and me." Una did not understand this fragile thing called life. She only knew that it had been strangled by a Higher Force, and it gave her great difficulty to breathe in the goodness she had once believed in.

Her husband, Keswa, died three years ago when Dahni was only five. Una was left as a widow by the age of nineteen. Sometimes Dahni would lie awake at night and become frightened because he could not remember things about his father. Una would cradle the boy in her arms and tell him stories that would make him smile. Keswa was a good man.

Bale was wonderful with Dahni. He taught him how to hunt and fish and how to play the drum. Bale, who had no children to call his own, was a father figure to the boy. Una was grateful to have such a caring and loving older brother.

Dahni was all Una had left in this world, and her love for him was immeasurable. She would have to think about heading back to the Clan soon for the sake of her only child. Yallowahii would be very unsettled with her. She thought about that fair-haired enchantress. Una was sure that she was sent by demonic Spirits. She thought of the way in which she sat and toyed with the idea of hugging her knees to her chest. She fought against the impulse, for she knew the gods were always watching from a distance. No one had hair the color of the sun or eyes as blue as the ocean. She had never before seen skin as pure and white as the tusk of an elephant. It was her enchanting character that scared Una so.

"Please, Mungo, O' Great Spirit of the Sky, send to me a sign that will speak to me through wisdom and guide me with your grace."

The rain continued to fall, and all was silent around her. Suddenly a sunbeam arc appeared in the sky, and a bateleur eagle swooped down from a parting in the clouds. She stood to her feet and watched as the eagle soared high above the gold and gray plains that unfolded all around her. The eagle flew in the direction of her home.

Una knew it was time to leave. She would wait until the rain came to a complete stop. She made a small hearth fire to keep warm and dry. Whenever rainstorms came on, no matter what time of day, it was customary to turn in and go to sleep until the storm was over. The custom was followed by young and old of all classes.

When the rain stopped and the sun rose high in its clutching skies, Una awoke from her nap to find Mazi and the Village Elder climbing up the rocks where she had taken refuge.

Una ran to them and told them all about the bateleur eagle and how she knew it was a sign for her to return to her home. She bowed before Yallowahii, fell to her knees, and begged him for forgiveness. She did this by putting her hands together, bringing them over her right shoulder, and then dropping them down to her knees. She repeated the action in quick succession. She kept her head down low for she was ashamed of her betrayal toward him.

Yallowahii placed his hand on her shoulder. "Come." He beckoned. "Your child awaits you."

The three headed back toward the village. During the walk, Yallowahii spoke to Una. "Woman, I am disheartened by your selfish actions. I gave you strict orders to tend to the needs of our Spirit Walker." Yallowahii spoke harshly. "If you ever lay a harmful hand upon her, I am afraid you will be disowned by the Clan and left to fend for yourself. Your only son will be taken away from you. Do I make myself clear?"

Una looked down at Yallowahii with hurtful shame in her eyes. "Yes, Chieftain. I understand."

Eden's Amulet

Eden lay in the hut alone, left with her fears and worried for the safety of Yallowahii. She knew that if he had returned, he would be at her bedside. She was beginning to feel stronger. Her thoughts were interrupted as a smiling Bale entered her hut. In his massive hands, he carried an array of mangoes, bananas, nuts, and berries. "You are too scrawny. The Swahili women are large and strong and healthy. Bale will fatten you up." He handed her a piece of fruit. "It is good, yes?"

"Yes. It is good." Eden smacked her lips, savoring the taste of the ripened and delectable fruit. "Has Yallowahii returned?"

Bale shook his head. "I have good faith in believing that they are heading toward the village. Una will return to her son. A mother does not leave her child." Bale watched as Eden's expression changed. "I am sorry, Edi. How insensitive of me to say such a thing when you may have children of your own."

Eden let out a sigh and handed the fruit back to Bale. Suddenly she was not very hungry. "I miss them so much."

"You have a mate?"

Eden nodded. "Yes. His name is Frank. We were high school sweethearts. Do you know what a sweetheart is? I know you do not know what high school is."

"You are a sweetheart. No? I must go now to feed Dahni. You will be all right for a while? I will return shortly, and I want to see that some of that fruit has been eaten." Bale flashed her a giant smile and winked at her. "I will see you later, sweetheart."

Eden could not help but smile. Somehow, something about Bale really made her smile.

The rain had stopped, and the village outside of her hut came back to life again. She heard the sounds of children, chickens, and dogs. She felt restless. The sacks of grain were uncomfortable, and she was bored. She had found a piece of plantain fiber and tied a knot in it for every day she was separated from her family. Four knots for four days. She tucked it in between the sacks so that no one would discover it. Yallowahii appeared at the entrance of her hut.

"You are back!" Eden's face brightened. "I was worried about you. Did you find Una?"

"Yes, Mazi has brought her to her hut. You look well today. There are many people who await your arrival. Today I shall take you around the village to introduce you to the people of the Heart Clan. Do you feel like you are up for such a thing?"

"Oh yes!" Eden clapped her hands together in delight like a little girl. "I was just thinking to myself how listless I am feeling. I would like that very much." She paused for a moment, and her eyes shone like crystals. "I am glad that you are back."

Yallowahii was charmed by her sincerity but was careful not to show it. "First, you must eat."

"I did eat. Bale brought me some delicious fruit."

Yallowahii raised an eyebrow. "Bale?"

"Yes. He is very nice."

"Bale is a true and sincere man. I have known him since he was born, and I have watched him grow into an upstanding man of the Clan. I worry for him. He has never taken a mate and brought forth children of his own. He would be a fine mate and father. It is very strange for a man of his age to be alone the way that he is. It is customary for a man to be married, usually by the age of fourteen. Bale has done a fine job with Dahni. For the sake of the child, we have made provisions for him to stay even though he does not have a mate." Yallowahii handed Eden a fresh tunic. "Change. I shall wait outside."

⁂

The sun was high in the sky and had already dried up any trace of rain that had previously fallen. Together they walked out in the brightness of the day. "You are limping. Did you get hurt?" Eden asked.

"It is my leg. Sava will look at it. He is the medicine man of the Clan. He will look at you also. The bandage on the back of your head needs changing."

The village was an array of color. Handmade baskets filled with maize were lined up in neat successions outside of the little thatched huts. The people were a collage of Arab, Swahili, and Portuguese. Most of the people wore the traditional white tunics or light-blue kaniki. Some wore turbans upon their heads. Everyone was of color, some darker than others. Bale was among the darkest, for his skin was of the deepest black. Others, like the Arabs and the Portuguese, were of a light brown. No one possessed the fairness of Eden.

The people of the village stopped what they were doing and stared at the one they had heard so much talk of. The first hut they stopped at was the home of Sava, (pronounced "Sah Va ") the medicine man, and his mate, Tama (pronounced Tame Eye). Yallowahii explained to Eden that the medicine man formed a most powerful body and that he was very feared and treated with reverence. Sava was a surgeon and saved the lives of men who had been wounded in battle or whose limbs had been amputated by their masters for whatever reasons. Sava knew how to deal with illnesses caused by ghosts. Priests and mediums paid the medicine man the highest respect of all. Sava walked toward Yallowahii and Eden.

"It is my leg, Sava. It gives me great pain." Just by glancing at the Chieftain, the medicine man knew it was his right leg that needed tending to.

Sava brought forth a sack tied on to a stick and opened it. He mixed three herbs together to form a thick paste and applied it onto Yallowahii's leg. Tama, his mate, tore strips of white cloth and tied it over the applied medicines. Both worked quickly and in silence.

"Sava. Tama. This is Eden, who was sent to us by the Spirits."

Eden felt foolish at such an elaborate introduction. It made her feel too important. At home, she was just plain old Eden, mother and wife. End of story.

Sava was old. As old as Yallowahii. When he smiled, he displayed a mouthful of yellow-stained, rotted teeth. His skin was dark, and his face was wrinkled and lined with years of wisdom. His nose was long and pointed, and his eyes were tiny in comparison to his elongated features. The whites of his eyes were as yellow as his teeth. He greeted her with kindness and acceptance.

Sava had horns of antelope and buffalo of all sizes. In each case, he had filled the hollow of the horn with exotic herbs and clay. The opened end was stopped by a wooden plug that was decorated with pieces of brass and iron. "These horns," he explained, "are vehicles of the Spirits, and the powers they possess are of the highest magic." Sava opened one of the horns and blew into it. Then he administered a mixture of the herbs and clay into the open wound on the back of Eden's head. He removed the old bandage while Tama prepared a new one. Sava placed his hands over Eden and recited a chant. He tied an amulet around her waist. "This amulet will protect you from disease. Wear it always, Spirit Walker." Almost every ailment known to the medicine man was treated with some type of amulet.

The amulet that Sava had given her consisted of a piece of wood, sewn in a small cat-skin bag. It was intricately decorated with cowrie shells. Sava mixed a red powder with a liquid substance and instructed Eden to drink. Eden glanced over at Yallowahii apprehensively. He nodded to her reassuringly.

"Continue to walk with the Spirits!" Sava called to them as they left.

When they were a safe distance away, Eden spoke in a whisper. "He scares me."

"Sava is a sacred man. He has earned the respect of all his people and from the people of distant Clans. He is an old and dear friend to me. When I came to this land, Sava and I were young men. I have learned a lot from him. Sava has five mates. Tama is the first and the only one allowed to live in his hut."

"Five of them!" Eden declared. "I do not understand. He is not handsome in the least bit."

Yallowahii found himself laughing, which was something he did very little of. "Respect, child, is a far greater achievement than what you refer to as handsome."

Christmas Stars of Zanzibar

Christmas Stars of Zanzibar

Walking around the village with Yallowahii was quite an extraordinary occurrence. Eden was amazed as she watched this universe of wonder unfold around her. She could not distinguish if she had actually traveled back in time or if she was perhaps in the most remote corner of the world. One thing was for certain, this place was unspoiled by the hands of the progressive man, a place of purity and modesty and uncanny fascination. She remembered Yallowahii's words to her: "The Spirits have taken you to a place long ago and far away." She gazed over at him and saw the profound wisdom he held in his eyes. In those eyes, she sensed a truth, a truth so painful it hurt her eyes to look at him. His face was lined with stories like words carefully written across the pages of a classic. Eden shifted her gaze from Yallowahii up to the brilliant indigo sky, so vast and endless. Yallowahii turned toward her and followed her gaze. He could feel her confusion as they studied the clouds passing over the sun.

"I am so far away," she said wistfully. "Tell me the truth, have I traveled back in time?"

"Timeless traveler, that is you. I will tell you only this. In the course of the next two suns, an extraordinary event will take place far off to the East. A happening that will change the beliefs of all men. You are here in this state of Tanda. Do not look forward, do not look back, only to the here and now. There will be a time when you will want to look back. I am here to tell you, child, that you must not. You will know the time when it is upon you. For you will see a vision that will lead you and guide you to your final destination. When your father died, his soul went straight to the heavens. He came to me in visions and asked me to watch over you. That is what happens when people die and move on to the state after. A guardian is appointed for each of the remaining loved ones who are left alone to suffer. My destiny was here. I have waited a long time for you. Your fate has been rolled out for you from the time you came into this world as an infant. You have the capability to change the road you are traveling, yet you will always end up at the place you were intended. You are blessed more than most because you are here among the living. It is not your time to die; however, it is your time to live and to learn." Yallowahii looked at her and saw the little girl on the beach with the pale braids blowing across her face.

"So, you *do* remember seeing me when I was a child. Is my father here?"

Yallowahii placed his hand over her heart. "He is here inside of you. He has always been with you, as I have been."

Eden touched his hand over her heart. "I can barely remember him. I think that I do, then, when I stop and really try, my memory of him fades. I remember loving him so much. So, you are an angel. If my father came to you in dreams and appointed you to be my guardian, you must be..."

"Your keeper. The angels are up there." He pointed up to the distant sky. "I am here with you in this land...Together we shall walk."

Eden shook her head. "If I had died, I would be in Heaven with my father. Instead, I am here with you."

"Perhaps...you are only just beginning the journey of your life."

"You spoke of an event that will change the history of mankind."

"Yes, my child, close your eyes, and tell me what you see."

Eden closed her eyes and immediately saw the water globe with the Holy Family. Her eyes flew open and grew wide. She was speechless as she watched Yallowahii slowly nod his head.

"We are time travelers, you and I. We are the Spirit Walkers. We are Christmas Stars."

Eden moved close to the old man, threw her arms around him, and cried upon his shoulder. He let her. Then awkwardly, he placed his arms around her and patted her reassuringly on her back.

A brightly colored butterfly flew above them and landed on Yallowahii's hand. He showed it to Eden. "It is a sign to us both," he explained. "Someday our colors will be displayed freely for the sun and the moon to witness."

Eden watched as the colorful wings spread themselves wide and flew away. "Someday, you shall spread your wings and you shall fly, too," he said. "I promise."

A young girl ran over to the Village Elder and the fair-haired one. She seemed impatient as she waited eagerly to be introduced to the one who had the entire village talking. "Eden, please make the acquaintance of Zinga..." Pronounced ("Zing Ah.") "She is a daughter of Sava's." Yallowahii sighed. "Zinga is a fantasy child. Young and bright with many foolish dreams."

Zinga did not seem to mind Yallowahii's contrite introduction. She was tall and lofty with a plump, round face and generous wide eyes that danced across her cheeks. Like Una, her hair was cropped close to her scalp. Her lips were full and lifted into a smile that brightened her childlike face. "It is my greatest honor to meet you, Spirit Walker." Zinga smiled sweetly and bowed before Eden. Zinga's formality made Eden somewhat uncomfortable. Zinga genuflected before her and looked up through long, dark lashes. "I have had dreams of distant lands where white stars fall from the skies. Yallowahii has explained to my people that you have traveled with the Spirits. Spirits of Brightness, Spirits of Light...for my eyes have never seen anyone as radiant as you. I am just an ordinary girl. Forgive me for my common appearance."

Eden looked her in the eyes. They studied each other for a lengthy time. "Please, do not apologize to me. Where I come from, I am quite ordinary."

Zinga shook her head in amazement. "No. You could never be the ordinary one. People say that I am a dreamer, that I am ruled by a foolish heart and childish dreams. There is nothing that I would like more than to hear your tales from the far corners of the lands. When I close my eyes to dream, you will be able to supply me with visions that I desperately seek."

Eden smiled. "I would like that very much, Zinga. Where I come from, a girl like you is called a teenager. And that is what teenagers do, they dream and fantasize...just like you."

Yallowahii helped Eden to her feet. Zinga remained on her knees and clasped her hands under her chin. She was mesmerized by Eden's remarkable essence. The sun cast a halo of light around her albescent hair.

"Bale says you are a sweetheart." Zinga giggled.

"Bale is very kind."

Zinga watched over her shoulder as Eden and Yallowahii walked away. *She moves like the wind and walks in elegance*, thought Zinga. She ran to her friends to tell them all about their strange and astonishing new visitor.

During the walk back to her hut, Yallowahii spoke. "You must rest. For tonight when the moon is full and rises in the night sky, we will have music and dance in your honor. The people of the village await you. Tonight, my child, you shall be officially inducted into the Clan." Yallowahii escorted Eden to her hut, fetched her an animal horn filled with medicine tea, and left to check on Una.

Eden sipped the potent tea and nestled her body on top of the sacks of grain. She thought about all the people she had met: the little boy, Dahni; Sava, the medicine man, and his mate, Tama; their daughter, Zinga; gentle Bale…and Una. She had not seen Una since the incident down by the ocean. She would have to face her tonight. The thought of it frightened her. Then of course, there was Yallowahii. Eden felt unscathed in his company. Perhaps, it was because they shared a sacred bond and a similar experience or perhaps because through him her father was very much alive. Perhaps, it was because they were Christmas Stars. Her heart was filled with admiration for this mentor.

New York
(Present Day)

The doorbell rang. Frank Salina extinguished his cigarette and ran toward the door.

"Hey, Frankie."

Frank did not mean to look disappointed to see Annie on his front porch holding a tray of baked ziti. "Annie, come in, come in." He followed her into the kitchen and pulled out two stools at the butcher block counter.

"No news yet?" Annie asked while placing the foil-wrapped tray into the oven.

Frank reached for the coffee pot and poured two cups. "This is crazy...I don't get it. It is two days before Christmas, the kids are scared out of their minds thinking that their mommy is...I don't know. My wife is missing. No leads, nothing. It is like she just vanished off the face of the Earth!" Frank ran his fingers through his long, shaggy hair and paced back and forth. "I'm falling apart here. Where can she be?"

Annie took a seat and wrapped her hands around the warm mug of coffee. "I'm so scared. I can't help but feel guilty. She called me, you know, and asked me to go shopping with her." Annie shook her head. "Dean was working and..."

"Don't take the blame, Annie. Don't do that to yourself. How were you supposed to know any of this would happen?" Frank patted her hand reassuringly. "We really have to be strong now...for the kids...and for Eden."

Annie nodded. Frank was right. Tears and guilt would not bring her best friend home. The police were notified, and family and friends were out combing the area. Frank had called all the local hospitals. Someone was bound to find her and bring her safely home. The phone rang, and they both jumped. It was Eden's mother.

"No, Ma...nothing yet...Yes, yes, of course they're eating. We're OK. I'll talk to you later," Frank slammed the phone down and lit another cigarette. "I can't take this! Where the hell can she be?"

Ben entered the kitchen. "Who was on the phone, Dad?"

"It was Grandma, partner."

Frank rubbed his hands across his face. He looked so tired. "She just wanted to make sure that we were OK. You know Grandma; she's worried too. Jeez, I shouldn't have been so rude to her." Frank looked down at his son. Ben was nine years old and looked so much like Eden. The same honey-colored hair, the same wide blue eyes, the same small and striking features.

Ben hung his head, and Annie put her arms around him and rubbed his back as she forced a smile. "Benny, your mother is fine. I can feel it. She's going to come home to all of us...and when she does, we are going to celebrate and have the best Christmas ever. You'll see." Annie kissed him on his forehead. "I promise you, baby."

Ben looked up at Annie with shining eyes and a quivering lip. "But what if she doesn't?" he asked in a trembling voice.

Annie and Frank exchanged glances. It was a valid question, and they both knew it.

Frank stood in front of the big bay window and watched the snow fall by the light of the lamppost. It was three o'clock in the morning, and there was a hush throughout the house. The room was fully decorated for Christmas. He could feel his chest tighten. "Where are you, babe?" he said out loud. "I know you're out there somewhere. I just need to know that you're OK."

Frank saw a figure in the dark beneath the lamppost. He strained his eyes to see. Who would be out there at this hour? Through the blinding snowstorm, he saw a man—an elderly Asian man dressed in an old black suit with a mink pelt around his neck. Upon his head, he wore a tattered fedora. He walked with a cane and looked directly at Frank in the window. Then he was gone.

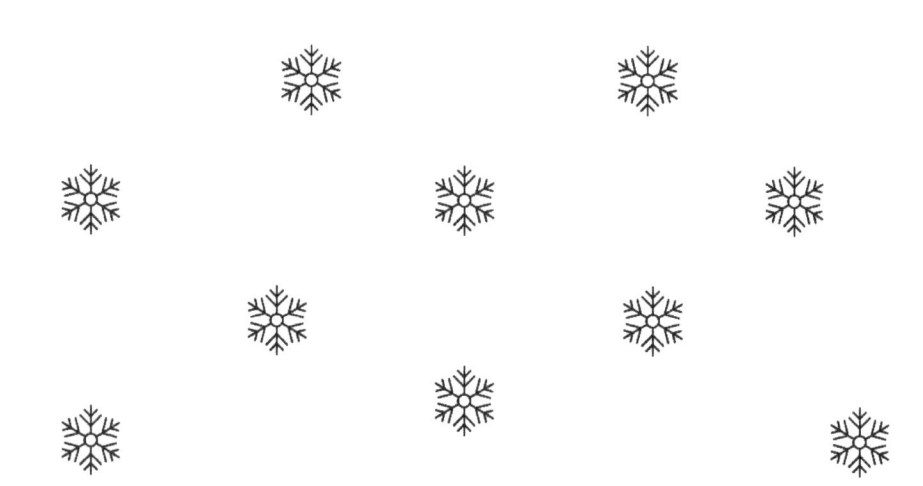

"And there won't be snow in Africa
this Christmastime.
The greatest gift they'll get this year is life
where nothing ever grows
no rain or rivers flow;
do they know
it's Christmastime
at all..."

Feast of the Python

Eden squinted and stared into the fiery glass lantern. She could see the snow that was falling back home. She stared into the glass for a good long while. It had been days since she saw her children and her husband. She found herself humming the tune to "Do They Know It's Christmas?" Eden heard a voice. "Who is there?"

"It is I, Zinga." Zinga walked over to Eden. "You look so sad, Spirit Walker. Tell me, why are you woeful?"

"I miss my family...I miss my home. I know how worried they all are." Eden's eyes grew wide and solemn. "I wish I could just see them and tell them that I am all right."

"You do not like it here?" Zinga asked.

Eden sat up. "Oh, I do. This is an extraordinary place, and you all have been so kind. Except for Una. You know, it is strange; I cannot be angry with her. In some ways, I feel we share the same pain. A loss for our loved ones. I just want to go back to the place where I belong."

"Yallowahii says that you belong here, with our people. Tonight, we hold festivities in your honor. You should be happy. For we are overjoyed that the Spirits have blessed us with your arrival. Here. I brought a wrap for you to dress in. It belongs to Nalinya; she is small like you."

Eden fingered the soft white garment and smiled. "Thank you, Zinga. You are very sweet; however, I cannot wear this. I cannot go out there to be honored. I feel very foolish and undeserving of all this attention."

"Oh, you must, or my people will be very insulted. They have gone through so much trouble for tonight's feast. If you do not come, they may believe in the things that Una has said. I know in my heart that you were not sent by the demonic Spirits. If you do not show your face tonight, I am afraid the Clan will turn against you and savagely destroy you. Besides, Bale would be terribly disappointed if you do not arrive. I see such a glow in him that my eyes have never seen before." Zinga continued, "Bale is too old to be without a mate. He will be thirty-two in one more full moon. Our people are expected to marry and produce children by the time they are fourteen or fifteen. That means that I have only one year. Love sometimes does not enter into the Swahili marriage. More often than not, it is a marriage of convenience, one that is set up by the parents. A woman will cling to her mate in times of danger. A woman will always respect her mate. When Keswa died, Una mourned for him with great sincerity. I believe she truly loved him."

Zinga stood close to the lit torch and touched the glass that surrounded the fire inside. The firelight flickered upon her face as she spoke. "Bale never took a mate. Nalinya wanted to marry him. She is a fine woman and very beautiful. You shall see tonight. Bale refused her and she became my father's fifth mate. Bale insists that his destiny is to take care of his sister, since she is a widow, and to be a father to Dahni." Zinga wrinkled her nose. "There is so much about Bale we do not know. He is a mystery to us. He seems to admire you."

Zinga sat next to her new friend. "I do not want a marriage of convenience. Sava and Tama already know this, for I speak my mind and say what I feel. I want to feel real, deep, and true love. I want to find my love...and look him deeply in his eyes. Sava tells me that there is no such thing. He is my father and the medicine man, yet I know he is wrong." Zinga's eyes grew wide by the light of the lantern. "There is a boy who makes my heart dance. His name is Kimu." (Pronounced it "Key Moo.") "I have prayed to Mungu at great lengths for Kimu to see me. Anyone can see with their eyes. That is easy. To see with your heart, I believe, is the truest love of all. So, you see, I can feel all you are feeling about being apart from the ones you love the most. If Kimu were to go far away from me, I do not think I could go on living. You must dress now. My people request your presence. I will wait for you if you would like."

The music started, and Eden could feel her heart pounding. It sounded eerie, primitive, and wicked to her ears. Eden reached out and touched her young friend. "Do not leave me, Zinga. Stay with me. I am so afraid."

Zinga smiled. "Tonight, you become our Spirit Walker. Tonight, you become a part of the Heart Clan. We shall dance to the music in our souls. We will eat. We will drink. Tonight is the night that Kimu will finally see me."

Eden changed into the wrap that Zinga had given her. It was different from the traditional tunics. It was softer and enveloped her, clinging to the curves of her shape. Swags of material hung below her shoulders, exposing the paleness of her skin. It fit snugly around the lower half of her body. She fastened the amulet around her slender waist.

Zinga's dark eyes glistened like melted chocolate hearts. "You look like a Queen!"

On the outside, instruments were being set up for an evening of dance and music. The men of the Clan maintained bands that were known as busoga bands. They made trumpets or horns from long bottle-gourds and covered them with skins. They had learned to blow them in such a manner that with a number of eight or ten, they managed to produce different sounds, and by blowing them at intervals, they made up tunes that were not unpleasant, though they were somewhat weird. By making instruments in different shapes and sizes, they attained many different tones.

The madinda was a favorite instrument of the Swahili people. It was formed of two logs that were placed over pieces of wood from three to four feet long and three or four inches square. These pieces of wood were scooped out underneath, laid across the ridge, and graduated to produce a very melodic sound. There were twelve pieces laid on the logs for the scale.

Bale and Mazi sat on each side of the instrument, opposite one another. Each man had two short sticks to beat upon the pieces of wood. There were harps and fifes, hunter's horns, and drums. The sounds of the busoga band were not like the music Eden was used to hearing. It was primitive and bewitching amid the lit torches of fire that surrounded the musicians.

She stood in the entrance of her hut feeling nervous. There were so many people out there, all waiting to witness the Spirit Walker. They were dressed in their finest wraps. They ate and drank and danced and laughed. Eden turned toward Zinga. "There are so many people in your village."

"Yes, many people make up our Clan." Zinga placed her hands on Eden's shoulders. "Look. It is Kimu. Does he not look like a dream?" Zinga pointed to a young boy sitting off by himself. He held a fife in his hands, which he had made from reed wood.

To Eden, he looked like a child, not much older than her own son, Benjamin. "Yes, Zinga, I see him. He is very cute." Eden turned toward her young companion. "What if your people do not accept me?"

Zinga's young face took on a pensive look. "Yallowahii will speak to the Spirits and ask them for a sign. If the sign is a good one, my people will know that you are true and genuine."

"What if the sign is not good?" Eden asked with panic in her voice.

"It will be. You must believe."

The music grew louder and more intense. It was the same steady beat playing to climaxing grunts and screams coming from the Clanspeople. Eden's heart pounded wildly. Zinga gave her a friendly shove and followed her out to the ring of people. As soon as she came into sight, every bit of music, laughter, dance and chant came to a complete and abrupt halt. Everything fell to a deafening silence.

Eden looked at all the strange and foreign faces. Some wore masks that looked evil and ominous. Though she was racked with fear, she stood as still as she could. She spotted Bale sitting behind the madinda. He sat tall and proud and gave her a nod. That gesture put her at ease.

Yallowahii stood. "Five sunsets have come to pass since the Spirit Walker has found her way to our people. We, the people who proudly call ourselves the Heart Clan, have been blessed. She comes to us in peace. She walks in eminence. We pray to Mungu as we look forward to living and moving to the next state. Oh, Spirit Walker, you have entered into the state of Tanda. Walumbe, the god of death, has breathed into you a new and fulfilling life."

Yallowahii knelt and raised his arms above his head. "Your Spirit has set us free, and forth to the people of this land, we hail Zanzibar. We welcome you, O Fair One. We honor you and ask you to join with the people of the Clan. Forefather, Namiegera, who lived and died by the sea, we ask of you to send a sign to show us that our Spirit Walker is true and pure of heart and worthy of our never-ending dying devotion."

The rest of the Clanspeople fell to their knees. The only sound heard was the crackle of the fire. Eden felt her body go numb as they all awaited the sign. A paralyzing feeling overtook her as she tried to remain standing. Time was passing before her as the people bowed close to the ground. After a lengthy time, a python appeared out of the hollow of a log. Its long and thick body slithered slowly over to the spot in which Eden stood. The snake then curled its body around her ankle. It felt tight and heavy around her. She placed a hand to her forehead and fainted. Bale threw his sticks down and ran behind her to cushion her fall. She fell into his strong arms. Finally, the snake detangled itself, rested its head upon a stone, and milk began to leak from the rock. The snake drank the milk and then quietly moved away and off into the blackness of the night.

Yallowahii stood to his feet with the rest of the Clanspeople following. "Selwanga, the great and powerful python god, has delivered to us a sign. We believe in you, Spirit Walker. We believe in our hearts that you were sent to us by the gods of goodness. May your destiny be one of great fates."

Sava ran over to Bale and handed him a pouch full of spices to revive Eden. Bale stroked her hair and her face and held the pouch beneath her nose. "Edi," he whispered in her ear, "open your eyes. The sign has been one of virtue."

Eden opened her eyes and gazed into Bale's soothing face. "What happened? I feel so strange..."

"The python is a sacred animal to my people, Edi. The Spirits sent such a promising sign, as I knew they would. I pray that Una will see this as well. Drink the milk from the stone."

The music began to play, and the Clanspeople danced all around them. She felt drunk from the stone milk as the swirls of people encircled her while they chanted and grunted louder and higher over the music.

Yallowahii pushed his way through the crowd and sat beside Bale and Eden. "The music. The drink. The food. The dance." He pointed to the starry night. "The moon. Tonight, it is all for you, my child." The Chieftain handed her a hollow piece of wood that was filled with more of the powerful and potent stone milk. "Drink," he commanded. Eden sipped it slowly.

Bale stood and helped Eden to her feet. "Come. There is someone I would like you to meet."

Eden felt unsteady as she held onto Bale's arm. Bale brought her over to the madinda and watched as Mazi played with flair and flamboyance. Eden looked up at Bale, who was smiling down proudly at his friend. "He is a wonderful music man, the finest in the Clan." Eden watched in amazement as Mazi took control over the instrument, playing crazily while jumping in rhythm between carefully selected notes. He was truly spectacular. Bale motioned to him. Mazi put his sticks down and ran over to them. His body was covered with sweat, and his face was painted with the fiery colors of the sun. His hair was worn longer than the others and matted into rows. He was as tall as Bale. His eyes were light and clear and gray. Through his nose, he wore a small gold ring.

"This is my dear friend, Mazi. We are not brothers in the true sense of the word; however, we are as close as brothers could ever be."

Eden immediately thought about Annie and how much she missed her.

"Bale speaks very highly of you. If you are his friend, I hope you will think of me as one. I welcome you to our land and into the Clan."

Eden felt dwarfed standing between such towering men. She caught sight of Una, who sat alone on the other side of the fire. Mazi caught her eye.

"Una is not a happy woman. It is for Wanyenya that she mourns. For the loss of Keswa, as well. I have prayed for peace for her. Una is a fine and upstanding woman, though you may not think so. Please do not judge her harshly. She will come around, you will see," Mazi explained.

"I do not judge her. I know how she must feel. For I too have suffered a severe loss. My family is so very far away." Eden bit her lip and spoke gallantly. "I will see them again someday."

Bale and Mazi exchanged glances. A woman joined them and waited politely to be introduced. "Edi, please, make the acquaintance of Nalinya." (pronounced Nay Lean Ja) Mazi made the introduction, and Bale seemed to grow uncomfortable. Nalinya was dissimilar to the typical Clanswoman. Her hair was long and straight, and her complexion was olive. Her features were fine and chiseled. She looked more like a Navajo Indian than a woman of the Clan.

"I have heard talk of the one who looks like me. Your hair is long and straight like mine." Nalinya studied Eden closely. "I am of Arabian blood. My family came by canoe. I am the fifth mate of Sava. I am told that you are Bale's sweetheart." Nalinya glanced up at Bale. "It is good to meet you."

Eden avoided the remark about Bale. "It is nice to meet you, Nalinya." Eden's eyes fell upon her swollen belly.

"I am expecting Sava's twenty-first child. However, it is the first for me. Revered men such as Sava are allowed to take as many mates as they are able to support and protect. Fathering twenty-one children is not unusual." She seemed as if she were speaking directly to Bale. "Sava is a good provider and would not turn me away from his hearth."

Bale shifted his weight from one leg awkwardly to the other. Nalinya excused herself and walked over toward Sava and Tama. Eden stood on her tiptoes, and Bale leaned down to meet her. She whispered in his ear, "Nalinya is young and beautiful. Sava, he is so old."

Bale responded, "Sava is very respected. It is an honor to be the mate of such a powerful and mighty medicine man."

Eden was drunk and felt brazen as she asked Bale a question. "She likes you, Bale; it is obvious that she has been hurt by you. Why did you not take her to be your mate?"

"Edi, it is a very long story. Perhaps, someday I shall tell you."

CHRISTMAS STARS OF ZANZIBAR

Eden stayed close to Bale and Mazi. She felt safe in their company. Mazi excused himself and went back to playing the madinda. Aside from Yallowahii, Bale was the only person she trusted completely.

Dahni was busy playing and running with the other children. His face lit up as he ran over to Bale. "Kojawe!" he called to Bale. "Kojawe" was what the boy called his uncle, meaning mother's brother. Bale caught the child and lifted him up. "Put me on your shoulder, Kojawe. I want to touch the sky!" Dahni sat tall on his uncle's shoulders.

"Dahni, can you reach up to the stars?" Bale teased and began to spin to the music. Around and around. Faster and faster. Around and around. Faster and faster. Dahni held on and threw his head back in delight screaming, "More, Kojawe, more!" Eden clapped her hands to the music while Bale danced with the child on his back.

From across the fire, Una watched her son, her brother, and that one her people called the Spirit Walker through narrowed and suspicious eyes. Jita, Una's brother-by-marriage and the mate of her late sister, whispered in her ear, "She is evil. Do not be fooled by her magic." Una studied Jita's face.

He was gruesome, grotesque in every way. Jita was tall and had little flesh upon his lanky bones. His black skin was speckled with unsightly spots due to the lack of pigmentation in his coloring. The whites of his eyes were as yellow as his long, claw-like fingernails. His brows were sinister, looming over his dilated eyes. Within the pupils of his dark eyes glowered flecks so red they resembled the flames of doom. He hissed his words when he spoke and licked his dry and cracked lips, which caused Una to wince. When he opened his mouth to speak, venomous words dripped from his fang-like teeth. Some of the Clanspeople believed that he filed his teeth and nails in order to produce such finely sharp and tapered ends. Others believed that Jita simply became that way.

When Jita was a boy of six, as the legend goes, he wandered away from the village and lost his way in the thick of the night. There, Jita, normal looking at this time of his young life, met up with a leopard cub who was stricken with disease, ill, abandoned, and left to die. The cub was lifeless as it heaved its final breaths. Jita became curious at such an animal who seemed to be clinging desperately to its final moments. Never before had he been so close to a leopard. He was fascinated and intrigued by it.

Feeling a sudden surge of dominion over such a helpless creature, he began to torment and tease it, knowing full and well that the powerless animal did not possess the will to retaliate. Jita decided he most definitely liked this feeling of power.

Jita poked his fingers into the leopard's eye sockets and beat upon its body with sharp and jagged rocks and sticks. The leopard produced a sharp, sibilant sound, and with every ounce of strength in its feeble body, he reached out a claw and swiped it across Jita's forehead, which left an imprint of a shape that resembled a half-crescent moon above Jita's right eye. The blood trickled down the young boy's face. It dripped into his eyes and fell into his hands. Jita became malevolent, and in a fiendish rage, he continued to beat the animal until he was sure it was dead.

A thick substance oozed from the animal's mouth. Jita knelt down on all fours and drank it, lapping it up like a dehydrated dog. He devoured every ounce of the foamy matter and realized he was thirsty for more. He nuzzled his face into the fur of the animal and began to rip open the animal's skin with his teeth. He stuck his entire face inside of the leopard and consumed the blood and the raw insides until his insatiable appetite was fulfilled. His face, neck, and hands were bloodstained as Jita fell into a state of unconsciousness beside the mangled and disfigured carcass of the leopard cub.

It was his own mother who had found him. In a state of panic, she dragged her son down to the water's edge and cleaned him frantically. She picked up the child in her arms and ran toward the village. By the time she reached the plantain grove, she was half crazed and babbled insanely about what she had surmised had happened. In her state of delirium, she confessed to the Clanspeople the sight she had witnessed and then later changed her story to protect her son. The Clan did not know what to believe. As the days drifted, the story had changed so completely, to the point that Jita's mother said that he had never left her side. Jita's mother's testimonial became more and more abstruse, and everyone began to think she had gone completely crazy.

Jita's appearance began to change slowly, so slowly, in fact, it was hardly noticeable to the people of the village, who simply became accustomed to Jita's ugly and unsightly features.

On her deathbed, when Jita was twelve, his mother whispered the words for only her son to hear, "You are not my son. I lost him the night his soul was traded with that of the leopard." From that day forward, Jita knew and believed that he was the devil's child, the evil one of the Clan.

"Wanyenya was not ready to die," Jita droned on. "The Spirit Walker killed her. I saw her in the garden the night your sister died. I saw her with my own eyes. She took a rope and tied it around your dear sister's neck. I tried to stop her, but it was too late. Poor Wanyenya was dead by the time I got to her."

"Jita, find another ear to talk into," Una said quietly.

Una had never cared for Jita. She never thought he was good enough for sweet Wanyenya. He was rough and hostile and not liked by many. Una knew that Jita had taken another woman to his hearth because Wanyenya had confided in her. Jita was known to slap and beat his mate. Una was always afraid for her sister's well-being. She did not have to worry about her any longer. Jita continued to madden her just the same.

"I will teach that Spirit Walker a lesson the hard way." Jita rubbed his hands together. "In the loving memory of my beloved mate and your dear sister, I say we should make her suffer. This attention that she seeks is absurd."

Una looked at her brother-by-marriage. He seemed half drunk and half mad. He had the look of an insane man and the soul of the devil himself. "It is your unfaithful act that killed my sister."

Jita laughed and spit into the fire. "Woman, it is true that I was unfaithful. What you do not know is that she was the woman I was with." He pointed directly toward Eden. "She came to me and took possession of my soul. Then she killed your sister with her very hands. She will get what she deserves."

"That is not possible, Jita. Yallowahii found her one day after Wanyenya's death."

"No, Una. You are wrong. She came to my hearth looking for trouble. I tried to run away from her, but she cast an evil spell on me. She took my soul, and I will prove it to you. Nine full moons from now, she will produce a child who will look like me. Then you shall believe."

"For the sake of my sister, I pray that you are wrong." Una held Jita's stare. "If what you tell me is the truth, then I promise you this, Jita, I shall murder her with my own bare hands."

The Dance

Zinga placed her hands behind her and leaned against a tree. From a distance, she watched young Kimu's every move. Kimu sat in a circle of boys. Some banged upon beautifully handcrafted drums, and some played a game known to them as Weso. Some of them played upon their harps and horns. Kimu did not notice Zinga. He laughed and wrestled with his friends, and every now and again, he picked up his fife and played. Zinga closed her eyes and imagined he was playing love songs composed in the notes for her ears only.

"Kimu," one of the boys teased. "Look, over there by the tree. Zinga is looking at you."

Zinga watched as Kimu's eyes met hers. She walked to the other side of the tree and continued to stare at him from behind its trunk. Kimu stood and walked toward her. The rest of the boys laughed and slapped each other on the shoulders in jest. Zinga lowered her eyes to the ground and dug her foot into the soil.

Kimu placed his hands on the tree and peered around to face her. "It is a lovely night, Zinga. Are you having a good time?"

"Oh yes, I am having a splendid time. I was listening to you blow your fife. Your melody is like bells ringing and awakening my soul." She leaned her body into the bark of the tree and looked into the eyes of her love. Zinga then surprised herself by saying, "I have dreams about you, Kimu, dreams about you and I. I hope this does not shame you."

The laughter of his companions rose above the music. Kimu looked over his shoulder and felt embarrassed by their behavior. A man does not want to be mocked when he is talking to the woman that he desires. He ran over to them and wrestled them down to the ground. Zinga's eyes filled with tears.

They were laughing at her! She ran off crying. When Kimu looked up at the tree, Zinga was gone.

Yallowahii sat with his legs crossed and took another sip of the stone milk. It was very intoxicating. He watched the way Eden moved through the crowd. She was gracious, friendly, and valorous. She was welcomed by all; he was pleased to see. He watched as Bale stayed close to her side. Big, strong Bale. He looked like a colossal silhouette walking in her shadow. Eventually, Eden would have to take a mate of the Clan. Yallowahii felt sadness for her. He knew that she believed that she would one day return to her own family. He decided he would not mention this to her for some time.

Sava took his place next to Yallowahii. "Your leg, Chieftain, does it feel better?"

"Yes, Sava. Perhaps, it is the drink. Perhaps, it is your powerful medicine. Perhaps, it is a little of both. Our people have welcomed her; for this, I am grateful. However..." Yallowahii took another sip of his drink. "I fear that Una and Jita feel differently. Look at them, the way they sit together. I am an old man, Sava. I cannot look out for her forever. We must find her a mate who will protect her. I feel very strongly that she is in danger. A woman of the Clan must be protected under a man. Our Spirit Walker is no exception."

Sava took the drink from Yallowahii's hand and raised it to his lips. "My hearth is large enough for a sixth mate. I will look after her if it is in accordance with your wishes. She is ravishing like Nalinya. She will bring forth beautiful children."

"I have deep respect for you, Sava, my friend. Yet, I am afraid that six mates may be too much, even for you."

Sava smiled, displaying a mouthful of serrated teeth.

"Nonsense. We shall pray for a sign. If a diamond-shaped star should appear in the blackened sky, we shall know that it is a blessing from the gods."

Yallowahii heaved a sigh. "This would be fair. We shall wait and see."

Zinga took her place at the fire next to her younger sister, Bukiwa (pronounced Boo Key Wha). Kimu watched her. He constructed a mask from the root of the plantain. He hollowed it out, so that his head was completely enveloped inside. He had cut out holes for his eyes and his mouth. It was customary for a young man to dance in such a mask, in front of the nubile girl whom he desired when the moon was at its highest pinnacle.

Kimu looked up at the sky. It was time. His heart began to pound as he slipped the mask over his head. The music was mesmerizing, and it took great control over his body. He jumped up into the air with a scream, leaned his body as far back as he could, and shook his arms dramatically above his masked face. His friends banged furiously upon their drums as Kimu leaped in front of Zinga and danced only for her. Bukiwa leaned into her sister and nudged her. Zinga stared up at him. She knew in that instant that Kimu felt a powerful love for her. Eden watched as Kimu performed his dance of passion.

"Bale, why does Kimu wear that mask? Why is he dancing in front of Zinga?"

"He has desires for her, Edi. Kimu is showing her that he has a love for her. This dance that Kimu performs will bring on a cycle for Zinga. Tonight, she will become a woman. If they receive the blessing, they shall be married."

"Married? They are just children."

"If she is ready to produce a child, then she is ready for marriage."

Eden continued to watch Kimu's exotic dance and wondered what deep and dark secret Bale was trying to keep from her about Nalinya. The festivities lasted until the earliest traces of dawn. Yallowahii escorted Eden to her hut and laid her down on her bed. She was drowsy and let out a yawn. "Your people are all so nice." Half asleep and half drunk, she rolled over to her side and mumbled, "Tomorrow, I must go home."

Yallowahii covered her with a piece of bark cloth and watched her as she slept. "Christmas Stars belong together in the heavens, child. I feel you shining...Your soul someday will be free."

Bale's Secret

The following day, the people of the village slept until high noon. A smoldering fire was the final trace of the previous night's festivities. Eden opened her eyes to Zinga's smiling face.

"Oh, Spirit Walker, did you see Kimu dance for me last night?" She twirled herself around like a dancing light. "When I awoke, I found myself lying in a pool of blood. Today, I have become a woman!"

Eden sat up and held Zinga's hands. "That is wonderful. Tell me, were you surprised to see Kimu dance for you?"

"I have prayed for him for so very long. I have dreamed of a Prince who lives inside an enclosure inside of my heart. Kimu is a Prince if ever there was one. I love him so. I heard my father speak of a marriage. If a diamond should appear in the blackened sky, there will be a joining. We must pray for such a sign. Then my love and I shall be together." Zinga flopped her body on the bed next to Eden and rolled over on her stomach. She rested her chin on her hands. "Tell me about your marriage day."

Eden was startled by her question. "It was a perfect day in June. Where I come from, every girl dreams of being a June bride." Eden thought for a moment. "June is a time, a season, when the weather is warm, and the flowers are in bloom."

Zinga wrinkled her nose. "Every day is like that. The days are all the same."

Eden nodded. "For you, that is true." Her face brightened. "It was a day much like today. We had a large wedding with many guests with music and dancing, just like last night. Really, our traditions are not as different as you may think. Customs are different, times certainly are, but people are people. We live for love."

"Your mate, tell me about him. Did you love him?"

Eden took on a faraway look in her eyes. "Very much. The way that you love Kimu."

"Then you produced children?"

"Yes. Three. Their names are Benjamin, Tara, and Nicholas."

"Hmmmm, such strange names."

Eden laughed. "Yes, I guess to you they are. To me they are names of pure joy and happiness."

"I must go. I must tell my mother the good news. I came here as I wanted you to be the first to know." Zinga gave Eden an affectionate hug and ran to spread the news of becoming a woman.

Eden reached down deep in the sacks of grain, retrieved the plantain fiber, and added another knot. It was Christmas Eve. She thought heavily about Frank and the children and decided that today was the day she would find her way back to them. But how?

She walked out into the sunshine and made her way through the grove down to the water's edge. The sun shone ribbons of silver upon its cradling waves. She slipped the tunic over her head and dove down into the rolling rushes of the crystal-blue sea.

She felt inebriated as the water engulfed her and gently rocked her upon its shimmering waves. She dove deep into the surf and no longer could she feel the sandy ocean's floor beneath her feet. She could not remember a time when she swam naked beneath the ardent rays of the sun on Christmas Eve. As the sea continued to exhilarate her, she bobbed upon its flapping ridges. She cleansed her body and allowed her mind to think as freely and openly as the Indian Ocean, which flowed over her.

She had heard talk of a city called Dar es Salaam. A city of progress and melioration. Perhaps this city was more advanced than the simple village she had stumbled into. As the water caressed her, she thought about heading toward that city. Maybe there would be someone there who could help her. She would talk to Yallowahii and perhaps persuade Bale to take her there. She continued to wade in the water and looked up at the towering rocks. She saw Bale watching her.

Eden called out to him, "Bale! I did not expect to see you there." She stayed down low so that the water covered her like a blanket.

"Good morning, Edi!" Bale waved. "I will turn my back while you dress." Eden came up from the ocean and threw her tunic on. She stood behind him breathlessly and then said, "You may turn around."

Bale smiled at her modesty, something he was not accustomed to. "Sit, Edi. I would like to have a word with you." He sat beside her and reached down for a blade of sweetgrass that grew between the rocks and placed it in his teeth. They sat in silence for a few minutes, each taking in the scenery that surrounded them. Then Bale spoke. "Edi, last night, you asked me why I did not take Nalinya for my mate."

Eden looked into Bale's tender face. "I am sorry, Bale, I should never have asked you such a personal thing. Really, it is no business of mine."

Bale spit the sweetgrass out of his mouth and rubbed his gigantic hands over his face. "You are right by saying it is a personal matter, one that I have never discussed before. Not even with Mazi. As you know, there was a time when Nalinya took a fancy to me. She is pleasing, and I was flattered." Bale looked out into the ocean with sadness. "However, I had no desire for her."

Eden touched his shoulder lightly.

"Sadly, Edi, there is not a woman in all of Uganda for me."

"You just have not met the right one." She smiled.

"You do not understand. There is not a woman for me because..." His voice began to falter. He turned his face away from hers. "It is not a woman that I desire. I am so ashamed."

Eden touched his chin with her finger and turned his face toward hers. Their eyes locked together.

"I admire women very much. I do not understand these feelings inside of me. I am big, and I am strong, yet, I am afraid, I am not very much of a man... for my desires are for another like myself."

"Bale, you are bigger and stronger than any man I have ever met."

Bale fell into the blueness of her eyes.

"I will die a lonely man. It is bad to feel the feelings I have. Dahni is like a son to me. This secret I shall take with me to my grave. So many times, I have tried in vain to make such feelings go away. You must think that I am wicked, and perhaps I am. Tell me the truth, Edi, do you think Bale is a man of corruption?"

"I think Bale is a man of merit and distinction. I admire your courage. It takes a strong man to admit what you have finally revealed to me. I am sorry that you had to carry this burden for such a long time. Your secret is safe with me, Bale."

"If the Clan were to find out, they would mock me and disown me and possibly put me to my death. I would shame the name of my family. I am not normal."

"I know you cannot grasp all I want to say to you. This place and time in which you live is primitive. The future holds many great men who are exactly like you. Respected men. Successful men. In my world, it is nothing to be ashamed of. I am honored that you chose to confide in me. I do not think any less of you for it. I have great respect for you, Bale. I feel safe with you."

"You are a true friend, Edi. I am so glad that the Spirits sent you here to me, to the people of simplicity and modesty. You are very smart. I feel good with you."

"I feel good with you, too."

Bale and Eden sat on the rocks and talked for a long time. There down by the seaside, two people formed a bond, a bond so profound nothing could ever sever it.

"Bale, do you suppose you could take me to Dar es Salaam today? It is Christmas Eve, and I thought perhaps this city could be my only hope to lead me to my home."

Bale looked confused. "Christmas Eve? What is Christmas Eve? I do not understand. I have been to Dar es Salaam many times. By camel and canoe, we could make it in two sunsets. It is a big city, with many people, yet it is not much different than our village, I am sorry to inform you. If you feel strongly in your heart that we should go, I will ask Yallowahii for the permission to bring you there."

"Yes, I do want to go. I will talk to Yallowahii when we get back." She leaned forward and kissed his cheek. "If I should make it back to my homeland, I want you to know that I am going to miss you so much."

"And I shall miss you, too, Edi."

Eden had never been inside of Yallowahii's hut. She walked in and found him taking his afternoon nap. With closed eyes, he spoke. "Come, child."

"I do not mean to disturb you; I could come back later."

Yallowahii did not flinch. "Speak your mind."

Eden took a deep breath. "My journey has been one of great teachings. I have learned so much in the short time I have been here. My eyes have been opened, but my heart is broken. I cannot bear to be away from my family any longer. I want to be with them. I want to go home."

"I have explained to you, Spirit Walker—"

"I know what you have said to me," Eden interrupted. "And I will make a promise to you. If you allow Bale to take me to Dar es Salaam and if there is not a gateway home for me, I will return and never mention another word about going back. Ever." Then she softened her voice. "You must at least let me try. Surely, you can help me with all of your high powers and influences."

"Dear child, I hold no greater magic than you do. You will come to understand."

"No!" Eden shook her head. "I do not want to understand. It is Christmas Eve. There is no such thing as Christmas here. Do you not remember? Think back to the years that you were with your children and your wife. Please, Chieftain, please, I beg of you, let me at least try. If I do not make it, I will return here to you and to the people of the village and live here as your Spirit Walker." Her eyes shone like moonbeams in the celestial heavens.

Yallowahii sat up in his bed and admired the fire that ignited her soul. "Very well, child. Tell Bale to round up two of the finest camels. Then, come and see me before you leave for this journey so that I may administer my blessing."

Eden ran to Yallowahii and hugged him. "Now, go. Before I change my mind."

The First Noel

Bale saddled up the camels, and Zinga brought forth baskets of food. The word spread quickly throughout the tiny village of the Spirit Walker's journey. The people of the Clan gathered outside of Yallowahii's hut. Mazi shook Bale's hand, and Zinga wrapped her arms lovingly around Eden. No one was sure if they would ever see her again—no one except for Yallowahii.

Yallowahii picked up his walking stick and hobbled out toward the people. "Go in peace. Walk with the wind upon your shoulder and the sun upon your face. Journey with an open heart and shining lucidity in your soul."

Eden noticed he spoke his words without his usual dramatic flair. He looked tired. His faced looked weary. He walked over to Bale and whispered something in his ear that was meant for only Bale to hear. "Watch her every step of the way. In my heart, I fear there is a danger. I am trusting you, Bale."

Eden and Bale mounted their camels. She waved to the people she had come to know and like. She turned to take a last look at Yallowahii. He did not look at her. He turned his feeble back to her and hampered his way toward his hut. "She will be back," he said to his people quietly so she could not hear.

Una was relieved. Maybe Wanyenya had finally called the Spirit Walker to her grave. Perhaps it was time for the little village by the sea to get back to normal. Hopefully she would disappear as quickly as she came. It was Bale's safety Una worried about. She did not go outside to bid him farewell. She was not feeling well and summoned Dahni to fetch her some water.

Jita exploded into her hut. "Have you heard? The so-called Spirit Walker has gone to Dar es Salaam with Bale." Jita narrowed his eyes and pursed his lips. "I do not believe that she will get very far. Woman, you do not look too satisfactory."

"I am ill. If I do not feel better soon, I will call on Sava."

Jita paced back and forth and rubbed his jaw. "I will find her and make her pay for the grief she has bestowed on you and me." He looked down at Una with hatred in his eyes. "No woman shall ever shame the name of the mighty and powerful Jita!"

Una closed her eyes. "Wanyenya is dead, Jita. Let her rest in peace."

"You are foolish! It is no wonder there is no man at your hearth." Jita spit his words out at her. His venom cut deep into her as he spoke with a tongue as sharp as a razor's edge. Jita stormed out of the hut, leaving his sister-by-marriage alone in her discomfort.

Bale made the trip to Dar es Salaam fun and exciting. They rode along the coast at great speed, stopping every so often to water down the camels. Bale pointed to exotic sights along the way and for every picturesque moment, he told a story that made the instant come alive. Stories of his childhood and tales of historians before him. When they rode fast, they did not speak at all. He was mesmerized at the way her hair took on the highlights of the sun, and he was infatuated as he watched it blow wildly around her. Bale was charmed by her sense of freedom, her quintessence.

Together they traveled through the day and into the early stages of the night. "The animals need to rest." Bale announced.

They found a cavern at the summit of a hill. They climbed up exalting rocks and made a fire in the grotto. They ate chipato and drank water from a buckskin flask. Bale felt so at ease with his traveling companion. They made comfortable talk and enjoyed each other's company. The warm, tropical winds that blew off the ocean were relaxing, yet mysterious. They watched as the last traces of the sun was swallowed by the mouth of the hungry sea. Eden leaned her body against the wall of the cave and let out a yawn.

"Close your eyes, Edi, and dream. For tomorrow we shall make fast tracks to the city, which may guide you to your home."

Bale watched her as she slept with her amulet beside her. The moon was high in the sky, casting its glow upon the dancing, climactic peaks of the thunderous waves splashing below them. He was feeling restless. His large frame felt awkward in the little cave. The thought of an evening swim appealed to him. He leaned close to Eden and kissed her lightly on her forehead. He climbed down the moonlit rocks, slipped his tunic off, and dove into the blackness of the sea.

The water was cool and refreshing on his skin. All at once, the entire ocean became a beacon of light. Bale was startled; he had never seen the water glow like this. He looked up at the sky and had to cover his eyes. Above his head, beaming through the dark, was a light so gloriously illuminating he could not look at it. The glint was coming from a star high in the heavens so exalting, Bale could feel his body fill with a grandiosity he had never felt before.

"Edi! Edi!" he called from the water. He ran to the shore, threw his tunic over his wet body, and climbed the rocks with a vengeance. "Edi..." He shook her arm and woke her. "Come! Look!"

Bale pointed to the brilliant sight. Eden rubbed her eyes and looked up to the sky in marvel as she witnessed the miracle. "Oh, Bale, do you know what this means?"

"Yes, Edi." Bale nodded excitedly. "Sava spoke of a sign, a diamond in the sky. It is a blessing for a marriage."

"No, Bale," Eden said in a low voice that Bale had never heard before, a voice filled with praise, a voice filled with glory. "Tonight is the night that will forever change the beliefs of all men all over the world...from this day forward...until the end of time."

Bale watched as Eden dropped to her knees. With her right hand, she made the sign of a cross, and while doing so, she came to the realization that she, Eden Salina, was the first person in history to bless herself. She stared up at the flashing star that glittered like silver against the velvet of black. The magnificent star was the most splendorous sight they had ever viewed.

Its radiant sheen was so powerful Bale dropped to his knees and bowed his face close to the earth, uncertain of why he was doing so.

"Look!" Eden pointed to the camels. The camels dropped down to their front legs, looking as if they too were kneeling. Eden got up and climbed to the highest peak of the hill. Bale turned to watch her. Her body shimmered beneath the sky. The star shone silver in her eyes. She began to sing, and when she did, for that one instant, her own native language had returned.

Christmas Stars of Zanzibar

Silent night
Holy night
All is calm
All is bright
Round yon virgin
Mother and Child
Holy Infant
So tender
And mild
Sleep in heavenly peace
Sleep in heavenly peace

Bale listened to her words…and somehow…he understood.

Way off in the distance, Bale could see an entourage of camels and burros with royal Kings riding upon them. They traveled in a long, steady line following the star to the North. They carried torches of fire and pouches of treasures. Bale climbed up next to Eden. "There are Kings down there, Majesties of grandeur and greatness from far and distant lands. Edi, look… It is King Bursala!" Bale exclaimed. "The King of all of Uganda. He is a wise man. He is majestic and regal."

"Bale, do you remember earlier today you asked me what Christmas Eve was?" Eden's eyes were sequined rhinestones as she spoke. "We are here, Bale. We are here to witness the very first Christmas Eve."

Bale shook his head. "I do not understand."

Eden placed her hands on Bale's face and kissed him. "Merry Christmas, my friend. Merry Christmas."

Bale wondered if she had gone mad. "Edi, you wait here. I am going down to watch them as they pass. I have only been this close to royalty once when I was just a boy. Will you be alright? I will return shortly."

Eden nodded. "Oh, yes, Bale, I am fine. Go to them. I will wait right here."

Jita's Revenge

Jita moved through the night like a leopard after its prey. He was annoyed by the light of brightness in the sky. It was bothersome and a hindrance to keeping himself hidden. And so much commotion! King Bursala's royal entourage had just passed. He stayed low and concealed so he would not be sighted. He would not let the disturbance interfere with his plan. He would get to the Spirit Walker tonight. He would find her and give her what she deserved. With every step he took, his desire to destroy her swelled.

He did not think the Spirit Walker was beautiful at all. Her skin was not black like his. She was a deformity sent by the devil. She was unsightly and not fit to live among his people. Thoughts of Wanyenya filtered through his deranged mind. She was young and sweet, but the barren female could not produce a child. What use would he have for such a woman? Jita had held his hands tightly around her neck until she breathed her final breath. Then he tied a rope around her neck and hung her from a tree. He had staged the whole thing so well. Everyone believed she had taken her own pitiful life.

Jita continued along the water's edge. He stalked the land cautiously, like a madman beneath the full of the moon. He could feel his demonic desires increase inside of him. The thought of tasting her was more than he could bear. He wanted to swim in the warmth of her blood and leave her in the ocean to die. It would not be long now.

He came upon a hill. There she was in all her illuminating glory. She was alone. Jita turned his head. Bale was walking alongside the royal entourage, trying to catch the King's attention. Perfect. In the still of the night, he slithered up the rocks like a snake filled with bitter toxicans.

Eden was fascinated by the wondrous star. Her long blond hair cascaded to her waist. Jita watched her from behind. He could feel his manhood increase within him. Like an animal ready to attack, he began to circle her until his fangs dripped with an insatiable thirst.

Jita pounced upon his prey and covered her mouth with one hand. Eden's eyes widened in terror. She could not scream because his hold was heavy and strong. With his free hand, he ripped off her tunic, exposing the creamy white flesh of her skin. Eden tried with all her might to wiggle free from his powerful grasp.

"Tonight, you belong to Jita! I will take your body and your soul and leave your carcass for the animals to feed on. I will dominate and devour you. Tonight, Spirit Walker, is the night you shall die. And if for some reason I cannot kill you, at the very least, you will produce my child. The Clanspeople will hate you." His words hissed in her ear as his wet mouth searched savagely for her face.

With one hand still covering her mouth, he began to shred her tunic with his fangs. Jita wrapped the torn strips of cotton around her hands and feet and then gagged her mouth. Her body heaved in fear as he traced her breasts with his tongue, tasting the flesh of his fiendish desires.

Jita flipped her over on her stomach and sat on her back. His weight was massive as she lay face down on the rocks. Jita penetrated her from behind and pulled out fistfuls of her hair as he exploded inside of her. He howled and laughed wickedly as he felt his pleasures exuding from him. He laid his head down on the small of her back and proceeded to bite her brutally, ripping his teeth into her flesh and lapping up her blood, which trickled down his neck.

"They call you the Spirit Walker! Ha! You are nothing more than a repulsive witch! Nine full moons from now, you will bear my child. Then the Clanspeople will believe me when I tell them that you are the devil herself! If you should live!"

Jita pulled Eden by the hair and dragged her body down the jagged stones. Though bound, her hand was able to grab hold of her amulet. He pulled her listless body down to the water and viciously beat and kicked her until he was sure that she would die.

"I am the great and powerful Jita!" he shrieked to the moon. Jita gave her one last kick, and her body rolled over in the sand. Blood covered her. He left Eden to die…alone…in the night…beneath the heavenly star.

When Bale arrived at the rocks, he found stains of blood and shreds of her tunic. Panic overcame him as he frantically searched the surrounding area. The first thought that came to mind was that she had been attacked by a wild animal, a beast who mauled and ate her and left her to die. There were no visible traces of anything else. He reached for his spear, placed it down his back, and set out to look for Eden.

BURSALA

"Is she alive?"

"There's still breath inside of her, Your Majesty. She has been brutally beaten and left for dead." Bursala's medicine man took the gag from her mouth and removed the blood-soaked rags that bound her. Her body had been covered with sand, in the hope that nobody would find her. Her battered body was covered with deep gashes, pernicious teeth marks, and baneful contusions. Her once fine features were swollen to the point of deformity. She lay there still and listless in the wet sand.

"What kind of animal would harm such a creature?" The man jumped down from his horse and knelt beside her. He held the golden tresses of hair between his fingers. His name was Bursala (pronounced "Bursa La"). He was the King of the land.

Bursala's medicine man, Ali of Timbatu, worked feverishly cleaning her wounds and administering herbs and clays, which he retrieved from his traveling pouch. He smeared them upon her face and body.

Bursala stood and looked about. There was no one in sight except for his royal entourage. He discovered an amulet a few feet away, held it in his hands, and studied it closely. "The amulet belongs to the Heart Clan." Bursala looked down upon the woman and added, "Though she does not remotely resemble the people of our land."

Ali examined the amulet Bursala dangled from his hands. "Yes, that is the work of Sava," he said, recognizing the expert workmanship. Bursala placed the amulet in the sash he wore tied around his waist. He clapped his hands together twice and spoke to his Kingsmen. "She needs a wrap. Ali, keep her warm." Bursala stood in the sand with his feet spread apart and his arms crossed over his chest.

Bursala was an Arabian man with insane good looks. He was a native African; however, the royal family were of different stock from the rest of the aborigines. African Kings married only Bahima or Arabian women in order to produce children who would inherit straight noses, lighter skin and overall finer features than the rest of the people of the land. The people of every Clan looked upon the King as belonging to a different race than themselves yet held him in the greatest esteem and thought him of the highest and most superior intelligence. Bursala was ravishingly handsome. His ebony hair was straight, shiny, and worn long. His dark eyes were shark-like and magnificently mysterious, set deep into his exquisite face. His nose was straight and noble. His breathtaking face looked as if it had been chiseled by the hands of the gods themselves, like a statue carved from marble. Bursala's skin was an olive complexion, and his teeth were white and startling against his tanned face. When Bursala smiled, he lit up the world. His narrow face was accented with high and hollow cheekbones. Along his jawline, the shadow of his uncut hair fell deeply into the crevices of his skin. A sharp line of separation was drawn between the royal family and the commoner, and the blood royal was considered to be the most sacred.

Bursala continued to watch as Ali worked his powerful medicines on the belabored woman. He stood with his hands resting upon his lean hips and wondered where this strange and perplexing creature came from.

Ali looked up at his King. "Bursala, it is up to you to decide. Do we leave the woman here to die, or shall we take her with us?"

"Take her to my Kingdom," Bursala commanded and placed his hand to his chin. He turned to one of his Kingsmen. "Send word to the Chieftain of the Heart Clan. His name is Yallowahii. Inform him that she will be kept safe and well-tended within the Royal Enclosure."

The Kingsman obeyed his master's order and turned his steed around. He rode off toward the village of the Heart Clan, following the ocean's coastline.

Ali draped the woman on the back of his Arabian mare. Her legs and arms dangled gracefully over the sides of the animal as Ali fastened her securely with strips of garments. Bursala mounted his Arabian mare, and together, he and his entourage galloped off toward the Royal Palace.

MIRACLES

CHRISTMAS STARS OF ZANZIBAR

Bale returned to the area only to find prints in the sand of horses, many of them. He climbed on top of his camel, grabbed the reins of Eden's camel, and headed back toward the village. Yallowahii would tell him what to do. He was scared for Eden. Bale glided along the coast with the wind on his shoulder and the sun upon his face.

Bursala's Kingsman arrived at the hut of Yallowahii as fast as his horse could take him. He jumped down from his horse and was greeted by the Village Elder himself.

"Yallowahii, I was sent to you by the King. He asked me to inform you that we have found a woman belonging to your Clan, a woman as fair as the days are long. She has been badly beaten, I might add. Bursala has taken her to the Royal Enclosure, where she is certain to get the best of care."

Yallowahii stared at the messenger sent by the King. "I thank you for saving her. Ali of Timbatu is the finest medicine man in all of Uganda. I am confident that she is in superb hands. This woman is a Spirit Walker. She is sacred and must be guarded. Please tell Bursala that I am deeply grateful for his kindhearted gesture." Yallowahii spoke with brevity. "You must not let her die."

The Clanspeople began to gather around Yallowahii and the Kingsman.

"Look!" Zinga pointed down toward the grove. "It is Bale!"

Bale climbed off his camel and spoke to Yallowahii quickly with little breath left inside of him.

"She is safe, Bale, though she is in a critical state. King Bursala has her within the confines of his Kingdom. I am afraid the word is that she has been badly beaten. Ali of Timbatu is working on her." Yallowahii's eyes narrowed. "Where were you, Bale? Why were you not guarding her? Did I not make myself clear when I told you that I feared she was in some sort of danger?"

"I left her for only a moment. There was this light, a star in the heavens. I went to take a closer look at the royal entourage." Bale hung his head in disgrace. "She was gone."

The Kingsman sensed Bale's grief and spoke to him. "She is in the care of Ali of Timbatu. I will take you to her if you wish."

Bale turned toward the Chieftain. "I will go to her. I will not return until she is well enough to travel. It may be a while." Bale paused for a moment and then spoke loudly enough for all the Clans people to hear. "Upon my arrival, there will be a wedding. For I shall take the Spirit Walker to become my mate." In a humbler tone, he added, "If this is in accordance with your wishes, Chieftain."

Sava spoke up. "Bale, the star that you talked about, was a sign from Mungu for the Spirit Walker to be the sixth mate for me; however, I would be the first to bestow my good wishes onto you."

Sava continued, "Then it is settled. There will be two weddings upon your arrival. I give the blessing for Kimu to marry my daughter, Zinga."

Zinga's eyes brightened and locked onto Kimu's.

Sava turned toward his daughter. "You are a woman now. Kimu, he is a good man." He placed his hands upon her face. "My fantasy child, perhaps Kimu and you will complement each other in a good way. I am confident that you will provide your mate with a long and fruitful life."

Zinga kissed her father's hands. Her heart was filled with joy and sadness at the same time. She ran toward Bale. "Tell the Spirit Walker the good news. You will make a wonderful mate, Bale. Hurry back so that these marriages can take place, and please tell Eden we are praying for her recovery."

Una remained in her bed inside of her hut. Her illness felt extreme. She sent Dahni to bring Sava to her.

"You are with child, Una. You are not ill at all," Sava explained.

Una's eyes were full as she held tightly to her son's hand. Dahni stroked his mother's face and placed his cheek close to her. "Mama," he cooed, "you are having a baby!"

Una remembered a time, a very long time ago, when Mazi had come to her hearth. "My son, run and fetch Mazi and bring him here to me."

When Dahni returned, he was pulling Mazi by the arm. He led him over to his mother's bedside. Una smiled at her son. "Please, Dahni, let Mazi and I talk in private."

Dahni nodded and skipped outside. He joined the group of people who surrounded Yallowahii's hut. He felt happy. He liked Mazi, and he was his uncle's closest friend. Maybe, just maybe, Mazi would become his new father.

"Mazi, please, come to me." Una spoke softly and extended her hand. "I have news for you. I do not know if this news will bring you joy or sorrow." Una took a deep breath. "Sava just informed me that I am carrying a child. This child belongs to you, Mazi."

Mazi's eyes danced with joy. He reached for her hand. "I will make a good mate and an honorable father to both Dahni and the baby. I know, Una, that I could never take the place of Keswa in your heart; however, I am Mazi, and I will do everything in my power to make you proud to be my mate. This news you have given to me today, woman, has made me very happy." He tenderly placed his hand on her stomach and then gently laid his head upon it.

Una touched his long hair and stroked it. "You will be a fine father and mate. Dahni will be pleased. He is very fond of you. Call my brother, and let us tell him the news, together."

Bale was jubilant to hear the good news about Una, Mazi, and the new baby. "Dahni will finally have a real father," he said, his eyes shining, looking into those of his dearest friend.

He thought for a moment about telling them the news about his marriage day and then fought against it. This was Una's moment; she should be allowed to revel in it. Besides, Bale knew all too well that his plans to marry the Spirit Walker would only cause her grief.

The Royal Enclosure

Bale bid the Clanspeople farewell and stood alongside Bursala's Kingsman. Yallowahii walked slowly toward him. He looked to be in grave pain.

As if Yallowahii could read Bale's mind, he spoke. "The pain that I am feeling is partly from my leg, yet mostly from my heart. Watch over her, Bale. Take good care of yourself. I will await your arrival." Then he handed him the piece of plantain and tied another knot in it. "Please make sure that you give this to our Spirit Walker."

Bale took the piece of plantain rope and tied it to his amulet, which he wore around his neck. He saddled up his camel with soft pieces of garment, and together with Bursala's Kingsman, he rode off into the horizon.

Bale rode side by side with the Kingsman until he came upon the Royal Enclosure. He looked up and noticed a high fence barricading Bursala's fortress. The enclosure was oval shaped, lengthy, and wide. The part that was called the back was reserved for the King and his mates. Each mate was given her own large estate. The King also had a private entrance and road to the lake through these estates. The very top of the hill was reserved for the King's residence. Bale had never been so close to royal quarters before.

He was aware that King Suna (pronounced King Soon Ah) had died, and his youngest son, Bursala, had just taken reign. The thought of Edi being inside such a magnificent Kingdom was beyond Bale's comprehension. And that he too would soon be inside sent overwhelming chills throughout his body. He walked up to the entranceway of the great fence. The doors to the King's private entrance were strictly guarded at all times.

"Who wishes to call upon the King?" one of the guardsmen demanded.

"He is called Bale of the Heart Clan," Bursala's Kingsman replied. "His business stated is to see the visitor who is in the care of Ali."

One of the gatekeepers went inside to the King and announced Bale's arrival.

"Very well, send him in," Bursala gave his order.

Bale had never been in such grand quarters before. He followed one of the guards into a room of great wealth and splendor. King Bursala sat on the floor with his legs crossed. Before him was a tablecloth made from banana leaves. Leaves from the plantain were spread out nicely to be used as plates for his food. In the corner of the room was a woman with her back turned toward the King. Bursala ate the food with his fingers and took a sip of ale. Bale bent his knee at the sight of his King.

"The lion eats alone!" Bursala spoke harshly to Bale. "I am not to be bothered while I eat my meal." Bursala looked sharply at the gatekeeper. "Take him away. Put him in the next room. When I am finished, then we shall discuss your business." Bursala waved his hand to dismiss them both.

It was customary for the King to eat alone, and no one was permitted to watch him. The Queen had the duty of waiting on him. It was her job to cut up the food and taste it to show that it had not been tampered with. Having done this, she then turned her back while the King ate his meal in solitude.

There was not a Queen at Bursala's estate. He had no Queen to call his own. His reign as King was sudden, and although women were plentiful, there was no one he wished to marry. Suna had had many mates. After his death, Bursala was informed by his Guardian that his father's mates should be dismissed from the Palace.

"Where would they go? They do not have quarters in which to dwell. No. Leave them be. My father loved these women. I cannot send them away without a roof over their heads. They are not a bother to me. It is my wish that they continue to live comfortably within my Enclosure."

The woman in the room with Bursala was his sister Sanda (pronounced Sun Dah). Bursala was still in deep mourning over the loss of his father. There would be plenty of time to take a Queen. For the time being, Sanda was the closest woman to him.

Christmas Stars of Zanzibar

Bale waited with the gatekeeper in the next room while Bursala continued with his meal. After a lengthy time, Bursala, escorted by two guards, entered the room. "What do you desire from your King?" Bursala asked.

Bale knelt and spoke again. "It is my greatest honor to be speaking to you, my benevolent King. My name is Bale. I am nothing more than a simple commoner. I have traveled far and wide in hopes that my search leads me to my quest. I am in search of a woman who belongs to my Clan, Your Majesty."

Bursala raised an eyebrow and motioned to Bale to stand. "If you speak of a yellow-haired woman, I must inform you that my subjects and I have found her down by the sea. She has been badly beaten...I fear she may die." Bale lowered his eyes to the ground. Bursala continued, "I assure you that my medicine man, Ali, will give her the finest medicines in all of the land. I have a great and deep respect for your own Chieftain, Yallowahii, for he was a friend of my beloved father's. I will do all that is in my power to see to it that she is made well again."

"She is to become my mate." Bale was intimidated by such great wealth and power. "I am most concerned for her welfare."

Bursala was the newly appointed King of Uganda. His father, Suna, had reigned before him for many long years. Bale could remember watching Suna being carried on the shoulders of his royal entourage when he was just a boy. He remembered seeing Bursala that day, as well. He was younger than Bale and much smaller in height and stature. Bursala's eyes were etched in his memory. Bale had watched as a young Bursala walked alongside his father and the royal entourage.

The two young boys had looked each other so deep in the eyes that day. Bale remembered wondering and feeling what it would be like to be the son of such an important man of wealth. How handsome Bursala was even at such a young age. Bursala looked back at Bale wondering and feeling what it would be like to be a child free to play with friends, free to run and roam the land. As Bale looked at Bursala now, in all his grandeur, he was sure that he did not remember him.

When Suna died, he left behind him three sons and many daughters. Normally, the oldest son would be expected to take over his father's reign. Kiro (pronounced Cairo), the oldest son, was said to be devious and malicious. The next son in line was Junju (pronounced "June Joo"). When Junju was born, he arrived in the world with only one arm. When a child is born with a missing limb, usually he is burned to his death. Because the blood that flowed through the veins was royal, he was allowed to live yet never to serve as King. Many daughters were born after Junju, one more striking than the next. Suna had Bursala when he was quite old. Bursala was smart and quick as a child. His mother, when she was alive, was an alluring Arabian woman. Bursala inherited his mother's incredible looks and his father's profound wisdom.

When Suna died, Kiro was sure that he would be the one to take over the Kingdom. Suna had spoken his last words to his sons while on his deathbed. "Kiro, you are my oldest son. You were the first. You are foolish and unwise. Your mother and I were so very happy to have you. You were wanted, and you were loved. However, in my heart, I do not believe that you understood that love. For somewhere along the way, you became very spoiled and selfish. It breaks my heart to tell you that you would not make a fit King for my people. There is an anger inside of you. A sadness. A jealousy. A rage. These are not traits of a King; I am sorry to say. Many people in this land do not think fondly of you, my son. For this, I am truly disheartened.

Junju, kind, sweet, Junju. You are a good man. A man of virtue. A man of integrity. You have always walked with a happy heart and a light step. You possess an inner beauty that cannot be rivaled. For whatever the reason the great gods had, they sent you to me with this deformity. It never mattered to me or the ones who loved you most. For what you are missing in one respect, you make up for so many others. You are charming and witty and clever. Your smile has always warmed my heart. However, dear Junju, what

I am about to tell you should not come as a shock to you. You could never take reign as King. For this, I am truly sorry.

"Ah, Bursala, Bursala, my son. You are strong, and you are sagacious. You will turn the heads of many. You already have. You are revered by all. With the eyes of your winsome mother and the soul of a King, my wish is for you to take my reign, as I am sure you will continue to lead my people in peace and harmony, my child. My son, from the day you were born, I knew in my heart that you were born for greatness."

Bursala held his father's hand and stared. "Dear Father, I am honored that you think so highly of me." His voice began to soften, and his demeanor was sincere. "I do not want to lose you. Becoming King sounds so grand, yet, I would rather have you here with me all the days of my life than to go on without you. If I am anything at all, it is because of you." Bursala sat at his father's side until the Spirits took him away.

After Suna's death, the royal family brought forward the chosen Prince, leading him by the right hand in front of the spectators who crowded as near as they dared to hear and see the newly appointed King. Bursala's guardian spoke the words, "This is the King. His name is Bursala." Bursala then walked past the line of his brothers and sisters.

One of the head chiefs held a bundle of spears and proclaimed the King by saying in a loud voice, "Bursala is King. Those who wish to fight him, let them do so now."

Kiro stepped forward and took a spear from the bundle. The two brothers held each other's gaze. Bursala did not wish to fight his brother. He knew he was stronger and younger. He also knew he wanted to be King. Bursala spoke. "Our father has appointed me, Kiro. Do not be foolish. You heard his words. Please, I beseech you, do not fight me, Brother; I do not wish to cause harm to you."

Kiro spat on the floor. "We shall see, little brother, who is fit to be the King of the land! For today, right here and now, I shall kill you with this spear I hold in my hands. I shall not shed a tear for my own flesh and blood as I did not shed a tear when our father died, for this land rightfully belongs to me."

Junju tried to stop his brothers from bloodshed. "Kiro, our father has passed me up as well. I am not angry. Please, Kiro, I beg of you, let Bursala do what is right." Junju feared his older brother terribly and thought the world of his younger one.

Kiro stared straight into the eyes of Bursala and spoke. "Junju, you are nothing more than a disgrace to the blood royal. Look at me. I have two good arms, and with only one, I shall prove my worth, and I shall be the one who stands tall and proud leading the people of Uganda." Junju took a step back with his five sisters and watched in horror as the battle began.

"Come to me, little brother." Kiro beckoned with his hand and hunched his back like an archer. "Come to me, boy, and allow me to take you. I know I am strong enough." Kiro slowly circled his brother, their eyes interlocked... their eyes...so much alike...yet so different. It seemed, at first, to Bursala, that perhaps Kiro was only taunting him. Maybe he thought he would weaken under the pressure and hand his reign over to him without a fight.

Bursala squinted his eyes and blatantly stared into Kiro's face. "Over my dead body will you ever become King of my father's land." Kiro hurtled himself on top of Bursala, and the two men began their battle. Kiro, being the larger of the two, threw Bursala down to the ground and began to spit in his brother's face. Bursala tried to move his face to one side as Kiro's weight kept him pinned against the earth.

Bursala could visualize his father's face, and in his ears, he heard the clear echo of his voice. "My child. My son, from the day you were born, I knew in my heart that you were born for greatness." He could feel the strength of a hundred men swell inside of him. He pulled himself off the ground and straddled Kiro. They wrestled on and on, taking turns sprawling on top of one another. He held his spear close to Bursala's face. Bursala's eyes stared lethally into Kiro's profane expression.

"Your birth was an intrusion on my life. You were never wanted. You were never meant to be the King of my land. Prepare to die at the hand of your King," Kiro jeered and pressed the tip of his spear closer into Bursala's face. "You are a repulsive sight to these eyes." The spear prodded the skin by Bursala's left ear, and a trickle of blood journeyed down his face.

Christmas Stars of Zanzibar

With the edge of the spear still at Bursala's face, Kiro took his free hand and pulled his brother's face closer. He closed his eyes and kissed him first on his right cheek and then on his left. He opened his eyes and breathed into him, "I detest you."

Junju closed his eyes. Sanda stood beside him. "I cannot bear to watch," she whispered and moved her way quickly through the crowd. No one seemed to notice as she quietly slipped away.

After he kissed him, Kiro pushed Bursala off of him, climbed up on top, and mounted him between his legs. He held the spear up over his shoulders and aimed directly for Bursala's heart. Bursala looked him straight in the eyes and said, "You say you detest me. You spit on me. You kissed me. I will pray for you, Kiro, so that someday your soul will be redeemed."

Kiro held the weapon higher above his head. With eyes full of fury, he spoke. "Father and you do not deserve proper burials. I will see to it that your carcasses are left for the wilderbeasts to feed upon!"

Bursala watched as Kiro's eyes widened, and his body grew rigid and fell heavily upon him. He could not breathe beneath his brother's massive weight. He slid out from under him and witnessed an arrow lethally piercing Kiro's back.

Sanda stood to the side and hung her head in reverie. Her shaking hands clenched tightly around a six-foot bow made of yew wood. She dropped the bow to the ground and slumped her shoulders. She had killed him. She had killed her own brother. Simultaneously, the crowd heaved a sigh of relief. Slowly a clamoring ensued, culminating in a deafening chant. The crowd cheered as the virtuous Prince was proclaimed King!

Bursala's eyes met his sister's. Neither seemed to hear the chants that were coming from the commoners. He scrambled on his knees over to Kiro, who was lying in a pool of his blood. He placed his face next to his dead brother and wept. "Why, Kiro? Why?" He kept saying over and over, "Did you not know that I would have shared my wealth with you?"

Sanda stood in a state of shock as she watched Bursala crying over their brother. She walked over to him, slowly, and knelt down beside him. "Dear brother, what have I done? I killed him, Bursala. I killed him."

Bursala collected her and wrapped her securely in his clutches. Her shoulders heaved against his. "You saved my life, Sanda," he said tenderly.

She looked up into his face and touched the blood that rolled down from his ear. "I...I could not watch you die."

Junju ran toward them, and the three fell into an embrace next to their dead brother. "Sanda, Bursala...do not cry. This land rightfully belongs to you. I was at our father's deathbed. I heard his words. Kiro would have tormented the people of the land exactly the way he has tormented us for all of our lives." His face took on an inspired expression. "Come, Bursala... Face your public. You are the new King of Uganda. You are the new King of the land!"

Bale had heard about the battle between the brothers, for word traveled fast and far in the land of Zanzibar. And here he stood, in front of this man. This man who was younger than he and wiser than he. This man who captured the hearts of the people of the land.

"I am certain you are concerned, Bale, is it?" Bursala's face softened, exhibiting two deep-set dimples creased into his stone-like face. "She is in the very best of care, I assure you."

Bale nodded at the regally handsome man. His eyes had never seen a man enveloped in so much artistry before. It almost hurt to stare into the glamor of Bursala's radiant face.

"Of course, if you wish, I will take you to her. However, I must warn you that she does not look very well."

"I would like very much to see her, Your Majesty. I am both honored and relieved that she has found her way into the care of the hands of your medicine man. I have heard only wonderful things of Ali of Timbatu and the magic he administers."

"Come." Bursala motioned.

The King, two guards, and Bale exited from the back of the building and out into the garden. They walked in silence for a good long distance until they came upon a lake. Across the lake were more estates and the quarters of the Queen. They crossed the lake by a small bridge constructed from wood and thick, sturdy branches.

"She is inside," Bursala said, and Bale followed him in.

The Threat

CHRISTMAS STARS OF ZANZIBAR

When Una awoke that morning, she was immediately flooded with thoughts of Mazi, Dahni, and the baby that was growing inside of her. For the first time in a long time, she felt happiness. Una glanced over to a sleeping Dahni. He was getting big. Surely, he would look very grown up next to the new baby. Una felt a smile touch her lips. Mazi was going to make a wonderful father. A look of terror swept over Una's face as her eyes focused on a trail of blood covering the sweetgrass on the floor. Jita sprang up from behind her and cupped his hand over her mouth. Una's eyes grew wide as horror overcame her.

"She is dead! I killed her, Una, and I watched her die!" Jita hissed in her ear with dried blood encrusted in his clawlike fingernails. Una tried to break free from his hold. "The Spirit Walker is dead. And I shall kill you, woman, if you breathe a single word of this to the others."

Una broke free from his embrace. "You are a beast, Jita! You have gone mad!"

Jita threw back his head and laughed wickedly. "You stupid woman. Everyone knew how much you despised her in your own obvious way. Was it not you, dear sister-by-marriage, who tried to drown her? And you call me a beast. Ha!" Jita stroked his jaw and walked slowly around Una. "We could be good together...you and I. You are as deranged as I am." Jita's eyes narrowed with a glint of red fire inside of them as he grabbed Una forcefully by the arm. "I will set this whole thing up to make it look as if you were the one to beat and kill her. Yes, that is what I shall do."

Una spoke quietly and stared into the red glow of her brother-by-marriage's eyes. "I was afraid of her. You were the one to convince me that she was possessed by the devil. Now I can see clearly that you are the evil and demonic one. It was not her at all...It was you...It has always been you!"

Jita raised the back of his hand to Una's face and slapped her hard. She fell back and landed on the floor. "You hypocrite! I see through your innocence, Una. You wanted her dead as much as I did! How dare you stand there and accuse me of being the devil when you and I are so much alike! I will let it be known that you killed her, Una, and you will hang for your actions...just like Wanyenya!"

Dahni lay very still in his bed and pretended to be asleep.

Bursala's Rhapsody

The estates behind the King's quarters were reserved for his own family. Bale was enthralled to see that Bursala had allowed Edi to stay in such an honorable setting. He could feel his pulse quicken, and his heartbeat became more rapid as he approached the estate. Bursala led him past more guards and into an isolated room that was also carefully guarded. Bursala clapped his hands together twice. "Leave us."

Bale looked at her severely beaten body and the disfigured face that was once so delicate. He turned his head away and closed his eyes. After a moment of silence, he turned toward Bursala. "She does not remotely resemble herself. She is quite fetching. Will she ever be the same again?"

Bursala folded his arms across his chest. "I do not know. She has been mauled, almost to her death, by some sordid beast. Ali has high hopes for her recovery. We must pray and not give up hope."

Bale's face took on a boyish expression. "She is the Spirit Walker."

Bursala placed his hand upon Bale's arm. "Go to her."

Bale walked slowly to Eden's bedside and held her tiny, fragile hand in his own. "Edi, Edi…it is Bale." His voice quivered as he spoke. He sat beside her and stroked her hair. "I have good news for you, my friend. I have spoken to Yallowahii, and he has extended his blessing. You will never have to be alone, for I will watch over and protect you all the days of your life. You will not have to marry Sava."

Bale noticed that her breathing began to grow more rapid. He placed his face close to hers and whispered in her ear, "I will never lay a hand upon you. For you are the only one who knows my secret."

Bursala clapped his hands together and startled Bale. He hoped he did not hear the words he had just whispered into Eden's ear. In an instant, the guardsmen returned. "Set up a room for our visitor. He shall be staying with us for a while."

Bale stood and faced the King. "You are most kind, Your Majesty. I fear I am imposing."

"Nonsense. If this woman was the great love of my life, I could not bear to pull myself away. If she belonged to me, I would not leave her. You shall be our guest. Stay for as long as you wish. I will send my horsemen to inform your Chieftain of your stay."

Bale looked back at Eden. "Thank you, Sire. I do not know how a poor man like me could ever repay you."

Bursala smiled for the first time. "What good is all of this power and wealth if you cannot share it with the people of the land? I open my home to you. All I ask in return is that you open your heart to me. I have always been around lavish surroundings. It does not impress me in the least. It gets lonely here in such a Kingdom. I am happy to have fresh faces about."

A guardsman showed Bale to what would be his temporary quarters. Bale sat on the bed and rested his face in his immense hands. Eden did not look very well, and he feared she would die. He did not believe, as Bursala did, that an animal had mauled her. Wild animals were scarce in these parts, with the exception of small prey like rabbits and foxes. No. It was not an animal at all but a person made from the same flesh and blood of his own people. Who? Who would harm such a person? Who would do such a horrible thing to his dear and sweet little friend? He could feel the hate rise in him. This was an emotion he had never felt before. He would tear the person's limbs out one by one. The kind and gentle giant looked up and spoke. "Please, Mungu, I pray to you with all of the reverence in my heart. Please let Edi live." Wearily, he laid his body down on the bed. He remembered the song she sang under the light of the majestic star. "Sleep in heavenly peace… Sleep in heavenly peace."

The next morning, Bale was awoken by the sounds of oxen clad in bells. He looked out of his window to see a gathering of people. Bale questioned the guardsmen appointed to his quarters.

"Today," the guard explained, "the newly appointed King will go to his father's grave, and a ceremony will be performed in the honor of the late Suna and for the newly appointed King, his son, Bursala. If you wish to join us, I shall escort you."

"Yes," Bale agreed, knowing that it was an opportunity of a lifetime to be included in such a royal tradition. "First, I must go to the woman."

The guard sent word to Ali, and together, they went to look in on Eden.

"Ali, she looks better today. Your fine medicines and potions seem to be fast at work."

"Yes. However, she has not yet opened her eyes. Go to her, Bale. She may respond to the sound of your voice. She does not know who we are. Bursala spent most of the night with her, as did I. She must be frightened having gone through such an ordeal. Go to her, now."

Bale sat beside her like he had done the previous day and touched her cheek lightly with his fingertips. "Hello, Edi. It is Bale. You are looking rather well today. You are in a grandiose palace, and the people here have all been very kind. Do not be afraid, Edi. I am here with you now. You are safe, and you are alive. I will never leave you again. This is my solemn promise to you."

There was no response. Although her face was very swollen, he could see her dainty features trying to take their form. "Ali, why does she not wake up?"

"It will take some time. The powerful herbs I have administered give her vitamins and nourishment like the food we eat. Soon, very soon, she will become stronger. You must have patience."

Bale spent the morning with Eden with Ali looking on. Bale's eyes never left her for a moment. He continued to stroke her face with the back of his hand, feeling such a closeness with her. She could not die and leave him alone to live his secret in silence. He would not let her. Two guards interrupted his thoughts and announced that it was time to go.

CHRISTMAS STARS OF ZANZIBAR

King Bursala was carried on the shoulders of the royal bearers to Budo Hill. Crowds of people followed them across the lake for a quarter of a mile until they came upon the spot. "Great Spirits, we are gathered here today, out under the sky, to pay our last tributes and respects to Suna, my father, the late King of Uganda." Bursala's face was somber, and his thoughts were heavy. "You have blessed my father with a long life, a good life, a prosperous reign as King." Bursala lowered his head. "I shall miss him dearly. Give to me the strength you have instilled into my father, so that I may continue to lead my people in peace and harmony. I ask this, O Great One, that I may think with my mind, see with my eyes, and feel with my heart." Bursala shocked the people with the following words: "Today, we pray for my brother, Kiro, as well. Lest we forget that he has died in the battle...a battle fought against me...for the reign of King. Let us remember him today so that the Spirits may put him gently at rest. My father and my brother walk together in an after state. I ask them for their blessings, as I have loved them both."

It was customary after the ceremonial speech for the newly appointed King to choose his Queen. The crowd watched as Bursala stared obliquely in front of him, his dark eyes shining in the sun. He looked majestic and regally handsome as silence fell over the people. They waited patiently for his announcement. Each and every woman held her breath, secretly wishing and hoping she would be picked. It took a long time for Bursala to speak, and when he did, his words startled everyone.

"I choose you, my sister Sanda. You are kind, you are gentle, and you are fair. You have cared for me since I was a small child. I believe that our father smiles down upon us today and approves of my decision."

Sanda moved out from the crowd and walked slowly toward her brother. She held out her hands to him and spoke quietly. "Bursala, I am flattered that you have asked me to be Queen, but I am your sister. Surely, there is a woman here among the crowd, a woman whom you shall love in the way a King loves a Queen."

"'Tis true what you say, you are of my own flesh and blood. However, I am afraid that the true love of my life exists only in my dreams. I can see her, yet I fear she is not real. So, for today, I ask you to stand beside me and look after me the way you always have. I shall look after you as well. If there is a woman who deserves to be Queen, dear sister, indisputably so, I believe it to be you."

Sanda's dark eyes shone. "It will be my honor, Bursala, to serve you as King until..." She paused for a moment. "Until you find the love of your life."

The King and Queen were carried on the shoulders of the royal bearers up to the top of the hill, so they could be taken into the Kingdom according to tradition. Bursala and Sanda faced crowds of people and publicly disrobed. Bursala's tunic fell to the ground. His lissome body was a series of rippled muscles that descended to a V-shape around his chiseled abdomen. Bale thought he looked like a warrior, so toned and lean, yet strong, and manly. Sanda was certainly statuesque, yet all eyes fell upon Bursala. The remaining sisters draped two white cloaks over their shoulders, which were then tied around their waists with a braid of gold and jewels. A fire was set before them to commemorate the new King and his Queen.

Bursala's guardian spoke. "We have brought forth a Prince who is our new King. For long may he reign!"

The people cheered.

The Weddings

Yallowahii had given much thought about the contamination that had manifested in his leg. Sava had explained to him that he was struck with an infection so severe his leg would have to be amputated. "If we do not remove the leg, the disease will spread, and you shall die."

The Chieftain decided he would live with the pain until he saw the Spirit Walker alive and well again. How he ached to see her face. Then, when she was safe and married to Bale, he would convince Sava to give him a poisonous potion that would take him to his final resting place. Yallowahii had already received word that Bale was staying with her at the royal Kingdom. He felt a great relief for if Eden would respond to anyone's voice, he knew it would be his own or that of Bale. He placed his feet on the floor and gritted his teeth. The pain had become almost unbearable. Sava and Yallowahii had decided that today was the day that two marriages were to take place. He wished that Eden and Bale were here to witness the weddings. It was the wedding day of Una and Mazi and Zinga and Kimu. It would be a festive celebration. Yallowahii and Sava agreed that Bale and Eden would have their own wedding day as a celebration upon their arrival.

Zinga's sisters cooked for her all day and fed her. It was customary for a Swahili woman to be made as plump as possible when preparing for marriage. Then her body was rubbed with butter to make it look soft and radiant. Una did not need too much feeding, as she was already swollen with child. Nalinya came to her hut to rub her down with butter as well.

The two women were veiled in bark cloth, which was thrown over their heads and cascaded down to their feet. The bridal party consisted of the bride's oldest brother and a number of friends. Una wished Bale was here on this very special day. She decided that Dahni would take the place of his uncle. Representing Bale would be such an honor for the child. Una knew the sun was at its proper setting for a marriage to take place. She looked up to the scarlet heavens and made a promise to Wanyenya. "If this child proves to be a girl, I will name her after you, dear sister." This sudden realization pleased her as she placed her hands upon her belly.

Una requested that Nalinya and Tama take part as her bridesmaids. The three women decorated each other with tiny ornaments made from exotic shells and handcrafted beads. Una wore a majebu, which was a gold pendant worn under the chin. Nalinya constructed a wreath made from wild berries and green ivy and placed it around Una's neck. She glowed against the soft white kaniki that softly draped around her and hung over one bare shoulder.

Zinga had many brothers and sisters, twenty-one in all. Each and every one of them fulfilled an obligation in their sister's ceremonial ritual. They wore their finest wraps with ornate headpieces. Her gown was trimmed with shells and small bells that tinkled when she moved. She felt elegant and very grown up beneath the swags of soft material. In her earlobe she wore many wooden ornaments.

The brides were placed on the shoulders of two strong men of the Clan who carried them down to the sea. The rest of the Clanspeople followed as Yallowahii and Sava led the traditional bridal march. Kimu's young friends played upon intricately handcrafted drums. The music cast a spell on the people as they marched to the same steady beat. No one spoke as their feet carried them to the spot where Mazi and Kimu stood anxiously awaiting their brides. The bridal party marched slowly until they arrived at their final destination. The musicians dropped their drums in the sand, and the two strong men lowered their bodies as Una and Zinga climbed off their backs.

The grooms stepped forward and handed the brides each a clay pot made from powdered stone and filled to the top with ale. The neck of each piece of pottery was rolled and smoothed on the inside and worked with a pointed stick until the lip was in accordance with the potter's taste. Una and Zinga held their pottery in their hands and stood before their bridegrooms.

"Shall we drink?" Mazi asked, looking Una in the eyes, searching her face with his own twinkling expression.

Una and Zinga looked at one another. "Drink," they replied. They handed the grooms each a jug. This was the legally binding action in marriage, and nothing could afterward cancel the contract once the men had drunk.

Kimu held the clay pot high over his head and placed his lips upon the finely crafted neck. He drank the ale, feeling its potency, and handed it back to Zinga. His lips looked moist. Zinga held the pottery and wrapped her arms around it, holding it close to her. Kimu looked generously handsome. Soon, very soon, she would taste his mouth.

Mazi drank also. He held the pot up and drank almost three times the amount as his young companion. He could feel his head getting lighter as he too handed Una back the jug. The wedding was then ratified.

Yallowahii began the ceremonial wedding speech. "The little village by the sea and the people who make up the Heart Clan gather today to join our fellow mates in the most sacred vow of marriage. Bow your heads, people, as we witness these weddings. Bestow upon them greetings and fair tidings. Una and Mazi, Zinga and Kimu, walk forth. Add to our ever-growing Clan the children for our future generations."

Yallowahii walked over to Sava and placed his hands on his dear friend's shoulders. "Sava, do you give to this marriage your innermost blessings? Will you accept Kimu as a son of your own family? Will you honor and respect their life together as eternal mates? Do you welcome grandchildren brought forth from your daughter?"

Sava responded, "Yes. Kimu and Zinga, you have my deepest heartfelt blessing for this marriage. Kimu, my son, you are welcomed into our family unit. I will bestow on you the teachings of becoming the medicine man for future generations. You shall be revered. I hold great and genuine respect for you. The children you produce will have a special place in our bloodline. The fruit of life grows from a seedling of your love. Nurture this gift, my children, and I shall pray for a long and fruitful life for you both. For us all."

Yallowahii walked over to Dahni and placed his hands on the little boy's shoulders. "Do you, Dahni, acting as man of the family, give to your mother and Mazi the blessings? Will you accept Mazi as your father? Will you honor and respect their life together intertwined with yours as mother and father and child? Do you welcome brothers and sisters?"

Dahni stood straight and tall, feeling suddenly much older than his eight years. "I extend my blessing to you both. I will never forget my own father, Keswa. I believe today he smiles down upon us all. It is for his blessing we must ask. Mazi, I accept you as my father-by-marriage. I wish to please you and make you proud of me. It is my duty to honor my father and my mother, and I promise you this: I will not fail you. The baby that grows inside of you, Mother, is most welcome and wanted by me. I will teach him and love him, just as my uncle Bale has taught me and loved me. Today, I feel complete, as I am now a part of an intact family. My only wish was that my uncle Bale was here to witness such an occasion."

Mazi smiled down at the boy.

Yallowahii spoke again. "We shall join hands in prayer and ask Mungu to protect you and give you all of his blessings, the highest blessing of all, in His name. I hereby declare Una and Mazi, Zinga and Kimu, shall all live as life mates under His glorious sky."

The Clanspeople gathered around, folding their hands high above their heads. Yallowahii picked up a handful of rich earth and anointed each woman on her forehead. "Kigori," he said to Zinga, which meant "young girl." "Mwari," he then anointed Una, "you are the maiden."

Mazi took hold of Una's hand and opened it. In it, he placed a sack filled with salt and another filled with shells. These were the customary gifts from a bridegroom.

Kimu called to his brother, who made his way through the crowd and brought forth a young, healthy calf, which he offered to Zinga. The Clanspeople were in amazement over such an extravagant gift. Zinga's eyes were full of love and appreciation.

"Kimu," she said softly, "you are so generous and so kind. As you stand here before me, I feel your love, which flows through my heart."

Kimu was swept away by her gentle words, and he could feel the heat rise to his face.

The musicians began to play, and the people journeyed back for a traditional wedding feast. Back at the village, a large meal had been prepared by the women of the Clan. The newly married couples were seated at the head of the circle, and Dahni sat between them. Mazi placed a loving arm around the boy, for he was so touched by the speech Dahni had spoken earlier down by the sea.

Slaughtered wild boar, curried shark, rock cod, and barracuda were served on giant green leaves of the coconut palm along with fresh fruit and plenty of the potent ale and milk of the stone. They sat beneath mango trees and date palms and ate. The festivities went on well into the night.

Rejoicing young women danced around Zinga using strong and vibrant bodily movements to welcome the nubile girl's period of menstruation. They fanned her with sunshades as they performed the exotic Kungwwia dance. The girls danced and swirled around her to the beat of the drums played by Kimu's friends, until they were dizzy and fell all around her laughing.

Yallowahii hushed the musicians and rose to say a few words of his own. "I am gladdened that we are gathered together to take part in these weddings tonight." His face took on a somber expression. "It is unfortunate, however, that we are not *all* here. Two very important links are missing from our circle. Although Bale and the Spirit Walker are not visibly with us, they are indeed in our hearts. We must take a moment to bow our heads and pray for their safe return. We must pray that our Spirit Walker gets well, and when she does, we shall gather together again for another joyous wedding."

"She is dead! That Spirit Walker, I tell you, she is dead!"

The Clanspeople turned to the sound of Jita's voice ripping from out of the darkness.

Yallowahii remained calm. "You are wrong, Jita. Word was sent from Bursala's fortress that she was badly beaten. Ali of Timbatu is caring for her. He has great faith to believe that she will be returning to us."

Jita's face was covered in sweat, and his eyes of fire glowed. "Una killed her. I tried to stop her. You must believe in what I say to you. She tried to drown her once down at the water's edge, and she tried to kill her again. I watched her with my eyes."

Una held onto Dahni as Mazi stood to her defense. "My mate is not capable of such an act. It is true, in the beginning, Una was afraid of the Spirit Walker. She was distraught over the death of poor Wanyenya." Mazi's eyes searched the crowd. "Come, speak up if you think she did it," he provoked them. "I dare any of you to stand here in front of me now and tell me otherwise."

"Mazi," Una whispered, "please, sit. It is all right."

"It is not all right!" Mazi's gray eyes met hers. "I love you, woman, and I defy anyone to question your innocence."

"It is you who tried to murder her!" Dahni blurted out and pointed his finger at Jita.

Una moved close to her son to protect him.

"I heard him tell my mother so. If our Spirit Walker is harmed, it is because Jita tried to kill her!" Dahni looked around at all the horrified faces. The child's eyes grew wild by the light of the fire. "And if she is not dead..." He took a deep breath. "She will produce a child from the devil's hell!"

The Clanspeople gasped and spoke at once to one another with fear in their voices. Una pulled Dahni toward her and cradled him. "Hush, Dahni," Una whispered in her son's ear. "You have already said too much."

Yallowahii looked directly at the boy. "Our Spirit Walker is not dead, child. As I have stated before, she is in the care of our King."

Jita took on a crazed expression and lunged toward Yallowahii. He placed his hands tightly around the Village Elder's neck. "Una killed her, I tell you. The boy is a liar. She is dead. Your precious little Spirit Walker is dead!"

Kimu threw himself on top of Jita and began to wrestle him to the ground. Zinga put her hands in front of her face and hid behind them. Mazi and Sava ran to the aid of Yallowahii while Kimu and his friends assisted each other in pinning Jita down. "I am the great and powerful Jita! No woman shall shame my name!"

"Take him away!" Yallowahii instructed, feeling his throat tighten. "Take him down to the grove and keep him there. Tie him up with vines. He has been possessed by the leopard ghost. Look at the way he growls and rolls his eyes like a wild and evil beast. Be gone with you." Yallowahii spoke with fury and disgust.

The boys and the men of the Clan carried Jita off kicking and screaming until his howls could no longer be heard.

The Awakening

Bale sat across from Eden and watched her as she slept, never taking his eyes off of her. Ali came in from time to time to check on her as well. He had left Bale strips of bark cloth dipped in medicines to administer upon her legs, face, and arms. Bale was patient as he continued to stroke Eden's hands and hair, as he always did when he was by her side. Bale watched her closely. He thought he saw her head move, and he held his breath and waited. "Edi, Edi, it is I, Bale." He spoke quietly and only to her, in hopes that she would respond to the sound of his voice.

Her head began to roll slowly back and forth as she was waking from a deep sleep. Bale moved as close as he could. "Edi, I am here for you. It is Bale," he repeated. "You have been hurt. You will be better. Nod your head, Edi, if you can make sense of my words."

After a moment, Eden nodded. Her eyes began to flutter, as she tried with all her might to open them. When she did, Bale could only see the whites of her eyes. He placed his cheek upon hers and whispered in her ear, "Please, Edi, please wake up."

Eden's eyes rolled down from beneath her lids as she tried with difficulty to focus them. "Bale." Her voice sounded dry and raspy but was like music to his ears. "Bale. Is that you?" She spoke in the Swahili language.

Bale's face lit up with a broad and ponderous smile. "Yes, it is I."

"Where am I?" Eden's words were lagging and slow. "Where is Yallowahii? What happened to me?"

"You are in the palace of the King. His name is Bursala. It is the most opulent place my eyes have ever seen. Yallowahii is fine. He is back at the village. They are all praying for your safe recovery and return, my friend. You have been attacked, they say, by a beast."

Eden shuddered, suddenly flooded with the memory of Jita. She could still see his face upon hers. She could feel his teeth penetrating through her skin. She could hear his wicked laughter ringing in her ears. "Oh, Bale, it was awful." Her body trembled with fear as she grabbed hold of his hands. "It was Jita! He did this to me."

"Jita?"

"He raped me, Bale. He raped me and left me to die."

Bale let go of her hands and rose to his feet. "No." He shook his head. "No, Edi, not Jita." He was in a state of disbelief that his brother-by-marriage could be responsible for such a cruel and inhuman act. "No, Edi," Bale cried and collapsed to the floor. He looked into the blueness of her eyes and knew she was telling him the truth. Bale wrapped his bulky arms around her and held her tenderly. His behemoth tears rolled down his face and flowed over her shoulders like a river in springtime. Her own tiny tears streamed down her face. Together, they cried in each other's arms.

Bursala entered the room to find the two in an embrace. He cleared his throat to make his presence known. "You have awakened from your dreams," he said in amazement. He turned to one of the guardsmen and summoned him to fetch Ali.

Bale wiped away his tears with his hand. "Yes, Your Majesty, though I am afraid it has been more like a nightmare. Edi, please, it gives me the greatest pleasure to introduce you to the King of Uganda. Please make the acquaintance of our sovereign King. His name is Bursala."

Bursala gazed down at the fair-haired lady. Never before had he seen eyes the shade of a robin's egg. He was taken in by them, allured by such a color.

Eden looked up into the face of the one who was known as the King. He was divine in every way. His face was like a painting on velvet, so smooth and so dark. His deep-set shark eyes sparkled like jewels. The strong and noble chin and profound dimples were abysmal, and his unshaven jaw shadowed his face and fell deep into the crevices of his skin. In his smile, she detected a courageous and generous spirit. And like in her first encounter with Yallowahii, she could see this radiant light all around him. He took her breath away. Bursala's face was the most ravishing face she had ever seen. His hair was worn long and parted in the middle. So black was his hair, it shimmered with navy highlights beneath the torches of fire that lit the room. His ivory teeth gleamed against his olive coloring. He was small and slight, yet brawny and authoritative. Tiny creases of wisdom lined his deep and intense eyes. He was a sight of magnificence. She was in a state of ineffectuality as she sat mesmerized by his immense sexuality.

"Thank you for taking me into your home." Eden smiled graciously.

He was fascinated by her. Positively spellbound. He had not realized the beauty she possessed, for when he found her, she was battered beyond recognition. She was the most enchanting creature his eyes had ever fallen upon. Her creamy skin was as translucent as the white sands along the African coastline. Her hair was the color of wheat that grew wild on his land. Just by looking at her, he could feel her warm winds blow through him. Her radiance filled him, like no one else ever had. He was transfixed by her loveliness and felt his pulse quicken as he spoke. "Bale has informed me that you and he are to be married." There was a hint of jealousy in his tone.

Eden looked quizzically over to Bale. "Married? I do not understand."

"Sava said that if a diamond should appear in the night's sky by the light of the moon, he would take it as a sign for you to become his mate. When I learned that Yallowahii had given him the blessing, I informed them both that I would be the one to take you as my bride. It is not what you think, Edi. It is only until we find the gateway back to your people. This, my friend, would be a marriage of convenience. In order for you to live among the Clan, you must be protected under a man who is your mate."

Eden flinched at the mere mention of Yallowahii. "How is he?" she asked. "Does he know that I am safe and alive? He must be so worried. It is funny." She sighed. "At first, I was concerned that my family knew that I was well... and now...I feel the same way for Yallowahii." Her blue eyes shone. "I really do think of him as family now."

Bursala looked perplexed. "I am only hearing small fragments of a large story; however, you must excuse me for I say what I want. If this is not my business, Bale, feel free to stop me at any time. My question to you is why would you marry such a startling woman and not desire to take her to your bed?"

Eden could feel the blood rushing to her cheeks. She felt a surge of compassion for Bale and did not want his secret to become divulged. Eden ignored Bursala's question and proceeded with her own statement. "Bale, I understand that your intentions are good ones; however, you know I cannot marry you. I must go home to my family. I have already come this far. I will not give up now." Her words began to trail off as she closed her eyes.

"Shhh, Edi, you are tired. Rest now. We shall talk more later," Bale said and kissed her on the forehead.

"You do not love or yearn for this woman?" Bursala asked. "Then why do you wish to marry her?"

"I do care for Edi, as if she were my sister. Just as Sanda is to you. It is true I do not love her in the traditional sense. But I will provide for her, look after her, protect her all the days of my life, and keep her free from harm."

"Yet," Bursala said and stroked his chin, "you do not wish to make love to her." He turned his head toward her and watched her as she slept. "To kiss her lips and thighs and breasts. To feel the heat of her skin next to yours. To dive down deep inside of her where any man, even a commoner like yourself, would feel like a King. My estate is grand. I can provide for her one hundred times better than you. My bed is empty and I am waiting for a lovely lady like her."

"I am not an award to fight over!" Eden's eyes snapped open, and her voice startled both Bursala and Bale. "How dare the two of you speak about me as if I were not here in this very room. Is marriage such a casual decision for you both? I do not need to be provided for. In case you have forgotten, I am already married. With children of my own. My only desire is to leave this God-forsaken place and return home to them...where I belong. I do not want to stay here with either of you!"

Bale had never seen Eden so upset. He had only tried to please her. He never meant to cause such an insult. The colossal man felt small as he hung his head in shame.

Bursala could not help but smile. He did not feel embarrassed like Bale. Instead, he found himself in admiration of her feisty spirit, her independent bounce. It was a trait in a woman he was not familiar with. "My dear, no one meant to affront you. You have been through such an ordeal. Sleep now." Bursala spoke in his most regal tongue.

Eden looked at each of the men. He was right. She was tired. She closed her eyes and wished that Yallowahii was there beside her. She wished that she was far, far away.

The Leopard Sleeps

Zinga nestled close to Kimu. "I am frightened, Kimu. Yallowahii says that Jita has been possessed by the leopard ghost. You are brave, and you are strong, and you are my life-mate. I know you will protect me from him."

"I am a man now. I will always protect you, Zinga. I am not afraid of this Jita. He has gone crazy; I take pity on his soul."

The wedding reception was coming to an end. Despite Jita's intrusion and the void of Eden and Bale, the day was everything Zinga had ever dreamed it to be. She headed toward the grove over to the well. There, she drew some water into a pot, gathered some firewood, and cut a bundle of sweetgrass. Then she took these gifts to her mother, Tama.

"I thank you, Mother, for taking good care of me. I am no longer your little kigora but the life-mate of a great man. I will make him so very proud." She smiled and gave her mother a long and loving hug.

"Zinga, Sava and I are honored. So quickly you have grown. However, I understand all the love you have in your heart for your new mate. I pray that he will always stand by you, Daughter." Tama accepted the gifts with open arms.

"It is time for me to leave. To my new hut with Kimu." Zinga wrinkled her nose and smiled. "He is waiting for me." Although she was only moving across the grove, suddenly she felt as if she were going to the other side of the land.

"Remember, Zinga, if this marriage is to be blessed by the Spirits of Goodness, then you are not to consummate this marriage until the moon shines silver in the heavens on the third night."

Zinga nodded. She knew and understood the Swahili traditions. It was arranged that her closest sister, Bukiwa, would stay with them until the third night. Then, Kimu would take her to their hearth. The thought of it frightened and excited the thirteen-year-old.

Kimu's relatives escorted the newlyweds to their new home. This was the final act in the marriage ceremony. The bridal party walked slowly to the small, thatched hut, which was nestled cozily beneath giant coconut palms. When they reached their newly constructed dwelling, Kimu's family bid the couple and Bukiwa good night.

"This is it, Zinga. This is our home." Kimu and his brothers had built it themselves. Kimu stood erect next to his new bride. "Before you enter, I have something for you." He extended his hand and offered Zinga a number of colorful exotic shells.

"Oh, Kimu, you have given me so much already." Zinga took the shells and held them close to her heart. Bukiwa, who was eleven, was happy to be caught up in the romance. "Let us enter our new home," Zinga pleaded.

Zinga was the first to enter. Her eyes scanned the dwelling. "Kimu, it is so lovely." The floor was covered in freshly cut grass, and there were garlands of flowers cascading down from the thatched ceiling. Zinga remembered the tradition and immediately changed her look of enchantment to one of dismay. It was customary for a new bride to look sad and miserable and to speak only in whispers until the night of consummation. This was difficult for Zinga. She wanted to pull the flowers from the ceiling and wrap them around her. She wanted to dance and sing and shout out from the deepest mountain. She wanted Kimu to take her in his arms and kiss her. How she wished she was alone with her new mate. She did not want her marriage jinxed by the evil Spirits, so she obeyed the tradition and sat in the corner with her back toward Kimu and Bukiwa. It was going to be a trying three days.

Una and Mazi did things differently. When Una had married Keswa, she was a young girl like Zinga. Una looked back on the day with fondness. She was older now and certainly wiser. Una was hardly a virgin bride. For her and Mazi, it was not as complex. Una and Dahni already had their hut, and Mazi simply joined them.

Una did not think that Mazi loved her in the traditional sense, although he did proclaim his love for her earlier when Jita was filling the Clanspeople with his malicious lies. Still, Una was not sure. Mazi was a good man and a true friend of Bale's. He would provide for them. A boy of eight needed constant care and guidance, and Una was sure that Mazi was capable of that. This new baby she was carrying gave her new light, new dreams to dream, new hopes, and a feeling of inspiration. It was all going to be fine. Una went to Dahni and wrapped the bark cloth tightly around him. "Mazi is a good man, Dahni. We are blessed to have him now."

Dahni nodded and smiled up at his mother. "Soon I will be a big brother, and I can teach the baby how to swim and hunt and fish just like me."

"Yes, child, you will be a very good teacher. I am sure of that."

"Mother?" Dahni looked up with questioning eyes. "What is going to happen to my uncle Jita? He is a bad man, is he not?"

Una kissed her son on the forehead. "He is a troubled man. Do not worry so much about him. Dream of nice things like your uncle Bale."

"And the Spirit Walker?"

Una smiled down at him. "Yes, Dahni, pray that she gets well. I am afraid I misjudged her."

Una waited until Dahni was fast asleep and then walked to the divided side of the hut where Mazi was waiting for her.

Mazi spoke through the darkness. "Come, Una. I am waiting for you."

When the moon hung high in the sky and all was peaceful among the village, Yallowahii met with Sava down by the plantain grove. Together they walked in silence to the spot where Jita was tied with vines to a tree. Sava untied the cloth from Jita's mouth. A white, thick foam dribbled from the sides of Jita's mouth, and Sava was careful not to touch the substance. For if he did, it was believed that he too would become possessed. Jita's eyes stared lethally into the eyes of the medicine man.

"Drink, Jita." Sava pushed a buffalo horn filled with human urine up to his lips. "Drink," he commanded. Jita tried to turn his face as Sava forced the liquid down his throat.

Yallowahii prayed aloud, "Take this beast to the next state. The leopard ghost has invaded his soul. He no longer exists in this Clan as we know it. His soul shall descend to the demons who await him."

Jita's face looked malformed beneath the brightness of the moon as he screamed, "I have hate for you, the both of you. And hate for the one you call the Spirit Walker. She is the one who is possessed. How dare you treat a member of your own Clan like this. It is your souls that need to be redeemed." Jita's eyes were wild with rage, and sparks of red glowed deep beneath the scar of the half-crescent moon. He tried, with all his might, to shake his body free from the hold of the vines that bound him.

Sava handed Yallowahii a lighted torch, and the Chieftain touched the flame to the branch of the tree. The branch was set ablaze, and the fire spread quickly. Jita's face was fiendish, and the red glow in his eyes was as intense as the glow in the leaves. Jita's iniquitous screams grew louder. His wails were heard throughout the village as Yallowahii and Sava ran from the inferno. His barks and growls howled through the still of the night, mimicking the sound of a sabotaged, wounded leopard. The sounds that came from within him vibrated throughout the land, piercing the souls of the Clanspeople like the blade of a dagger.

Finally, a deafening muteness fell over the village. The people of the Heart Clan, as they lay awake in their beds, knew that Jita was finally put to his death. Tomorrow they would go to the spot to gather the charred remains of the human flesh and sprinkle the ashes over their crops. This was believed to further ward off the ghost from invading upon their industries.

MAGIC POTION

Christmas Stars of Zanzibar

*E*den sat up suddenly. Her body heaved and trembled as she sat in the darkened room of the Palace. She called out to Bale, who rushed to her side in only moments.

"Edi, you had a bad dream."

Eden's voice grew tremulous as she spoke. "It was Jita! I saw him so clearly in my dreams. There was fire and smoke, and I could hear him screaming. I could feel him inside of me. Oh, Bale, I cannot erase him from my memory. I will never forget the stench of him...like some hungry and frenzied animal gauging and pawing me." Her face grimaced with pain.

"You are safe here, my friend. I am here with you, and Bursala's Kingdom is securely guarded. Jita is far away from here. When Yallowahii finds out that he is responsible for this, he will be put to death, if he has not already been."

"Bale, what if I am..." Her hands covered her stomach, and her face was devoid of color.

"Edi, I know what you are thinking, and I shudder to think such thoughts. My sister, Wanyenya, took her young life because she could not produce a child. Jita made her feel inferior in every way. It would not surprise me if it were, in fact, Jita who could not produce the child. It would be just like him to blame someone else for his own incapability. The Spirits have a way of blessing the good and taking away from the evil.

"Bursala informed me that on the night you were attacked, he was following that star to the North. He spoke of a Babe, a new King...a sacred Child. He is very wise, Edi. He believes that it was not he who saved you but the radiance of that star. You must believe in it also. No harm will come to you as long as you have that faith. Sometimes it is all that we have." He touched her chin with his finger and smiled at her. "I must opine to you and tell you that I take credence in his words. Accept and trust. It is all we can do.

"With great plausibility, I have high hopes that you will find the gateway to your home. You have not given up hope; you told me so. Edi, I would be nothing more than a liar if I did not tell you that when you go, I am going to miss you terribly. However, you are my friend, and I am committed to help you in any way that I can. Perhaps there is an answer still. I feel so strongly in my heart that our destinies were meant to cross. Yallowahii has already told you that your fate will be revealed if only you believe. I will fight for you all of the days of my life. Anything is possible. You will move onward and forward, perhaps if you do not try so hard.

"As I look at you now, I know that Jita's child is not inside of you. You must not think such things. If you do, then bad things will come to you. If it will be a comfort to you, I will ask Ali to make up a potion for you to drink to wash away any evil that has entered inside of you." He reached out his hand and held her tightly. "Bale is here with you now, and Bale will take you home. This is my promise to you, sweetheart."

Bursala clapped his hands together, and two guardsmen entered his private chamber. "How is the girl?" he asked.

"Bale is with her. She is awake. She laments for her homeland and for the pain that savage beast has inflicted upon her," one of the guards replied.

Bursala retrieved from his pouch the amulet and the knotted piece of plantain fiber he had taken from Bale. He stared out of his window to the lush hills of green and turned toward the guards. "That is all." He waved an arm in the air to dismiss them, and the two men returned to their posts.

Bursala continued to stare out at the starry night. Soon, she would be strong enough to head back to the Heart Clan—worse yet, to the gateway of her homeland. He knew in his heart that the time would come when he would have to bid the fair-haired maiden farewell. He held the objects in his hands. He had never met a woman with such fire in her soul. How could he let such a creature go like quicksilver slipping through his fingers? He would have to tell her what he was feeling, although she did not seem enamored with him. That made his desire for her all the more. He was King. Women were lined up waiting patiently for him. He could have anyone he wanted. He wanted her. Perhaps, he thought, he was attracted to her lack of interest. His thoughts were interrupted with an announcement of Bale's wish to speak to him. Bursala gave the order to bring him in and carefully placed Eden's belongings back into his pouch.

"Ah, yes, Bale. What is it that I may do for you? It is late. It is about Eden, I presume?"

"It is, Sire. Edi is sad in the heart. I see that she is getting better. I am afraid for her. Understand, Your Majesty, the arrival of Edi is a mystery to us all. Yallowahii found her down by the sea. Clearly, she is not like the people of this land."

"Clearly," Bursala responded.

"Yallowahii has named her the Spirit Walker of our people. A very long time ago, he was sent to us in the same fashion. She is sacred and must be guarded and protected. That is why I offered to marry her."

"So you have explained." Bursala put his fingers together and looked up. "Why, then, do you come to me? What can I do for you? Ali has given her the best of care. I have opened my Kingdom to you and this one you call the Spirit Walker."

"She has been raped by a man of the Clan." Bursala's eyes widened as Bale continued, "If it is in accordance with you, I was wondering that perhaps Ali could make a concoction to wash away the evil that this fiend has delivered to her. Then, I feel, it will be time for us to depart and head back to our village."

Bursala thought for a moment. "This Kingdom is not suitable for you?" His expression petulant, his tone somber.

"Oh, no, Sire. Quite the contrary. Your Kingdom is that of grandness. It is time for her to travel, I feel."

"I cannot let you go." Bursala turned his back on Bale and placed a hand on his pouch.

Bale was confused. The King had been cordial and charitable up to this moment. Bursala's voice softened as he turned to face Bale again.

"It is like this, Bale. I do not believe that Eden is well enough for such a journey. It is her welfare that I am thinking of."

"I appreciate that, and I do tend to agree. She is not very well at all—emotionally or physically. I was thinking that perhaps one of your horsemen could ride her back, and I will ride my camel beside them. Once we reach our village, Sava will care for her. And when she is better and stronger, I have promised her that I would try to find the way back to her homeland."

"One of my horsemen?" Bursala raised an eyebrow. He threw his head back and laughed. His demeanor changed quickly to that of seriousness. "I suppose it has never occurred to you that perhaps you ask too much from your King?"

Bale shifted his weight awkwardly from one leg to the other and lowered his eyes. "Perhaps, I did not," he whispered.

Bursala studied Bale's face and held his gaze. "I am only thinking of the lady. 'Tis all. I demand that she stays put until I feel that she is ready to leave. Your Chieftain has placed good faith in me. I do not wish to fail him. As far as Ali goes, I will see to it that he administers a powerful ale for the cleansing of your Spirit Walker. That is all, Bale." Bursala folded his arms across his chest. Clearly, the conversation was over.

Bale let out a small sigh. "You are the wisest of all men. I do not wish to disobey your command."

After a few moments, Bursala peered over his shoulder to make sure that Bale was gone. He had not intended to be so severe with him. However, he could not bear the thought of releasing Eden from his chambers. Not yet...

The Manhunt

The Village Elder's eyes opened to the sight of a frantic Mazi standing at his bedside. "Yallowahii, sir, wake up...wake up!"

"Mazi, what is it? Is it Una?"

"No...no, it is nothing like that." Mazi took a deep breath and blurted out his words. "It is Jita! He is gone!"

"Gone? Mazi, what are you saying to me? Last night, Sava and I set his body on fire. There was no way for him to escape. I tied the vines around his hands and feet myself. I heard his cries. I watched him burn."

Mazi swallowed hard. "Sava and I went down into the woods this morning to collect his ashes. Sava sent me to tell you that there were no ashes to be found."

"Then they must have blown away." Yallowahii put his feet on the floor. The pain in his leg was insufferable.

"You do not understand. There were no ashes to be found, but there were tracks. Trails of a leopard that led from the tree into the thick of the wood."

"He is gone, Yallowahii!" Sava proclaimed.

Yallowahii studied the site. The tree had been burned to the ground.

Sava continued, "It is a mystery. The leopard ghost, I fear, may be stronger than we thought."

Yallowahii faced Sava and Mazi. "He is a danger to us all. He must be found. Mazi, make sure that one of our men takes the word to Bursala's fortress. Our Spirit Walker is in the greatest danger of us all."

The word of Jita's mysterious escape spread quickly among the Clanspeople. When the news reached Zinga and Kimu, Kimu kissed his bride goodbye and headed out to join the other men in the hunt.

"Please, be careful, Kimu," Zinga warned. "I could not bear it if anything bad was to come of you. You are very brave. Take my love with you, and I shall await your return."

"You and your sister should go to Una and comfort her. At a time like this, there is safety in groups," Kimu instructed.

Zinga nodded. Kimu, with all his fourteen years, left with a hunting spear and all the courage he could muster. After all, Kimu was now considered a true man of the Clan, and he would not let his fellow men down. Zinga and Bukiwa made their way across the grove to be with Una and Dahni.

"Mother, I want to go with Mazi," Dahni pleaded. "I am no longer a baby. I can be of great help to him."

Una shook her head. "Dahni, my son, you are big now; however, you are not yet a man. I need you here with me. I know what you are thinking. Mazi will return to us. You shall see."

Dahni did not believe her wholeheartedly. He wanted to. He had already lost one father and was not prepared to lose another.

Una could sense this in her young son. "Soon, my son, we will all be together. You and I and Mazi and the baby and your uncle Bale. You shall see."

Dahni's big brown eyes met his mother's. "I am frightened."

"Do not fear, child. Hush." Una cuddled her son closely. She could feel the baby moving inside of her. And while she embraced so much life, suddenly she was overwhelmed with a feeling of death.

Someone was going to die...

Zinga and Bukiwa appeared at the opening of Una's hut. They brought with them gifts of sweet potatoes and wild berries.

"Hello, Una, Dahni. Kimu said it was time for us to be together. How are you feeling, Una? You are looking well."

"Yes, I am fine." Una tried to cover up any fearful feelings she was experiencing. "Please come and join us. You are always welcome here. Kimu is right. It is time for all of the women of the Clan to be together. We must pray for our mates' safe return."

"It sounds so queer to me to think of Kimu as my mate. Una, tell me, how do you like being the mate of Mazi?"

"It is nice. It has only been a day, Zinga."

"I cannot lie. I must confess that I cannot wait for our marriage to consummate. I must wait for two more sunsets, and then I shall become a complete woman."

"And I want to know all about it!" Bukiwa reminded her.

"You will be going home to your mother and father," Zinga corrected her.

Una smiled at the girls. It was what she needed to take her mind off of the men who were in danger.

"Everyone must divide," Yallowahii commanded. "If we travel alone, we shall cover much of the land."

The men of the Heart Clan stood on top of a hill with the fire of the sun beating down on their backs. Each man packed with him his most prized weapon. The men split up and scattered themselves in different directions. Kimu decided to travel with Yallowahii, despite the Chieftain's words. He did not look well to him. He was very old, though very sharp in mind. He was faltering, his movements measured. Finally, though reluctantly, Yallowahii agreed.

The sun was fiercely hot, blazing high above the treetops. Each man moved cautiously, quickly, and silently on his hunt in search of the mad Jita—each man, secretly, in fear of what may lay ahead.

Kimu became Yallowahii's eyes and legs. The Chieftain would sit and rest a spell while the younger man combed the surrounding areas. Kimu moved quickly. His love for his new bride made him anxious to find Jita. Why, he would kill him with his own bare hands to protect her. The sooner he was found, the better. His desire for Zinga swelled up inside of him. The hunt could go on for days.

Kimu stood still. He heard a sound in the brush before him. He crouched down behind a shrub and grabbed hold of his spear. His eyes narrowed, and his heart beat fast as he waited breathlessly. The rustling sound grew closer. It was only a stray dog. Kimu stood to his feet, half relieved, half disappointed. He headed back to check on Yallowahii.

THE ESCAPE

Sanda took Bursala's meal to him.

"Dear sister," Bursala said after he had eaten, "come and sit with me. I would like to have a word with you."

Sanda adored her brother. When they were children, they spent hours together in the cornfields. There, surrounded by the lofty stalks, they shared their innermost secrets and childhood fantasies. Sometimes Junju would join them and make them laugh, as he was always the prankster of the family. Sanda always knew that Kiro would never become King. Even as a child, he was devious and stingy. Bursala was the prodigy of the family, and Sanda was in awe of him. She marveled at his intelligent wit and tremendous integrity.

Sanda, Bursala, and Junju spent a lot of their time together. Kiro and the other sisters were jealous of their bond, their pact, their unbreakable chain. They laughed at secret jokes and made up a language in code that only they could understand. The three hid themselves away from the others and found sheer delight in taking refuge in each other's company.

It was not always easy for Bursala. He had duties to fulfill, things he had to accomplish at such an early age. There was little time for him to be a child. Junju and Sanda always welcomed his companionship. They treated him kindly but gave him no special attention. This was what Bursala loved most about them.

Bursala was relatively close to all his sisters, yet it was Sanda whom he favored. The other girls fawned all over him. They were giggly and giddy and charming. Sanda had an inner beauty that touched him more. She was playful and not likely to fuss over her appearance as much. When she was a child, chasing the chickens and the pigs was among her favorite pastimes. Sanda was only two months younger than Bursala, which was possible because they were born to different mothers. They did not resemble each other so much on the outside. The insides, Bursala was convinced, were identical.

"What is it, Bursala? Why do you wear a frown upon your face today?"

"It is that enchantress. I cannot seem to get her image out of my mind. I am obsessed with her loveliness. She is the pinnacle of intrigue. She is all I can think of. Soon, Sanda, she will be well enough to travel back to her Clan." Bursala placed a hand upon his chin. "I desire her so."

Sanda's eyes sparkled like jewels. "She is so dissimilar from our people. I peeked in on her when she was asleep," she confessed. "What of Bale? The word is that he is to marry her."

"Hmmm, yes, so I am told." Bursala raised his drink of ale to his lips and then set it back down. "When I found her down by the water's edge, she looked like nothing more than a drowned river rat. I was not sure that she would live. Bale tells me that Yallowahii found her down by the sea, as well. There is a connection to this woman and the ocean, although the vision is not clear to me as of yet. Ali, as you already know, is a truly amazing medicine man. He worked his powerful medicines and magic on her, and every day, she lights up my Kingdom and holds a special place here." Bursala's shark eyes met his sister's. "Why was she placed in my path? I believe in destiny's fate, and we are told that everything happens for a reason. I fear that she does not like me very much."

Sanda laughed. "Bursala...you are King!"

"'Tis true," Bursala said sadly. "I am King. What good is all of this wealth and power if your heart is breaking and crying out for the love of someone who does not want you?"

Sanda studied her brother's incredible face. Did he not know how painstakingly handsome he was? She had never seen him so distraught. "Bursala, Bursala, dear brother, what can I say to you to make you feel better? Why don't you ask her to become your Queen?"

Eden lay on her side and thought about Yallowahii. She wanted to see him again, one last time before her journey. She wondered what Bale was doing.

Christmas Stars of Zanzibar

She thought about Bursala, the way his eyes haunted her. She gazed upon the entranceway of her room and was surprised to see someone watching her. "Who are you?" she asked.

"My name is Junju. I am the brother of Bursala." He moved toward her, and she noticed he had the same hauntingly soul-searching eyes. He lowered them to his tunic sleeve as it hung loosely without a limb to fill it. "I know I am ugly. Please do not be afraid."

Eden smiled. "Why, I was just thinking how startling your eyes are. I do not think you are ugly in the least."

Junju's face took on an ear-to-ear grin. "I hope I am not imposing. I had to come and see you for myself. There is so much talk of you throughout the Palace. Such chatter. You should hear everyone, especially Bursala. He was quite taken with you, and now I can see why."

"Thank you. You are very sweet, Junju."

"May I?" he asked and pointed to a spot on the floor. Eden nodded, and Junju sat cross-legged on the floor. "How has your stay been here at the Royal Enclosure? I know you are recuperating from an ordeal. I know you are not feeling well." Junju bit his lip and studied Eden's face. "You are extremely fascinating. For as long as I have lived in this land, my eyes have never seen anyone who looks quite like you. You remind me of a swan. All poised and graceful. And I am nothing more than the ugly duckling."

"Why do you keep referring to yourself as ugly?" Eden sat up on her elbow and leaned closer to him. "If you go around and tell everyone you are a ghastly sight, people will start to believe it. If you hold your head high, even on your lowest days, people will look up to you. They will admire you."

Junju thought about those words. "I have never heard such words. They make great sense to me."

He was friendly. He was funny and endearing. Eden liked him immediately.

Bale heard the laughter coming from down the hall.

"Bale, come here." Eden's eyes looked clear and bright, and her face was radiant. "Have you met Junju? He is such a delight."

"We have not been formally introduced. It is nice to make your acquaintance." He studied Junju's face. He had seen him from afar around the Palace, and he was amazed at how much, in fact, he looked like Bursala.

Junju's face was not quite as extraordinary but almost like a caricature of his younger brother's. In Junju's eyes, he sensed a spark of warmth and sincerity. There was a twinkle in them, like that of a child.

Junju beckoned Bale to come closer to him, and he lowered his voice, speaking in a tone that was just above a whisper. "My brother is a very kind man, though he would probably place his hands tightly around my neck if he were to hear what I am about to tell you."

Eden and Bale exchanged glances and moved in closer toward Junju.

"I heard that you, Bale, came to my brother and asked him for permission to take Eden back to your village. He does not want to let her go because… because…" Junju looked directly at Eden. "Because he is in love with you."

Eden's mouth fell open. "In love? With me? How could that be? We've only just met."

"It is true!" Junju nodded, his eyes were devoid of any hypocrisy. "Bursala could have any woman he wishes. It is you that he desires."

"This makes sense to me," Bale explained. "He spoke to me with such severity. I told him it was time for us to leave, and he would not hear of it."

"Yes." Junju was in agreement. "Please, I beg of you, keep this secret between the three of us, or Bursala will have my head." Junju watched Eden's expression change to one of terror. "I am only making a joke. Bursala is very tolerant of me. He has never laid a hand upon me. He is good and true. But this must remain a secret. "Do you understand me?"

Eden and Bale nodded.

"Now, I must leave you. I will be back shortly. Ali has a drink he has made for you, Eden. I will fetch it and bring it for you." Junju flashed a smile and left.

He returned shortly, carrying a potion in a hollow piece of wood.

"Drink, Edi. Now you will be free from any wickedness Jita has bestowed upon you," Bale coaxed.

Eden held the drink to her lips and drank. She did not truly believe that there could be a substance to wipe such fiendish memories away. She had to believe. It was all she had left in the world.

Junju sat on the floor and told funny stories that made Eden and Bale laugh. The sounds of their cackling echoed down the halls and into Bursala's ears. Above the hardy burbling of the two men, Eden's cachinnation was light and melodic, like music to the King's ears. It reminded him of a strand of bells or shells hanging from a vine blowing into the sea winds. When he walked into her room, a deafening silence fell among them.

"Please, by all means, continue your talk, Junju, as I am sure you are taking such delight in entertaining our guests."

"Brother, join us." Junju beckoned. "Yes, indeed. I was telling them stories. Like the time you were chasing the pig and you slipped and fell into a pile of its waste."

"Junju, I was just a child. I could not have been more than seven."

Junju's eyes danced. "And what about the time Sanda and I told you that we made you a delicious meal, and then later you realize you ate cooked worms, beetles, and leeches. I will never forget it. You were green for three sunsets."

Bursala did not seem amused by Junju's gossip, and a look of chagrin came over his face. "My dear brother, I am afraid that you are making me look like quite a fool in front of our visitors." He shot Junju an innocuous look.

"I think it is wonderful to laugh and feel happy again," Eden announced cheerfully. "Junju, I think you are quite a welcome distraction."

"Yes, a welcome distraction," Bursala repeated sarcastically. He was happy to see the gleam in her eyes, a gleam that was placed there by the gods. He felt as if he had waited all his life to see the sparkle in her eyes. Junju could always bring out the incandescent light in people. It was a gift he had possessed since he was born.

"Oh, Bursala, we are only having fun." Junju's playful expression changed to a grave one. "I have to be different. I have always felt the need to make up for my hideous deformity. Laughter replaces the ugliness. This I believe to be true."

Bale knew what it was like to feel different. All his life, he had lived a secret life, a lie so deep and forbidden it scared him. He liked Junju. He felt an immediate connection.

Junju stood, and his face brightened. "I will go now before my brother takes my head and puts it on a stick. It was such a pleasure. I believe, Eden, that laughter is the medicine you need. The horses need grooming. Though we have servants to do such things, I enjoy them so. The animal's love is very unconditional. I feel very at home in the stables. Look at me. I am rambling my tongue once again. Bale, would you like to come to the stables?"

Bale jumped to his feet and then sat back down. "I must stay with Edi."

"Go, Bale. Really. I am sure they have beautiful and exotic horses. Go with Junju. I am fine."

"Well, then, yes, I would like to go with you, Junju."

Bale and Junju exited the room, leaving Bursala and Eden alone.

Bursala felt his heart quicken to the pulse, yet he remained poised on the outside. He had never been left in her presence alone. There was so much he wanted to say to her. An awkward silence fell between them. They both spoke at once.

"Please, my lady, speak first."

"It is Junju. He is such a pleasure. He is truly a man with a free spirit and a good heart."

"I am amazed by him as well. His stories make me feel foolish, I am afraid."

"Do not feel foolish. You may be the King of Uganda, but you are real inside. My father would say to me never forget where you come from, because it is the place that makes you who you are today."

"Your father, he was a wise man." Bursala was struck by her friendliness. "You are looking well." Could he tell her that she was the most enchanting vision his eyes had ever seen? Could he tell her he wanted to place his hands upon her sweet face and kiss her long and hard? Could he dare express to her the desire he felt inside? That he wanted to hold her and make passionate love to her?

"Thank you. I do feel better. Your Majesty, I would like to take this opportunity to thank you for your hospitality and for your generosity; however, I have to tell you, I want to go back to see Yallowahii. He is very old and not feeling well. I know he must be worried about me. I feel so helpless here when, in fact, I could be there with him, tending to him and helping him." Her blue eyes looked into the darkness of his own.

"I cannot let you go. 'Tis true that you are looking better, yet I do not imagine that you are strong enough for such a journey. When Ali gives me the word, then, and only then, shall I release you." Bursala lied straight-faced and crossed his arms over his chest. "My dear, it is your health I am concerned for. Yallowahii would be most upset if anything were to happen to you. Rest now, my lady. We shall talk further, later." Bursala spun around on the heel of his foot and left Eden alone.

She was tired of being hushed. She sat up in bed and dropped her chin into her hands. She had to get to Yallowahii, and if she had to escape from Bursala's chambers...she would.

Late in the day, Bale came to visit with Eden. When he arrived, he immediately noticed a strange and pensive expression on her face. "Edi, what is it? Talk to me."

Eden placed a finger to her lips and motioned him to come closer. She whispered in his ear. "Tonight, we escape."

Bale's eyes grew full. "Escape?"

"It is time for us to be on our way. First, we must get to the village to see Yallowahii. Then we shall figure out a way for me to go home. I cannot do this alone, Bale. I feel well enough and strong enough only if you are by my side. You said you would protect me and guard me. I am pleading with you to take me home."

Bale delighted in living in the King's Enclosure. He too missed the tiny village by the sea with all his friends and family. However, he knew he was going to miss the magnificent Palace in all its splendor. Above everything, he was going to miss his new friend, Junju. Although they had just met, Bale could not remember a time he connected with anybody so quickly on the spot, except for Eden. For Junju, the feeling was mutual. Bale remembered his promise to her and spoke. "I apologize, Edi, if I have gotten so caught up in living like a King. Of course, you can count on me. I will think of a plan."

Eden and Bale acted as natural as possible for the rest of the day. They took their meals in private and in separate quarters, careful to roll their food into strips of bark cloth, which they hid beneath their tunics. Bale gave Eden instructions to follow. "Tonight, when the moon is at its highest summit of the sky, wait by your window, and I shall come to you. Do not sleep, Edi, for tonight, we shall ride."

She too would miss the confines of the Royal Enclosure. She would feel the absence of Junju and all the servants who had been so kind to her. Bursala's eyes weighed heavily upon her. They touched her deep in her soul—his esoteric look that he bestowed only upon her, his recondite aire. Yes, she would miss Bursala more than she dared to admit.

The Palace security was severe. There were at least two guardsmen in every room of the fortress. There were gatekeepers keeping posts on the outside continuously. Kingsmen surveyed the site. Escaping was not going to be a facile task.

Later in the evening, when all was quiet and still, Bale lay in his bed watching the clouds pass over the moon. He rose from his presumed slumber and met with the gatekeepers at his door. "I am having a difficult time sleeping," he lied. "The night is fresh and crisp. I am sure the evening air will help to clear my mind."

"Are you ill?" one of the men questioned. "I will fetch Ali."

"No. Please do not disturb him, as I know he is a busy man and needs his rest. It was a bad dream. I am sure if I walk through the garden and smell the wetness of the dewed grass, it will help me to ease my mind."

"Bursala does not like visitors to be strolling his land unaccompanied by a guard. I am sorry, Bale. We have strict orders to follow."

Bale smiled. "I understand. Please, join me, if you wish. I could use companionship on such a night."

"That is impossible. We are assigned to our posts." The guard who was talking turned toward the other. "Shall we let him walk in the garden?"

The other guardsman replied, "I am sure it would not be an issue. However, there is a condition. We shall let you pass if you give your word that you will only be a short while."

"I give to you my word."

Quickly and quietly, Bale went to Eden's window, looking over his shoulder all the way. He saw her yellow hair shimmering by the light of the moon. "Edi, Edi, it is I," Bale whispered to her. He braced one foot on the stone wall and held up his hand. She grabbed ahold of him and climbed down through the shadows of the night. The rays of the bright moon cast a glow like a lantern for the wayward midnight creepers. Hand in hand, they flew to the stables where Junju was waiting for them.

"Junju!" Eden sounded surprised.

Bale placed a leviathan hand over her mouth. "He is here to help us."

Bursala paced back and forth in his chambers. He was bothered over the harsh conversation he had had earlier with Bale. He had no claims on Eden. Perhaps he would tell her in the morning that she was free to go. Keeping her like a hostage would only make her despise him, and the thought of such an idea made Bursala shudder. However, there was a more important issue at stake. After the King had taken his meal, a messenger from the Heart Clan had arrived. The word was to be known that the savage who had tried to murder his beloved was on the loose and probably headed this way. Bursala had already conducted a manhunt for the sordid and feral beast. His command was to expropriate him and bring him back to the Palace, where Bursala would scalp him alive. He was prepared to lay down the claim for Eden's right to live. First, his men had to arrest him and take him into custody as his prisoner. He had not mentioned anything to Bale and Eden. As long as they were in the confines of his Enclosure, nothing would come to them. He would make sure of that.

Bursala thought it best to keep this secret under wraps, as he did not want to cause fret of any kind to Eden and Bale. Sleep was impossible. All he could do was think of the fiend at large.

The Chase

Christmas Stars of Zanzibar

The moon was rising, and darkness was unfolding all around the grassy plains. Everything was still and deserted. The short grass fields were the calving grounds for zebras, sheep, and hyenas. Jita knew he could have his pick of any of the wilderbeasts. He was feeling lucky and decided to wait for the blood of a human. He saw a gazelle through the heavy mist and thought it might be fun just to terrorize it, perhaps to its death. He whirled about and charged the graceful animal. He brought it to the ground with one fast swipe of his mighty claw. He zigzagged back and forth with his tail twitching nervously. He was hungry, but he would wait—wait for the creamy white flesh of a mortal.

Beneath the moon, the cat glided across the plains at a swift, smooth trot. His trim and muscular black body glistened beneath the African skies. His large, round yellow eyes were keen. His pupils contracted to narrow vertical slits with flecks as red as the flames that were igniting inside of them. He let out a bloodcurdling roar that pierced through the plains like the shrill scream of a train whistle. The mighty and powerful Jita was warning other predators that he was the ruler of the land.

He found a cave and dozed for a while. Every now and then, he would open his eyes and survey the land around him. Slowly, he yawned, taking great pleasure in doing so. He opened his jaws and extended his tongue, which was covered with sharp, pointed bumps that allowed him to lick the last bit of flesh from the bone of any animal he chose to feed upon.

It was believed by the Swahili people that leopards had breath as sweet as sugarcane. It was that very sweetness that drew other animals closer to him. The sweetness would then wear off, leaving the animal helpless to die in front of the ferocious cat. Jita nestled himself in the dark cave and fell asleep. For this night, he was going to have a splendid feast all for himself.

"We shall take these two horses," Junju whispered. "This one is mine. Bale, you and Eden take the other. They are saddled and ready for flight. Time is of the essence, and we must be swift. Now, listen to my plan…"

Junju instructed Bale and Eden to wait upon their horse. He lugged piles of hay away from the stable and out onto a field. He made dozens of trips until he was satisfied with the mound before him. He ran back to the stable, snatched one of the lit torches, and held it to the hay. Instantaneously, a blaze was ignited, and sparks of fiery flames rose into a conflagrant inferno. He stepped back, grabbed a chicken by its belly, and squeezed the animal, careful not to harm it but causing it to cluck and squawk wildly. He then threw the chicken back into the barn. Looking over his shoulder, he yelled, "Ready? Follow me!" Junju galloped past the comburent fire with Bale and Eden following.

"Hold on, Edi! Junju has gone mad, and we must keep up with him!"

The guards ran toward the fire with the thunderous sounds of horses blowing past them. "It is thieves!" one of the guardsmen cried. "Run and call for the King and his men!"

Junju, Eden, and Bale flew over the fence of the Royal Enclosure as the bounding gait of the quadrupeds beat as fiercely as their hearts. They were free! The three cheered and howled as they watched the lights of the Palace fall further and further away. By the time Bursala was notified of all the commotion, the three were well on their way.

"It was thieves, Sire. They flew right past here on two of your finest steeds. They cleverly set a fire to distract us."

"Did you see their faces?" Bursala demanded. He did not wait for an answer. He turned to one of his men. "Quickly, run and check on Eden and Bale. Be hasty about it," he commanded.

Sanda came running as fast as she could to her brother's side. "Bursala!" she said breathlessly. "It is Bale and Eden...They are gone. And Junju as well!"

Bursala placed his hands upon his sister's face. "No." He shook his head. Sanda's eyes pleaded with his. "No!" he screamed. Sanda handed him his bow and arrow and draped his cloak around his neck. In a moment, he was surrounded by an entourage of Kingsmen who were mounted on their horses and supplied with their finest weapons. Bursala ascended upon his horse and led his men. "Eden!" he shouted in fury as the wind whipped him across the face. "Eden!"

"Kimu, I am afraid that I cannot go on any longer. Listen to me, my son. Find the others. I do not want you to survey the land by yourself. You have a mate to think about, and I am worried about your safety. This is your first manhunt, and although you are now a man of the Clan, I feel very strongly that there is danger in the air."

"Chieftain, sir, I cannot let you go back to the village on your own." Kimu's eyes scanned the surroundings. "Jita is out here...somewhere. You are in just as much danger as I." The remote blare of a hunter's horn sounded off in the distance. "It is Sava. Perhaps he has found something."

The men of the Heart Clan met on top of the hill with spears at their sides and torches of fire in their hands. There was a gathering of thirty or forty of them, but no one had found any signs of Jita. Mazi was the first to speak.

"We have been out all day, and there has been nothing, not a trace nor a sign of the mad Jita. We have left our women alone in the village. I am afraid for their safety."

"Yes," Sava agreed. "Perhaps we need to divide. Some of us will go back to the village, and the others will continue the hunt."

"Yallowahii is in great pain. However, I am young and virile, and there is an unstoppable force inside of me that is pushing me to continue. Whoever wants to follow me, then do so. If I must go alone, I will," Kimu announced.

The men of the Clan nodded and talked among themselves until they came up with a fair decision of who should continue and who should turn back. It was agreed that Mazi and Kimu would be among the ones who would resume.

"Twenty men shall go, and twenty men shall stay. However, for those of you who are journeying forward, I must warn you. I had a vision earlier today, a vision I must share with you all. I do not think it is a man that you are looking for. In my vision, I saw a beast, a wild and ferocious beast like that of a true leopard." Yallowahii could see the terror in the faces of the men by the glow of their torches.

"It has not occurred to me that he could have changed into an animal. All this time, I was looking for a man!" Kimu exclaimed.

"As we all were," Sava added. "That is why our Chieftain is the wisest man among us. We must listen to what he says."

"Be prepared for anything." Yallowahii warned the men who were eager to conquer. "I will pray for all of you so that you will all be protected beneath the glow of the moon and return to our village as an intact Clan." Yallowahii clasped his hands together and looked out into the vast sky. "We must also pray for Bale and the Spirit Walker."

Blood Brothers

Junju, Eden, and Bale flew along the coastline at great speed. Eden held tightly to Bale, though she could feel her grip start to weaken. "May we rest a spell?" she called into Bale's ear. Bale slowed his pace to a trot and then finally came to a complete stop.

Junju called out to them, "We are not far enough."

"Edi must rest. For her sake, we must travel slowly. Let us splash some cool water on our faces to refresh us. Then we shall continue."

Junju moved closer to Bale. "My brother is not a fool. He is probably only paces behind us. He will be traveling with many of his men. They will divide, and one of them is bound to find us. The only way to outsmart them is to outrun them," he explained.

"I cannot." Eden sighed. She looked up at Bale. "What are we going to do?"

Bale felt confused. He knew she was counting on him. He also knew Junju spoke the truth. "Junju, your brother will be angry with you. Please, do not feel obligated to travel with us. I know the land rather well. I can take the responsibility of taking Edi back to my people. Turn your steed around, my friend. Tell them anything. Tell them we have simply vanished."

Junju looked hurt. "We are in this together."

Bale smiled. "I was hoping you would say that. Regardless, we are wasting valuable time, and our dilemma remains. Edi must rest."

Junju looked over his shoulder, expecting to see Bursala and his men at any given moment. "If the woman needs to rest, then we shall do so." Junju hopped off his horse, and with his one good arm, he helped Eden down. "This is why I would not make a good King. I am ruled by a foolish heart."

Eden walked toward the water and squatted. Her long blond tresses hung in front of her as she cupped the wetness to her neck and forehead. "Thanks, you two...for everything."

"Bale, if you ask me the only reason my brother would be angry would be because Eden was taken away from his quarters. If he finds us, I am sure he will be so delighted to find her he would overcome any such anger and simply just bring her back to his chambers."

"But then I would not get to see Yallowahii. And my family." Eden let out a moan. "I have such a long journey ahead of me."

"You must not be overwhelmed with such thoughts, Edi. You must take one step at a time. If you can accomplish one thing by sunset at the end of a period of time, you will have gotten so far. One step at a time. Look how far we have already gotten. You must not give up now."

"Bale, you are my strength." She looked him square in the face. "I do not know what I would do without you."

Junju watched as the two friends exchanged one of their frequent moments of friendship. "I must confess, it is peculiar and funny at the same time. For I have only known you both for just one sweet moment in time, yet I feel this strange closeness to you. It is as if we have been friends for a lifetime. Perhaps, it is because for the first time in my life, I feel as though I am not being judged on the way that I look or who I am or what I am not. I have been, for all of my life, different from the others. If I had been born to commoners, I would not be alive today. And that makes me sad because I would not trade this moment here with you right now for anything. It is the blood royal that flows through my veins that has saved my life, or so I thought. Somehow, oddly enough, as I sit here with the two of you, I feel like you have saved me a little. And I have saved you, as well."

Bale was touched by Junju's sincere words. "Friend, it has just dawned on me that the three of us truly do share a sacred bond, a feeling of nonbelonging. It is a critical emotion when you feel that you do not belong somewhere or to someone and that perhaps you are left all alone. Edi does not belong here. Just to look at her, it is obvious. I will never belong to a woman or have a child or a family at my hearth. You, Junju, should have been blessed with two good arms instead of one. Because of your deformity, you felt ugly and not worthy to call yourself Royal. We are unique, yet very much the same. I am confident that we shall all find our place. Though, at times, I must admit, it is difficult to see and understand when you are living with a heaviness in your heart."

"We shall be saved. We shall all be saved," Eden remarked.

"Bale, forgive me, why is it that you shall never marry a woman or have a child? I do not understand," Junju inquired.

It was at that moment Bale confided to Junju about his troublesome lifelong secret. "So, you see, I am not at liberty to pass judgment on anybody else," he concluded.

Junju stood, walked over to a nearby bush, and picked a large, plump berry. He then sat across from Bale. "Tonight, the three of us shall become united in a sacred bond of blood brotherhood. With this, we shall never be divided. We will always be joined with unspoken words, and nothing will ever tear us apart from one another. No matter what paths lie ahead, our roads will forever cross in unity." Junju withdrew his knife and cut the berry in half. He then pinched a mound of his skin on his stomach and made two profound gashes into his flesh. Junju dipped the two halves in his blood and then placed them in the palm of his hand. "This fruit is stained in the blood that runs throughout my body." He leaned forward and placed one half of the berry to Bale's lips and the other to Eden's. "We are people from different Clans, of different races and different heritages and different times. Tonight, we are united as one and the same."

Bale took the berry and swallowed it whole. Eden opened her mouth to receive the fruit and closed her eyes as she ate it.

Junju handed the knife over to Bale. He repeated the action in silence and held the berries in his own massive hands. "We belong to this night...and this night holds a special magic for us."

Junju and Eden consumed the berry that was covered in Bale's blood.

Eden lifted her tunic and held the cold stone blade to her own stomach. She flinched as she marked a generous incision into her flesh. She picked up the berry, sliced it in two, and covered the halves in the warmth of her blood. "Tonight, we are not so different from each other. Tonight, there is a feeling of finally belonging. Tonight, Bale and Junju, I am happy to receive you as my brothers." She then placed the berries into the mouths of her companions. The three sat beside the water like apprehensive drifters waiting to be rescued.

Sleep in Heavenly Peace

Christmas Stars of Zanzibar

Jita had been asleep in the cave for hours. He stretched out his front paws and licked them with his large, panting tongue. Suddenly, he was hungry, hungrier than he could ever remember being. It was the skin of the Spirit Walker he ached for. He peered out of the darkened cave and let out a yawn. His eyes adjusted immediately to the night, and flecks of red glowed from within.

His pace was sluggish as he sniffed the ground for the scent of man. His dilatory pace quickened as his desire to eat had enhanced. He heaved and gasped as a thick white foam dribbled from the sides of his mouth. The spotted cat pranced along the water's edge at an extreme and powerful speed. Jita's nine-foot-long, two-hundred-pound body was agile and graceful as he glided along the shoreline. His three-foot tail swooshed above the water, splashing him across his arched back. He stayed low to the ground as his front paws met his back ones in his fearless race and rapid chase for stealth. Jita's ears perked up as he heard the faint murmur of voices off in the distance. He crouched down close to the sand and quickly blended into his surroundings.

There she was, the cursed Spirit Walker. Jita's ferocious and insatiable appetite swelled from within. He remained motionless as the short, spotted fur on his back rose in anticipation. The imprint of the crescent moon over his right eye throbbed like a volcano ready to erupt.

One of Junju's horses sensed that there was a prowler nearby. The horse began to rear onto its hind legs with a spooked and terrorized look in its eyes.

"There is something out there," Junju whispered. "Quickly, mount your horses."

Junju leaped on top of his horse. Frenzied panic sent the horse high in the air, kicking sand.

Bale helped Eden onto their horse, which also became frightened and out of control. "Hold on, Edi!" cried Bale as he leaned forward and held on to the animal's neck.

Jita silently scaled a tree preparing for his brutal attack. He hunched his body upon a branch and dug his powerful claws into the bark of the limb, waiting to pounce upon his victim.

Out of the corner of his eye, Bale noticed movement in a branch above their heads. "Junju! Quickly! Grab hold of Edi and flee!"

Bale pushed her off the horse, and she tumbled to the ground. Simultaneously, as the leopard lunged toward them, Bale received the full impact of the beast while Juju pulled Eden up with his one arm, and together, they ran for their lives.

"Bale!" Eden and Junju screamed together.

The last thing Bale remembered was the shape of the crescent moon above the animal's right eye. "It is Jita!" Bale shouted loud enough for Eden and Junju to hear. "Do not let her watch, Junju. Turn around and run as fast as you can!"

Jita's sharp and mighty claws began to tear and slash into Bale's flesh. The sinister animal mauled and battered him, injuring and abusing Bale with every honed score of his paw. Jita, then seizing his prey by the shoulder, dragged Bale's body by his pointed teeth with the blood of his brother-by-marriage trickling down the sides of his mouth.

Bale tried to fight off the sordid beast as best he could. The untamed animal was too powerful, too wild, and too wicked to fight against. Jita dragged Bale up to the branch of the tree. With a powerful gnash, he sank his teeth into the weakened man, gnawing at him and butchering him. The mighty leopard slaughtered and massacred him until Bale's lifeless body hung from a branch of the tree, just like Wanyenya on the night she too was murdered.

Eden covered her eyes with her hands and cried into Junju's back. He cradled her beneath his arm. The only sound was the shrill, baleful wails and grunting yowls the leopard made as it howled up to the half-crescent moon, which hung low in the sky. Suddenly, silence filled the air. Everything seemed to come to a complete and utter stop. Eden lifted her head from Junju's shoulder and watched as Jita fell to his death with an arrow plunging straight through his heart.

Bursala sat on top of his Arabian horse, holding his bow.

Eden ran over to the tree, and with every ounce of strength left in her feeble body, she climbed until she reached the lowest branch. "Oh, Bale," she cried. "Please, Bale, you cannot die. I will not let you." She reached down and grabbed hold of his head and arms, which were draped over the branch, and laid him straight on the appendage of the tree. She did not think of falling as she crawled on top of him, cradling his massive body in her arms.

"Edi...E-d-i..." Bale breathed in her ear. "My time has come...Please do not be afraid for me..."

"No!" Eden cried. "I cannot let you go. Who will protect me? Take care of me? Listen to my words, Bale..." She held him by the shoulders, and his eyes opened for a moment. "You must hold on. You must, Bale. You have taken care of me. Please let me take care of you." Her eyes locked into his. Big, strong, gentle Bale. She placed her warm face next to his and traced the features of his face with her fingers. Her tears covered him, falling like the rain from the heavens. She could feel his rapid breathing heaving against her chest. "Three hearts cannot be wrong, my friend. You and I and Junju made a pact, only moments ago. We promised that we would always be together."

"E-d-i...I...will...always...be...a...part...of...you..." Bale's final words trailed off, and his body fell limp beneath her touch. His head cocked to one side, and with her fingers, Eden closed his eyes. She would never look into those eyes again. Eden buried her face in his chest and wept.

Sleep in Heavenly Peace

Sleep in Heavenly Peace

Bursala climbed up the trunk of the tree and held his hand out to her. "Come." He motioned. "Take my hand; it is all right." His eyes were comforting and inviting. "Please, come to me." Bursala helped Eden down from the tree, and she ran to Junju, who threw his arm around her and cried.

Bursala's men came charging over the horizon and gathered around the tree of death. Bursala touched Bale's hand. "You are very brave, Bale. I was honored to have a man like you stay in the confines of my Kingdom. My promise to you, my friend, is that I shall help Eden find the gateway to her home. I give to you my solemn word. We are all going to miss you."

Bursala instructed one of his men to throw up a piece of bark cloth, which he wrapped tightly around Bale's body, covering him from head to foot. He then tied the body with twine and lowered him down to the ground to two of his men standing beneath the tree. Bursala jumped down from the branch and landed in the sand. "We shall give him an honorable burial, for Bale was truly an honorable man." His voice was filled with remorse. "If only I had arrived seconds sooner, perhaps I could have saved his life. I am deeply sorry."

Junju ran to him and fell into his arms. "Brother, I apologize for deceiving you. If I were not such a fool, this would have never—"

"Hush, Junju." Bursala held him close. "For the first time in your life, you acted with courage and bravery. Perhaps, I am the one who should apologize. The way you saw it, you had no other choice." Bursala bowed before Eden. His heart ached for her, for the sadness she was feeling.

Eden collapsed in front of the King. Her body rocked back and forth, filled with grief. "What will I do without him? It was ironic because I was prepared to say goodbye to him. Now...I do not think that I can go on."

Bursala placed his hand under her small and dainty chin. "I will help you. I will take you to Yallowahii. My men will transport Bale. Then..." Bursala's eyes brightened beneath the glow of the moon and the stars. "When you are ready, I will find the gateway to your home." Bursala gently touched the silkiness of her hair. "Believe me when I tell you that my heart cries out to your heart. Soon, my lady, you will be home, and this will seem like a dream to you. I promise."

Bursala stood to his feet and affectionately kissed Junju on his cheek. "Go home, big brother, as we prepare for a journey to the village by the sea."

The last traces of the night were beginning to fade, and the start of dawn was upon them. Bursala clapped his hands together and gave a command to two of his Kingsmen. "I want this beast burned at the stake. Take his ashes and discard them." He softened his voice and spoke directly to Eden. "It is time to ride."

"Kyojo, Taki, Jaleel, ride with Junju and escort him back to the Royal Enclosure. Do not argue with me, Brother. Now go. I shall ride with the lady."

Junju did not argue with Bursala. He looked deeply into Eden's eyes. "I know in my heart that you shall make it back to your homeland someday. I will miss you. I will miss Bale. You, Eden, are a true Queen, because the blood Royal runs through your veins now, as Bale's blood runs through mine and yours. He will always be alive inside of us. He spoke the truth when he told you that he will always be with you. Walk with the Spirits, Eden. Go with the gods."

Eden held him close. She was going to miss him too. She could not think of anything to say. Words seemed unimportant. She kissed him goodbye and wiped the tears from his face. Bursala guided her over to his horse.

Eden took one last look at Bale's covered body. The Kingsmen had placed him on a bed of tree trunks and covered him with leaves. They would take a different route and travel at a slower pace. For it is believed that if a dead man was transported in isolation, his journey would be a peaceful one.

Bursala mounted his steed and held out a hand to Eden. He lifted her up with great ease. She was exasperated. Eden rested her head upon Bursala's strong back and held on to his chest as they galloped away. Not one word was exchanged as the gold and silver morning unfolded all around them.

Taking Leave of the Dead

Yallowahii stood outside of his hut and reached down to feed the chickens. It was the earliest part of the morning, and already the sun was ablaze in the sky. He cupped his hand over one eye and watched as a horse with two people neared his village.

As he stood shakily on his feet, a thin and weathered smile crossed his face, and he realized it was his very own Spirit Walker. She was riding with the King! He waited patiently for them to draw near, and when they did, his smile faded as he searched the dark look she wore upon her face. Bursala helped her down off the horse, and she fell into the old man's arms.

"What is it, child?" He held her at arm's length and looked around. "Where is Bale?"

Bursala stepped forward. "I regret to inform you, sir, that Bale has moved onward and forward into the next state. I am deeply sorry for your loss."

"It is true," Eden blurted out with tears streaming down her weary face. "It was Jita. He came to us in the form of a leopard." She closed her eyes and relived the moment. "He was ugly and horrible, and he..." She took a deep breath. "He murdered our Bale."

Yallowahii closed his eyes. "Not Bale, please tell me it is not so."

"She speaks the truth. The leopard is dead. I destroyed him with a poisonous arrow that targeted his heart. My men are burning his carcass to dust, as we speak. No longer will he be a threat to your people. My entourage will follow shortly. I will personally see to it that Bale has a proper funeral."

Yallowahii managed a low, feeble bow. "Your Majesty, I am saddened by such talk. Bale has been like a son to me. We will all miss him deeply. I thank you for bringing the Spirit Walker safely to our village."

"Please." Bursala extended his hand. "Do not make such a fuss. It is I who should bow down to you. You were a friend of Suna's, my beloved father. He has told me many great tales about you." Bursala helped Yallowahii to his feet.

"Yes, I did know Suna well. And you, Bursala, have grown to be such a magnificent man, like your father. I can see that you will lead our people in his footsteps and care for the people of the land." Yallowahii studied the noble face. "It is your beguiling mother, Chamundeshwari (pronounced Kom Oonda Saharee), that you resemble."

The Chieftain placed his hands on Eden's face. "My child, it is such a tragedy that we lost one of the most upstanding men of our Clan. We will miss him terribly. Yesterday, he was a child at play. How fast the years have flown. Now he is gone. I cannot envision life without his gentle and kind ways."

"I will leave you now. I bid you farewell." Bursala climbed up on his horse and held his gaze over at Eden. She looked sad and lost in the pale morning sun. He dreaded leaving her; his heart craved her. However, he knew she wanted to be alone with Yallowahii.

"Come, child." Yallowahii took Eden's hand. "You are home now."

Eden watched as Bursala faded into the morning, with his long black hair blowing wildly behind him. She was going to miss the palace with all its drama. Junju. He could never be ugly to her. Bursala's eyes—they would always crush her. Eden felt her chest tighten, and her body grew heavy as she thought of Bale's smiling face. How happy he was at the Royal Kingdom. His peculiarity never frightened her. It was his kindness she would never forget. Eden looked up at the sun and thought it had no right to shine. How dare it rise over the horizon as if nothing had changed. She took Yallowahii's hand in hers and leaned upon him with a weighty soul. The old man was stronger that moment than he had ever been in all his ninety years. And on that sad, sad morn, the Spirit Walker and the Chieftain headed for home.

Later that day, for the very first instant upon opening her eyes, Eden's mind was blank. When that first instant passed, she was consumed with an abundance of sadness. She remembered his last words to her…"Edi, I will always be a part of you…"

Her hut seemed smaller than she had remembered, and she glanced around. She could envision Bale standing there, holding handfuls of fruit and smiling down at her with his head hitting the thatched ceiling. Yallowahii saw she was awake and moved closer to her.

"I feel like this has all been a bad dream."

"It is a dream, for now Bale glides along with the *Christmas Stars* up in the heavens," Yallowahii replied.

"Where are you going?"

"I must go to Una and Sava and the others. They must be told, Eden."

"Then I will come with you. Do not leave me, Yallowahii. Do not leave me ever again."

When Yallowahii and Eden arrived at the hut of Una and Mazi, they heard the woeful cries coming from within. Una turned toward them with eyes red and swollen. "I saw you riding with the King. Tell me, what has happened to my brother? Do not spare my feelings. Just talk to me."

Yallowahii started to speak.

"No, let me," Eden whispered. She walked over to Una, afraid of her still, yet so full of compassion for this distraught woman. "Una, Bale and I were staying with the King. It was all my fault, I am afraid. I convinced Bale to escape, not knowing that Jita was ready to attack. He was after me, I am certain. Your brother died a hero. I know these words do not comfort you, and I am sure your hate for me will only intensify. I am so sorry. I loved him, as well."

Una glared at Eden and turned her face away. "How did he die?"

Eden closed her eyes and saw the ferocious beast mauling and sabotaging her friend. "He died in battle."

Christmas Stars of Zanzibar

Mazi and Dahni watched Una as she turned around to face the Spirit Walker. Mazi was sure Una would slap her. He ran to her side, also startled by the news of Bale. The thought of Bale dead was more than he could bear. Dahni sat in a corner and cried. Yallowahii knelt beside him and comforted the child.

The tears were streaming down Una's face as she spoke. "Bale loved you, too," she said quietly. "All of my life," Una began, "I have been cursed. First, it was Keswa and then Wanyenya. Now it is Bale who was killed by my own flesh and blood. Jita was an evil man. He filled my head with malicious lies, and I, like a fool, believed him." She looked into Eden's eyes. "Understand this if you can: it was easier for me to believe Jita than to face the death of my young sister. Hate is an easier emotion than acceptance. I have misjudged you, for that I am sorry. However," Una began to wail, "nothing will ever bring my brother back. Nothing."

Eden wanted to hold this woman whose pain was so immense. She noticed, for the first time, how much Una resembled Bale.

"I would like to be alone, now, with my mate and my son. They are distraught as well. I must remain strong for the sake of my baby. Bale would have wanted it that way."

"Una has every reason to despise me," Eden said sadly as she and the Chieftain walked through the village. "Yet, I saw something in her today, a part of Bale inside of her, which I had never seen before. There is a strength inside of her that is very powerful. I did not take one moment to try and get to know her. Bale spoke highly of her. I should have known all along that she was a good woman."

"Una did a terrible thing to you down at the ocean when you first came to us. I do not blame you for thinking that she was evil. She is not. Her pain has been burdensome. You cannot take the blame for Bale's untimely death. The Spirits have called him. It was his time. This we must believe. The Mighty One works in a mysterious way. We are not equipped to understand or make sense of it. We must simply accept it even though our hearts are breaking."

Bursala's Kingsmen came galloping over the horizon. Two of the men carried Bale's body into the sleeping quarters of his hut. There they removed the bark cloth and laid him out on his bed. They crossed his arms over his chest. His legs were straight, and his two big toes were tied together with vines. Bale's throat and chest were so severely mauled they were covered by the thickness of leaves. While the Kingsmen prepared him for his funeral, the Clanspeople gathered outside to pay their last respects to brother, uncle, Clansman, and friend.

When the signal was given, everyone crowded into the small hut. There was a line of people waiting outside to view his body. Una wailed loudly and uncontrollably as her eyes fell upon him. Mazi and Dahni stood on either side of her, holding her as she cried. The women of the Clan beat upon their breasts and wept. It was believed that if the females of the tribe hit their fists to their chests the action would pacify the ghost of the deceased. The harder they hit themselves the better it was for the Spirit of Bale.

Sava placed pumpkin seeds in the palm of Bale's hand. Dahni removed them with his lips, and after chewing them, he blew them over his uncle's body. A pot of butter was placed near Bale's head, with some sponges made from the core of the plantain stem. Each member of the Clan rubbed a smudge of butter on Bale's forehead and then wiped his or her hand on one of the sponges.

"This ceremony," Yallowahii explained to Eden, "is called *'Taking Leave Of The Dead.'*"

The cries and grunts of the Clanspeople grew louder and more intense until they became somewhat of a chant. Eden stood next to Zinga and squeezed her hand tightly. The members of the Heart Clan stood around Bale for the remainder of the day.

As dusk began to fall, it was the duty of the men to dig the grave. The ditch was made wide and deep because many layers of bark cloth were placed in it for Bale's final sleep.

Kimu, Mazi, and Sava stood in the grave as the body was handed to them. Dahni stepped down into the site and was handed a knife with which he cut off the corner of the veil that covered Bale's face. Some of the women smeared ashes upon their breasts, and the ones who chose to do so had to abstain from sexual relations. Una and Zinga were among the women who did this.

Drums were beaten in intervals by the younger boys of the Clan as the women wailed to the music, sending eerie sounds to fill the air.

The relatives of Bale had to cut grass in order to thatch the grave. They first beat the earth and made the mound smooth and then polished it with wine. A layer of grass a foot thick was then laid upon the burial pit, and four stakes were driven into the ground at the corners to keep it up. The grass was tied down with rope to keep it from blowing away. Wine was then brought again to the grave; all the members of the Clan partook, and a quantity was poured at the head of Bale's resting place.

Yallowahii then spoke to his people in these words: "We, the people of the Heart Clan, are gathered here today to share in the deepest sorrow known to any man. My good friends, I hardly know what to say, for today I am at a great loss. I am the Clan Elder. Every day when the sun comes up over the horizon, I find myself amazed that I am there to greet her. I have seen and I have lived. So that when I am called to my Creator, I will accept it. Welcome it. Embrace it. At times, I wish for it." Yallowahii shook his head sadly. "Why then Bale? This, people, I do not know. In my eyes, I can remember him as a child. Quieter than other children. He would pretend with this imaginary mind of his." Yallowahii looked over at Dahni. "A boy of eight, like you, my son. Full of life, hopes and dreams. Bale has always touched me." Silence filled the air as he continued, "He grew into a man, a man with a gentle spirit and kind ways. Mazi, you were a great friend of his. Two brothers could not have been closer. To lose a friend so loved is frightfully devastating. There is a celebration of life that needs to be shared. It is a true sadness that your right to do so has come to an end." Yallowahii's eyes moved over toward Una. "He was your brother, woman. You never understand the way love dies until your heart has been tortured. Yet, this child that you carry is one small glimmer of hope for our future. We must not forget this. Your sorrow is felt by us all. Your pain is complicated. Bale now walks in the Spirit World."

Yallowahii looked at Eden. "We have known Bale a lifetime, yet some of us have only just met him. He had the quality to love in an instant, for he knew the good that people possessed. Bale could love quickly and hard. There was never any time to lose, for time was precious to our dear friend. Spirit Walker, he loved you with all his heart.

"Bestow in your heart this abundant loss to us all. We look forward to a reunion with him and the others before him in the next state. When Mungu calls our name, we shall follow Him, and we shall rejoice in His glory."

Yallowahii held his hands high in the air. In them, he held a water globe. As he shook it, Eden could see the tiny snowflakes whirling about. She tried to focus her eyes clearer. There were three letters inscribed into the wooden base: POE for *"Peace on Earth"*! She remembered. There seemed to be figurines in the center...the Holy Family? But how could this be? The water globe from the department store...here? It was not possible.

Eden rubbed her eyes and looked back at the object in the Chieftain's hands. It was nothing more than a simple pitcher inset onto a block of wood filled with salt water and tea leaves. She could hear Bale's voice, so loud and clear: "Do not be afraid, Edi. I will always be a part of you. This I promise."

As Yallowahii sprinkled the water over the grave, Eden fled from the graveside. Her breathing heaved inside of her chest. She ran down to the orchid grove, leaned against a tree, and slid her body down to the ground. Her hair fell forward, covering her face. Something on the ground caught her eye, something glistening. Her fingers reached out to touch it. It was her amulet and the knotted piece of fiber.

"This belongs to you."

Eden brushed her hair away from her eyes and looked up. It was Bursala's silhouette in front of the sun.

"Please, allow me." He helped her to her feet and fastened the amulet around her waist. She threw the piece of rope over her shoulder.

"Why, Eden, do you do such a thing? Clearly, it was of some great significance to you."

"Yes, at one time, I suppose it was. How foolish of me to think that perhaps there was a way for me to go home."

"So, you have given up. You surrender just like that." Bursala snapped his fingers in front of her face, causing her to blink.

"Without Bale, I am afraid I have lost my hope, my desire, and my will."

Bursala shook his head sadly. "Bale would not want you to talk this way."

Eden changed the subject quickly. "You have saved my life. Thank you."

"No, Eden, it is you who has saved mine. However, I was too late in rescuing Bale from that beast."

"You would have." Her response was quick. "This place will always remind me of Bale, how lucky I was to know such a man."

"As was I." Bursala squinted his eyes up to the setting sun. "I have come to pay my respects and also to bid you farewell. My duties take me far and away for quite some time."

"Where will you go?" Eden asked, looking into the most gallant face she had ever seen.

"My canoes are ready to set sail to the island of Karagwe. There, my men and I shall trade goods. Cotton and calico grow plentiful there. Perhaps a wrap of calico would help to cheer you?" Bursala reached out his hand and touched the silken threads of her hair. "There is a woman there who I am to meet. A daughter of a friend of my father's. It has been explained to me that she may become my Queen. I am to meet with her. It is funny how my entire life is so set up for me. I do not even know this woman, and yet I am supposed to love her and bring her here to my land."

Eden looked down at her bare feet in the grass. "She is a very lucky woman."

Bursala was touched by her sentiment and allowed himself to laugh. "I know what I want. It is not some woman on a faraway island. Look at me, Eden."

Her eyes lifted to meet his.

"My dear, I am ambitious as well as able. I shall return when the sun is high in the noon sky of the tenth day. Then I will help you to find the gateway to your people. Come to me, Eden. Let me at least hold you once in my arms."

She was hesitant at first. She walked slowly toward him and laid her head upon his shoulder. He nestled his face in the mane of her windblown hair and drew in its herbal aroma. He could have stayed there a lifetime, locked with her in an emotional embrace.

"Eden, we have all suffered terrible and tragic losses in our lives. I know and understand how you are feeling. When I was a baby boy, all of two years of age, I lost my first mother...my real mother." Bursala's long lashes were moist as he talked. "Evanli is my sister. My oldest sister. She has cared for me like a mother and loved me like a mother. Since I was a child, I have always looked over my shoulder in hopes of seeing her again. All of my life when I looked, I found myself alone." Bursala gazed up to the sky and shifted his jaw to one side. "Yet, I have never given up hope. For all of my days, I have been reared to become King, and yet, I feel I have never found a sense of belonging. Sometimes at night I have dreams of an embrace. Everything about those dreams is bright and warm. I believe it is my mother holding me near, holding me close. When I awake, I cannot remember her. Eden, aside from my family, who know the truth, you are the only one I have ever told this story to. I want you to see me as a man, not a King. I have let you inside a private place in my heart." Bursala smiled. "That woman in Karagwe, she will never know what I feel. I do not even know her, and I am ambivalent toward her."

A peculiar expression came over Bursala's face. He stared up at the twilight skies for a long time, and then he took Eden's hands in his. "Did you hear that?" he asked. Eden shook her head. "It was Bale. It was as if I heard his voice in the wind. He is with you, Eden; he will always be with you." He took a step back and drank in her beauty. "I gave Bale my solemn word that I would help you." He picked up the knotted piece of plantain rope and placed it in her hands. "I am a man of my word. I will go now." He turned to walk toward his horse and looked over his shoulder. "I shall miss you!" he called.

Eden held the piece of rope to her heart. She watched him gallop out of view. "And I shall miss you too," she whispered.

Part Two

New York (Present Day)

CHRISTMAS STARS OF ZANZIBAR

Benjamin Salina woke early and headed downstairs for breakfast. He made a glass of chocolate milk and grabbed a handful of graham crackers, which he stacked and balanced on a paper plate. He pulled the coffee table close to him, and with the remote control, he turned on the Disney Channel. The vertical blinds that covered the French doors that led to the backyard were open. The winter's light was gray and dim, and the snow cast drifts against the panes of glass.

Ben wiped his mouth with his sleeve and remembered how much his mom hated when he did that. Something out of the corner of his eye caught his attention. He walked over to the double-hung doors and pulled the blinds back. Ben's mouth dropped open as he yelled for his father.

"Dad, Dad, wake up!" Ben charged into his parents' bedroom and began to shake and shove his father. "Come downstairs! Quick!"

Frank opened his eyes and glanced at the digital alarm clock on the nightstand. Seven o'clock. Man, it was early. "Benny, what is it? Is it your mother?"

Benjamin shook his head. "No, Dad, but I think you better follow me."

Frank followed his son down the stairs and over to the doors. A heap of snow covered the ground, and there was that familiar winter's hush blanketing the dismal morning.

"Dear God in heaven!" Frank exclaimed. "There's a man out there!"

Ben peered out from behind his father. "He looks like he's hurt, Dad, or maybe even dead."

"Benny, call 911!" Frank called over his shoulder as he hopped and balanced on one foot, trying to put on his hiking boots. The bitter chill penetrated right through his flimsy pajamas as he crouched down to take a look at the strange man. Frank's first thought was that he was homeless. His skin was swarthier than any complexion he had ever seen before. The black skin against the shimmering brightness of the snow was as contradictory as the day was to the night. This person was covered in a thin, white cotton gown that was spread over his vast body, and as Frank moved closer, he saw that he was still breathing.

"Dad, the blizzard knocked the phone lines out again. Should I get some blankets?"

Frank nodded and studied the mysterious man. "Where on earth did you come from?"

Ben ran to his father's side and handed him blankets he pulled from the hope chest. "I think he's in shock, Dad. In Cub Scouts, we learned about this kind of thing. You should cover him and raise his feet and turn him over to his side." Ben instructed his dad and looked up at the sky. "Do you suppose he fell from up above?"

"No, I don't. We must get him to a hospital. I'm afraid to move him; I don't think I could if I wanted to. Keep him covered as best you can. I'll run and get Annie. She's a nurse; she'll know what to do."

Ben watched as his father darted across the snow. Frank had aged a little during the last weeks. His dark golden hair was highlighted with a few strands of coarse "tinsel," as he called it. "Cut your hair, Dad," the kids teased. "Long hair went out in the seventies." A couple of lines had formed around his eyes. He looked weather-beaten, like a piece of driftwood left out on the beach.

Ben remained still as he observed the peculiar man. Maybe he was a rapper like DaBaby. That would be awesome.

Frank punched Annie's doorbell several times until she answered with a yawn. "Frank, it's so early. Is it Eden? Have you heard something?"

"No, and I'm sorry for waking you. Someone needs medical attention. Is your phone working? Damn storm knocked my line out again, and my cell is dead. Call for an ambulance. And hurry!"

Frank guided Annie into his yard and lit a cigarette. "We don't know who he is. Benny found him here in the snow. I don't know how long he's been here. It could not have been too long, or he would have frozen to death."

Annie reached for the foreign medallion he wore around his neck. "He's so big!"

"Maybe he's a basketball player!" Ben said excitedly, thinking to himself that would be just as cool as a rapper.

"He's burning up," Annie said as she placed her hand upon his forehead. "Sir, can you hear me? You are going to be fine. We are going to get you to the hospital. Please hang on." She spoke loudly.

Frank paced back and forth and ran his fingers through his hair. "Can things get any weirder around here?"

Tara and Nicholas pressed their faces up against the glass panes of the doors. "Who's that, Daddy?" Tara asked.

"Is he dead?" Nicholas wanted to know.

Frank came inside and stomped the snow from his boots. "No, sweetie. He's not dead, but I think he is very, very sick. We're going to help him, and everything's going to be fine...just fine."

The Salina family somehow got through Christmas with a tree and presents, though the heartache they felt for their missing mother engulfed them with a heavy sadness. They got through the New Year with high hopes that a fresh beginning would reunite them back with Eden.

Annie and Dean were there every step of the way, offering their support and love by babysitting and sending over hot home-cooked meals. Annie missed Eden terribly. Not a day, not one single moment, went by when she didn't think about her friend who had mysteriously disappeared. Their evening jogs at the track, the constant phone calls...even though they were only two houses apart, popping in on each other. Annie missed the sisterly companionship that only Eden supplied her with, the meeting of the minds that only best friends shared.

Frank interrupted his nervous shuffle long enough to bend down to take a better look at the unfamiliar man who was probably dying in his backyard. Something so strong took hold of Frank—a feeling so compelling that it inundated him. The icy January winds whipped across his face and blew the long strands of hair away from him. "Who are you? And why are you here?" Frank's voice was as forceful as the blizzard's gales that blasted through him. He didn't seem to notice the glacial rigidness as he watched the man lie still in the snow.

Annie watched Frank. She was worried about him. He looked as unraveled as a ball of yarn in the clutches of a skittish kitten. Her thoughts were interrupted as a team of paramedics exploded onto the scene.

Frank turned toward Annie. "I'm going with him. Stay with the kids," he called out. He followed the body lying upon the stretcher.

"Frank!" Annie yelled out. "You're still in your pajamas!" It was too late. He was gone. Annie opened the French doors with Ben following. She took a deep breath and squared her shoulders. "OK, guys. Let's get you some breakfast."

At the hospital, Frank explained to the clerk at the admittance desk how he had found the man and that he did not know his name or anything about him. He took a seat in the waiting area. Jeez, he hadn't even dressed. After a while, a doctor in green escorted by a nurse and policeman took a seat beside him.

"He is in a coma. There has been extensive head trauma." He proceeded to explain that there were many different stages of a coma and that the stage he was in was certainly critical yet promising. "What really baffles me are the x-rays we have taken. The man's jawbone and skull region protrude in a fashion that I am not accustomed to. Almost archaic, like the bones of men who lived thousands of years ago." The doctor took off his glasses and wiped them. "He wears some sort of medallion that was constructed from shells and stones that are foreign and early...yet he looks to be about thirty years old. Mr. Salina, I am truly mystified."

Frank hung onto every word that fell from the doctor's lips in disbelief. None of it made any sense to him. "So what are you trying to say to me, Doctor? This man is from another dimension of time?"

"What I am saying, Mr. Salina," the doctor corrected, "is that this particular John Doe case must undergo further investigation. There is a lot of uncertainty. I have no answers." The white-haired man shook his head. A nurse and policeman explained to him their investigation procedures.

Frank watched as the doctor disappeared through swinging white doors. "OK. Uncertainty. Good word, Doc." A police officer on duty at the hospital drove Frank home.

Annie poured Frank a cup of coffee. "Annie, I just don't get it. What in heaven's name is going on around here? My wife is missing just like that. The cops have no leads on her whereabouts. And now I find a caveman in my backyard."

Annie listened as Frank rambled on about what the doctor had just told him. She studied his face as he spoke. He was incredibly handsome. His deep-golden hair glowed against his bronzed complexion. He was perpetually tan all year long, and the silver threads at the crown of his head glistened beneath the kitchen lights. He had inherited his light hair and eyes from his Irish mother and his dark skin and hot temper from his Italian father.

Annie cupped her coffee in her hands and took a sip. "You know, Frank, Dean and I have been talking. Why don't you take some time off? We're really worried about you."

Frank placed his hands on the kitchen table and leaned his weight upon his sturdy arms. His eyes blazed into hers. "I'm not crazy." He turned his face away, and one lone tear rolled down his cheek. Damn it. He didn't want to cry in front of her.

Annie stood and placed her arms around him. "Let it go, Frankie. Come on. Let it go. Cry to me. It's going to be alright." Annie's loving arms were a harbor; her gentle voice was peaceful and comforting to him.

He stayed like that for a long time with his face buried in her neck. His tears poured down his face like a little kid's. "I just want her home. I just wish Eden would come back to us." Frank sobbed.

Annie stuck around for most of the afternoon. She made sure the children had their lunch and straightened up the little country kitchen. "I've got to get to work. You'll be OK?" she asked, looking deep into his eyes.

Frank nodded and kissed her on her cheek. "Thanks, Annie, for everything. I know I've been a real mess lately. Hey," he added with a glint in his eye, "do you think you can check up on that guy and let me know what's going on with him?"

"Sure, Frank." Annie smiled and ran her fingers through the wealth of his sandy hair. She pinched his cheek affectionately. "I'll call you later."

He reached for his vape, closed his eyes, and took a drag. She was right. It was all going to be alright. Life had a strange way of working out. He thought for a moment about the words John Lennon had written in a song: "Life is what happens to you while you're busy making other plans." Those words made great sense to him at that particular moment.

Annie arrived at the hospital early. She got off on the second floor, the ICU. "Hi, Michaela. I wanted to check in on that John Doe case. Is this the weirdest thing to ever hit our hospital or what?"

"I'll say. He's still under. Dr. Charney reported some basic eye movements, but that's about it."

Annie bit her lip. "Michaela, see what you can do about changing my shift today. I really want to stay close to this man. My friend was the one who found him. You know, the one I told you whose wife has disappeared. He's acting mighty strange about the whole thing. But the more I thought about it, the better it is for him to concentrate on something other than his own problems."

Michaela nodded. "Tell the nurse on duty to change schedules with you."

Annie gazed down at the humongous man who had the entire hospital talking. He was breathing evenly without the help of a respirator, which was a hopeful sign. His skin was blacker than any other she had ever seen. Could he really be a primitive man? How could such a thing be so? His right hand began to twitch, which was a common involuntary spasm among coma victims.

Annie watched him closer. Poor Frank. She thought about his nervous energy. A smile came to her lips as she pictured him here in the hospital wearing his pajamas. Someday she would tell Eden the story, and they would laugh about it.

The man's hand twitch grew more rapid. Annie noticed that his breathing accelerated, and she heard a sound emit from his mouth. Annie reached her hand over the man's head and pressed the button to page Dr. Charney. She focused on him and spoke softly yet firmly. "You are in the hospital. You're going to be just fine," she said reassuringly in her comforting nurse's tone.

The man's eyes fluttered uncontrollably. He battled within himself to try to open them, but something was preventing them from seeing. 'I am in the after-state of Tunda, the space Yallowahii had told me about time and time again. There is a brightness so heavy...I cannot open my eyes to it. I am dizzy, and everything feels hazy. There is someone with me. Yallowahii? *No.* It is a woman. Edi! Edi! Is that you? It is me, Bale! Can you hear me? I am shouting! Edi! You cannot hear me. I am frightened...and yet I know I am not alone.'

Annie was edgy as she waited for the doctor. She pressed the page button again and watched as the man silently trembled.

'My beautiful family and friends. I can see you all so clearly. Look, it is me—Bale. Certainly, you could not have forgotten me already.' Bale watched from above his hut. He watched little Dahni blowing the pumpkin seeds from his palm. 'Dahni, boy, look up here. Una, Una, dear sister, please do not cry for me. It is not good for your child. Mazi. My friend. You are looking straight up at me. I see your familiar gray eyes; however, you are looking through me. No, Mazi, no. Please do not look away. Yallowahii...surely, if anyone can see me, it is you.'

Bale listened for a moment as Yallowahii spoke. He began to cry with gusto. Then he stopped. There she was. "Edi!" He called out her name. "Edi! Edi! Do not be sad. I am with you…I am always with you." Out of desperation, Bale screamed out to his King. "Bursala! Tell her I am right here. Please, Bursala, look up at me and give me a sign!" Bursala's face lifted to the sky. He stared up at the heavens for a lengthy time. Bale was sure they connected. Bale held his breath and whispered into the wind. "Bursala, tell her I am with her," he repeated.

Bursala looked away and held Eden's hands in his. "Did you hear that?" he asked.

Eden shook her head. "It is Bale. It was as if I heard his voice in the wind. He is with you, Eden."

Dr. Charney and a team of doctors and nurses burst into the room. "He looks so peaceful. But his hands were trembling. It wasn't your typical spasms. They were really shaking. I thought he was coming out of it," Annie explained. "I guess it was a false alarm," she added.

"Nurse Jurgens, you did the right thing," the doctor assured her. "Do not, under any circumstances, hesitate to page me," Dr. Charney announced as he turned to leave.

"Doctor…" Annie said in a small voice that was just above a whisper. "Something's happening."

Bale's eyes flashed open as he stared lethally into Annie's. The dark-haired girl who stood before him was dressed in white, though it was not the customary tunic he was familiar with. The bed he was lying on was not made of lumpy sacks of grain that he was accustomed to. The room was white and stark, with objects of silver that beeped and glowed. The bright article hanging over his head made his eyes hurt. There was an element of fear in his eyes that Annie had never seen before.

Annie smiled at him. "You probably cannot understand me. Please do not be frightened. We are here to help you."

"We are here to help you…we are here to help you…we are here to help you." Her words echoed inside his head. They were of no value to him. He did not understand. Bale's eyes left Annie's and focused on Dr. Charney. The doctor placed his stethoscope in his ears and placed it on Bale's chest. Bale scurried down to the foot of the bed and positioned his gangly body in the fetal position. He began to whimper and cry and babble words in a foreign language that sounded like a chant. The man to the left of Dr. Charney was taking notes upon his clipboard.

"This will not hurt you." Dr. Charney took the stethoscope and held it up in the air. "It is a device to listen to your heart."

Bale could not understand. He kept his head down between his legs so he didn't have to make eye contact. His body was so large that it was hanging over the sides of the bed. His massive body rolled off, and with a startling thud, he fell to the floor. Like an enormous fiddler crab, he crawled to the corner of the room and sank down low with his hands over his face.

"We'll have to sedate him." Dr. Charney turned toward Annie. "Mellaril, two hundred milligrams, IVQ4."

The floor was cold and hard. There were no sweetgrass coverings to cushion his fall. Bale hid behind his hands. He was as frightened as a child who was lost in the woods.

Two more nurses entered the room. It took six people to hold him steady while Dr. Charney administered the shot. Bale's arms and legs were kicking and flailing about as he let out a shrill scream. Finally, his body fell limp as the medication began to take effect. Bale's body floated into a dream. A dream so beautiful...so peaceful. He, Edi, and Junju were down by the sea...

The doctors and nurses examined him while he dreamed of gazelles running freely over the African plains.

Frank could not get the image of the man out of his mind. There was *something* about him that continued to gnaw away at him. He walked over to the fireplace and picked up a picture of Eden. He traced her face lightly with his fingertips and spoke out loud. "I miss you, babe."

"Daddy, what are you doing?" Nicholas charged into the room with a gun in his hand and a cowboy hat perched upon his blond curls.

"Just talking to Mommy's picture, partner." Frank seated himself on the couch, and his son planted himself on his father's lap.

"Can I talk to her too?"

Frank kissed his son on his cheek. "Sure you can. Maybe if we believe hard enough, she will hear us."

Nicholas took the picture frame and held it in his chubby hands. "Hi, Mommy. Tara's been really nice to me. Yesterday she gave me two Twizzlers and three Blue Slime Lickers. They're so cool because they make your teeth turn blue. I don't think you would like them very much. Ben's been kind of mean. Daddy says it's his age, but I think it's because he misses you a lot. We all miss you a lot, Mommy. And we love you. Please come home soon." Nicholas kissed the picture and handed it back to his father.

"She sure is pretty, huh, Nicky?"

"Dad!" Ben called from the kitchen. "Annie's on the phone."

Frank hadn't even heard it ring. Well, at least it was working. "Hey, Annie. What's up?"

"I'm still at the hospital. Things here are really crazy. He's agitated and totally freaked out."

Frank ran his fingers through his hair. "What's he doing?"

"Well, for starters, he won't let anybody near him. They are moving him to another wing of the hospital for psychological evaluation. You, my friend, have found some winner!"

"Ben, I'm heading out. I'm going to meet Annie at the hospital," Frank announced as he slipped on his coat. "What's the babysitter's phone number?"

"Aw, Dad, I don't need a babysitter. I'm almost ten!" Ben whined.

"Yeah, well, Nicky says you've been mean to him. Besides, I might be late." Frank reached into his pocket and pulled out a twenty-dollar bill. "You guys order a pizza for dinner. Now give me the phone number." Reluctantly, Ben rattled it off.

Frank kissed his kids and headed out to his car. The winter air was bitter as he waited for his car to warm up. It was 4:30 p.m. and already dark. God, he hated the winter, and this one seemed like it would never end. He turned on the radio and hummed along to an old Led Zeppelin song.

Frank loved music. When he was in high school, he had a band called Sabre Tooth. "Sex and Drugs and Rock and Roll" was the motto. Of course, if his kids carried on that way, he would break their arms! Eden and Annie were always hanging with the band. Frank dragged hard on his vape and peeled out of his driveway. "There's a feeling I get when I look to the west, and my spirit is crying for leaving."

At the hospital, he had a nurse page Annie. She came down to the lobby to greet him. "Hiya, Frankie. I'm on a break. Come on. Let me buy you some dinner." They sat in the hospital's cafeteria and ate.

"So what's going on with that guy?" Frank asked in between bites.

"It's really very bizarre. This guy is so strange. They're running all kinds of tests on him, and the last thing I heard is that he was strapped down onto a gurney."

"Maybe he's a crackhead."

Annie shook her head. "No, nothing like that. He's really odd. When he does speak, it's in another language. He's not from here, Frank. I don't know where he comes from. The investigators believe that he is not even from this time period." Annie sipped the last of her Diet Coke through two straws. "He has the whole hospital stumped."

"Can I see him?"

"He's under heavy surveillance, but I'll see what I can do." They finished up their meals.

Annie explained to the head of the psychiatric ward that Frank was the one who had found the peculiar man."

"I am sorry," was the reply. "He can only be visited by immediate family members at this time."

Annie turned toward Frank. "Nothing I can do. I have to get back to work." She turned toward the person in charge. "Please let me know of any further developments."

Frank kissed her goodbye and bunched his hands into his jean pockets. He did not understand why, but something so strong continued to eat away at him. He left the hospital feeling depleted. He just had to see the face of that man again.

Bale was showing little progress under the hot lights of the psychiatric ward. Mostly, he stayed in bed, curled on his side with his face buried in his hands. This land was too new, too modern, for him to absorb. The neon lights above his head penetrated through his skull. He was greatly relieved at night when the big lighted things somehow disappeared. It was at nightfall when he would open his eyes and recall his thatched hut beneath the starry skies of Zanzibar.

Yallowahii had talked frequently about the "state after." He spoke of a light brighter than the fire of the sun that would guide one to Mungo. Maybe he was in that "state," but he did not think so. Where were his people, with their skin so black? Everyone looked like Edi. Not in the face, of course. No one could ever look like her. Yet he knew somehow that he was now among her people. Could it be possible, though it seemed too strange to comprehend, that he was now a part of her Clan?

The people here in this forsaken land moved quickly around him. They talked fast and thought fast. As he lay there, he silently wished that morning would not enter. In the dark, somehow, he felt safe and secure. His mind began to saunter off into slumber as he dreamed of Bursala and his magnificent Palace. He could see his face clearly, the most extraordinary face he had ever witnessed.

In his dreams he could vividly see the faces of Junju and Edi. They were laughing. Then there was a fire. Flames and sparks flew into the night sky like an orange-and-red waterfall. There were Arabian horses. Bale could feel Eden's small hands tightly wrapped around his waist. There was darkness. And out of the blackness, perched upon the limb of a tree, was the demonic face of Jita. His crazed face charged closer and closer. Bale could feel the weight of an animal upon him. He could not breathe. He could not move. He could only call out to his loved ones.

Then there was this tunnel. His body was carried off by a Higher Force. He could not resist it. It called out his name. His body drifted toward a light that enveloped him. He wanted to stay with his friends, yet this brightness was so calming and so magnanimous that he wanted nothing more than to become a part of it.

As he floated into the light, he levitated above the people he would miss most in his life. He could see Edi. She was crying and cradling his body close to hers. He could see Junju kneeling beside her. He looked so sad. There was Bursala, sitting upon his horse. "I am up here," he shouted. "Do not cry for me. Look up. Do you not see me? Do you not hear me?" They did not respond.

He could see Jita, lying in a pool of his blood with an arrow sticking out of his back. Bale woke up in a cold sweat. "No. No. No!" he cried. "Edi!" He screamed out her name.

The lights were back, and Bale squinted his eyes. He could no longer see. He could no longer dream. A man stood beside his bed and pierced Bale's arm with something sharp. Bale could feel his body go limp. His eyes rolled back. The light, the tunnel, the horses, the fire, his friends, his enemy, the terror, the laughter stopped. Bale lay there in a complete state of numbness.

The following morning, Frank woke up early and went down to the kitchen to put on a pot of coffee. Frank loved Sunday mornings when Eden was home. The whole family would get dressed and pile into the car and head to Sunday services. When they got home, Eden would prepare a delicious breakfast with bagels, eggs, Jimmy Dean sausage, coffee, and freshly squeezed orange juice. After breakfast, Frank would retire to his couch with the Sunday paper strewn about as the kids hovered over the comic section. Later that day, Eden would make sauce, and by 2:00 p.m., the house would be filled with family and friends.

The men would congregate in the family room, yelling and screaming at the ball game, while the women gathered around the dining room table. There would be rice pudding and nuts, anisette, cakes, coffee, and bottles of red wine. The kids would run through the rooms with their cousins, laughing and playing.

Frank looked around. There hadn't been a Sunday like that since Eden's disappearance. The dining room table looked cold and empty, with a lace tablecloth draped over the shiny mahogany. There was still church and the Sunday paper, but the day lacked the festivities that Eden had incorporated. She never complained. She handled large crowds with finesse. Eden could work a room full of people with such ease. Frank held great admiration for his wife.

There were invitations given to him and the children by his parents and her mother, but Frank always declined. He didn't feel much like visiting. He didn't feel much like anything anymore. He took a sip of his coffee—black, no sugar. It was snowing again. The fifteenth snowstorm of the winter, and it was only January. He felt depressed. His mind drifted to the man he had found yesterday in his yard. He did not know what to make of the whole thing and wondered how he was doing. One by one, the kids drifted into the kitchen. Frank fixed them each a bowl of Honey Nut Cheerios and sliced up a banana.

"I want sugar on mine!" Nicholas cried. Frank took a teaspoon of sugar and flicked it onto his son's cereal.

"Mommy would say it already has sugar," Tara reminded her father.

"Well, Mommy's not here," Frank snapped. He was angry. Damn it. And why shouldn't he be? His wife was missing, and he was left to take care of a family, a house, bills, the shopping, school, and whatever else the day would bring.

After the kids' breakfasts and his third cup of coffee, he helped the two younger children get ready for church. A purple dress for Tara. Where were her tights? He pulled everything out of her drawer. Can't find them. Shit. He threw on a pair of green sweatpants under the dress. Eden would probably cringe. Frank could never get the hang of fixing a little girl's hair, but he managed a ponytail. There. He dressed Nicholas in a pair of slacks and a sweater. *It kind of matches*, he thought. *No law saying you can't match plaid and stripes.* Ben came down in a Knicks jersey and jeans. They piled into the SUV and headed off to church.

Frank sat in a pew with his kids and ran his fingers along his jaw. He had forgotten to shave. The church was serene. Frank glanced around to see many familiar faces. Women smiled at the disheveled bunch; their hearts poured out to them. He could feel a few of them staring. He got down on his knees and prayed. *Dear God, please give me the strength to carry on. Please, God, bring my wife home to us.*

Up on the altar, behind the crucifix, were words painted on the wall. It read, "All Who Suffer, Come to Me." Frank read those words over and over. When the Mass had ended, Frank made small talk with some of the women who came over to him, though if he could have avoided them, he would have.

"We're all praying for you and the children. And of course for Eden's safe return," they would say. "And if there is anything we can do…"

Back to the house. The quiet little house lacked the usual hubbub that Frank and the children had grown accustomed to. Still snowing. Frank lay on his couch with the Sunday paper strewn about while the kids hovered over the comics section. Thank God, some things remained the same.

Frank reached for the sports section first. Dean exploded through the front door. "Have you read this yet? Check it out, man." Dean tossed the paper over to Frank.

He sat up and read aloud, "A body was found at approximately seven a.m. at the location of 17 Wilson Street—"

"That's our address!" Tara exclaimed.

"The man, who appears to be about thirty years of age, was found by Mr. Frank Salina, homeowner and construction worker. The estranged man appeared to be in a coma. He was rushed to Memorial Hospital, where he received expert attention.

"Apparently, the unknown victim has awoken from his sleep. Dr. Charney, resident MD, has commented, 'We have reason to believe that this particular case has made medical mainstream history. His CT scan shows a discreet malformation of bones that does not exist in today's day and age.'

"The man has been moved to Memorial's psychiatric facility, where he will undergo several extensive tests under heavy surveillance. A social worker has been assigned to the case."

"We're famous!" Ben cried. "Dad, let me see your name in the paper."

Frank looked up at Dean. "Wow!"

"Tell me about it."

"Do you suppose..." Frank didn't finish his sentence as his eyes glanced over to the picture of Eden. "No. I don't know." He stood up and began his familiar pace. "I mean, my wife is suddenly missing, and this guy is suddenly found. It doesn't make any sense."

Dean watched as his friend nervously fidgeted. As far back as Dean could remember, Frank was always the cool one. The one the chicks dug. The one who excelled in sports. The guy with the guitar in his hand. The one who made the grade. Yet now, lately, he seemed to be nothing more than a bundle of nerves. Not that he could blame him. "Frankie, listen. Annie has arranged for you to go see this dude."

Frank stopped pacing and looked over at Dean. "When?"

"Tonight."

Annie and Frank arrived at the hospital at 7:30 p.m. The hallways of the psychiatric ward were dark and dismal as they made their way to the desk. Annie introduced Frank to the woman at the desk, and she called for the doctor on duty. His name was Dr. Mutebi.

Dr. Mutebi asked Frank and Annie to follow him to his office and asked them to take a seat. "I am told, Mr. Salina, that you have a great interest in seeing this man."

Frank nodded and studied the doctor's face. He was a tall black man who spoke with an accent.

"I am from Zimbabwe, and I have worked with the people of Africa before I came to this country. This man goes by the name of Bale. He is from Zanzibar, or Tanzania, as it is known to us today."

"If this is true, how did he get here?" Frank questioned.

"We do not know. Luckily, I speak the language, and I am able to converse with him somewhat, though the dialect is different. He speaks of Clans people and a King who goes by the name of Bursala. I have researched King Bursala of Uganda, and I have found that he reigned as King two thousand years ago."

Frank and Annie exchanged looks. "This...stuff...that you are telling me means nothing to me. I never heard of this place or this King," Frank said.

Dr. Mutebi continued. "This man you have found, Mr. Salina, claims to be a Spirit Walker."

Frank sat back in his chair and pulled out his vape. "Do you mind if I smoke? A Spirit Walker? What does that mean?

Dr. Mutebi shook his head. "I am uncertain myself. He speaks of a life after death, an after state. He speaks of a woman, a white woman, who was sent to his people through the same passage."

Annie looked over at Frank's face and noticed his expression had turned ashen.

"Come," said Dr. Mutebi. "You may see him now."

Frank's legs were heavy and numb as they carried him through a dazed and bewildered abstraction of emotions. A white woman was sent to his land the same way. Could it be? The long corridor seemed endless as his footsteps echoed through the obscurely lit hallway. Annie slipped her arm through his. "You OK?" she asked.

Frank felt paralyzed as he managed a nod. He had to be OK. Anticipation rose up inside him, expectations to meet the one who referred to himself as this Spirit Walker. The three entered the tenebrous room. "He does not like to have the lights on," Dr. Mutebi said in a low voice.

Frank could barely see the man who was lying in the bed. As his eyes began to adjust to the darkness, he could make out a silhouette. The man was strapped down by his arms and legs. To Frank, he seemed like a large trapped, frightened animal.

Dr. Mutebi spoke in his native tongue. "Bale, there is someone here to see you. Do not be afraid. They are friends of mine, and they come in peace."

Bale's body was still. He rolled his head to one side and looked up into Frank's face. In his eyes, Frank could feel the beat of his heart. There was a touch of desperation...an element of deadness. There was no desire or will in this man.

Annie let go of Frank as he approached the bed. Bale's enormous outline was defined by the glow of the moon, which streamed in through the blinds on the window. It started to snow again, and the white blizzard caused the room to brighten. Frank nervously ran his fingers through his hair. He noticed Bale's eyes following the trail of light his wedding ring gave off. Frank slipped the ring off his finger and held it in front of Bale's face. The lifeless eyes seemed to come alive as he examined the delicate gold band with its intricately etched fig leaves. Frank held the ring between two fingers only inches from Bale's face. The ring seemed to glow like an auricle of light as Bale felt a sudden urgent surge of power lift him. He opened his mouth to speak. Frank moved his face closer to the stranger's and tilted his ear toward him. Bale spoke the word. It was one solitary word: "Edi."

The moment Bale called out her name, Frank knew that this was the moment he had waited for. He stood before Bale transfixed, with the ring still in front of the man's face. "Her hair is yellow like the sun. Her eyes are as blue as the sky. She is alive and well and living among my people." Bale's voice sounded queer to himself. He remembered a time when Eden had been blessed with the "tongue." The same thing had just happened to him.

Dr. Mutebi felt dizzy as he listened to Bale speak English. Bale continued. "Yallowahii told me once that if you believe with your heart, you shall be blessed. The gods have blessed me with the tongue. My people, the people of Zanzibar, have accepted Edi as their Spirit Walker." Bale's eyes dropped down to the straps that bound him. "Yet"—he let out a wistful sigh—"Eden's people treat me as if I am a wild beast."

Frank did not hear the despondent tone in Bale's voice. His body swayed with faintness as he collapsed onto a nearby chair. His eyes were gripped onto the ring he still held in his fingers, and his words were sluggish and dilatory. "My wife is alive." Frank shook himself out of the dreamlike state, and his voice boomed throughout the room. "My wife is alive!"

Annie ran over to him and threw her arms around him. "She's alive! Oh God, she's alive!" He leaped to his feet and twirled her around. Frank's eyes glistened through the darkness.

"Edi speaks of her family often. I promised to be her protector so that Sava would not have to marry her." Bale swallowed hard and took a breath. "Jita tried to murder her. She was terrified. The mighty leopard killed me instead. Edi and Junju were forced to watch. It must have been terrible for them. Bursala pierced the animal's heart with an arrow. She is back with Yallowahii now. I assure you that she is safe from any further danger."

Frank, Annie, and Dr. Mutebi could not follow all that Bale was saying. Frank pressed his face close to Bale's. "I want to go to her."

"I am afraid that is impossible." Bale shook his head sadly. "You must see her in your heart, not with your eyes. I was sent here by the powers of the Spirits. Perhaps it was part of my journey to come here in Edi's homeland to inform you of her well-being. I am very tired. My soul has already died. My body must now follow."

"*No!* You must hang on." Frank was shouting at Bale. "You can't die! You are my only hope, my one and only connection. She has children who miss her. Family and friends! You have to tell me how I can reach her."

Bale closed his eyes. "I am tired," he repeated.

Frank grabbed ahold of Bale's face. "Look at me, Bale. Open your eyes, and look at me. I am reaching out to you." Frank's voice quivered. "You can't leave me like this! You just can't." He sobbed.

Bale did not open his eyes. Frank turned toward Dr. Mutebi.

"Mr. Salina, he is only resting," the doctor assured him.

Frank's face was beaded with perspiration as Annie and the doctor led him out into the hallway. "Doctor, you have to do everything in your power to keep that man in there alive. I mean *everything!*" Frank pounded his fist into his hands. His expression was heated.

Annie broke the tension. "I miss Eden too. And I am as happy as you are to hear that she is alive. But, Frankie, the man in there is a person. His eyes were full of sadness, confusion, and pain. He has been through a traumatic ordeal. Somewhere on the other side of the world, there are people grieving over his loss, just the way we are for Eden." Annie shot her eyes over toward Dr. Mutebi. "The way he is strapped down is cruel. To me, he seems so harmless. He was a friend to Eden. That alone should be reason enough to show some compassion for this man. He claims that his people have taken good care of our girl. We should be ashamed of ourselves. Now, if you'll excuse me, I am going back into that room, and I am going to sit with him until he wakes up. And when he does, I will be there to comfort him."

She was right. How could he be so selfish? "Will you join us, Doctor?" Frank said while holding the door. Annie's eyes brightened as the two men came back into the room.

Zanzibar, Cry of the Living

Una stayed in the confines of her hut all of the day and all of the night. Mazi and Dahni stayed with her, trying as best as they could to cheer her. They, too, were grieving over the loss of Bale. It was a burdensome time for each of them.

"Una, woman, you must keep up your strength for Dahni and the child that you carry," Mazi explained. He tried to feed her, but Una turned her face away from the food. The losses of Keswa, Wanyenya, and Bale were more than she was able to handle. Even the death of Jita had affected her. He did not ask to be possessed by the leopard ghost. She felt as though her soul and her heart had hardened far beyond her years.

Yallowahii was moving slower than ever. The heat of the day seemed somewhat unbearable. Eden picked up his daily chores and gave him strict orders to rest. The infection in his leg was spreading. If only he did not have Eden to think of, he would persuade Sava into giving him a poisonous ale so that he could lay his old and frail body to rest. He could not leave her now. The poor child was so alone.

Sava finally approached him. "Chieftain, I see the pain that you are living with. I urge you to consider surgery. If I amputate the leg, there will be no way for the infection to spread. It is your time, old man, to give me your decision."

"Sava, you speak the truth when you call me an old man. I am old, too old for such a surgery, I am afraid."

"Nonsense. Your mind is as sharp as the claw of an eagle. Why, then, do you insist on being so stubborn? I am as old as you. I am still active as the medicine man of the Clan. I am still fathering children," Sava replied.

"Another reason that brings me to call is the Spirit Walker. I understand that she is in deep mourning over Bale, as we all are; however, the issue remains. In order for an outsider to remain a part of the Clan she must be married to a Clansman. You know the law, Yallowahii. She must be married to Clansblood. The Spirit Walker is no exception."

Eden was just about to enter the hut when she heard their conversation. She placed the buckets of water at her feet and listened from outside.

"As I have explained to you before, I will be happy to take Eden on as my sixth mate."

Eden remained quiet. Her mind drifted for a moment as she thought about Frank and his American good looks. Without warning, Bursala's face burned in her mind—the way he looked at her with so much love in his eyes. No one had ever looked at her like that. Not even Frank.

"Sava, I will not bring this issue up to her at this time. She needs time to heal. Both emotionally and physically. As for my leg, I would rather live with the pain than have my limb severed. When the god of death calls out my name, I will be ready to meet with my Creator."

Eden picked up the pails of water and entered the hut. "Has there not been enough talk of death about?" she asked and blew a strand of hair away from her forehead. She turned toward Yallowahii. "Now what is this about surgery?"

Sava explained the necessity for the Chieftain to undergo such a procedure.

"Then it is settled." She looked over at Yallowahii with shining eyes of blue. "I need you. I will help you through this. I promise."

Yallowahii waved his hand in the air. He did not wish to discuss the matter any further. He turned his back on them and muttered something under his breath about taking a nap.

Eden followed Sava outside. "I will talk to him. He just has not been the same since Bale died. None of us have been, I am afraid."

"It would be in his best interest to convince him. If anyone could talk sense into him, I am certain it is you. He will listen to you. Sometimes the old man can be stubborn like a mule," Sava explained. "I must go now. There is an ill child over at the Bushbuck Clan. Word was sent for me to go to him. I shall return in one sunset, for the journey is a long one."

Eden bade him farewell and returned to the well for some more water. The village seemed unusually quiet. Even the animals were lethargic. She went down into the fields and filled her baskets with vegetables. The hours droned on beneath the burning rays of the sun. She took a moment to wipe the moisture from her forehead. She remembered a saying her father once told her when she was little: "Horses sweat, men perspire, and women glow." A smile came to her lips as she picked up her baskets and continued picking stalks of corn.

Eden cupped her hand over her eyes. Cornfields as far as she could see. Fields of lofty golden stalks that towered over her and waved their arms up to the sun. The only sounds were the sonance of birds singing and whistling in the rhythms that sounded like sweet music to her ears. A distant squawk of a crow called out to her. Her peaceful thoughts were interrupted as she could see someone in the distance, cutting through the fields and calling out her name. It was Mazi.

"Mazi, what is it?" Eden asked anxiously, running to meet him.

"It is Una! Something is wrong with the baby!" Eden dropped her baskets, hoisted her tunic up to her knees, and ran behind Mazi all the way to their hut.

Una was lying in her bed, doubled over in agony. "Please, run and fetch Sava. The baby...something is not right."

Eden turned toward Mazi. "Sava is not here. He left hours ago to tend to an ill child."

Mazi held out his hands. "What do I do?"

"Where is Dahni?" Eden asked.

"He is fishing with a friend."

"Good. We do not want him to see his mother this way." Eden rushed over to Una and grabbed ahold of the woman's hand. "Una, it is me—Eden. Can you make sense of what I am saying?" Una squeezed Eden's hand and nodded her head. "It is going to be fine, Una," Eden said as she wiped the glow from Una's forehead. "It is time for a baby to be born!" Una's cries were forlorn.

"Mazi," Eden instructed, "fetch some well water and fresh bark cloths. And hurry. There is little time to waste." Eden smoothed Una's hair away from her forehead and tried as best she could to comfort her.

Una shook her head. "It is not time for his baby to be born."

Eden's eyes met Una's. "Listen to me, Una. My aunt was with child for nine months before she knew she was having a baby. When she went into labor, she still did not know what was going on until the baby was born. This happens to women sometimes. Yes, it is rare, but it happens. You are much further along than you thought, and this child is ready to be born. Now I want you to focus on everything I am about to tell you."

Una closed her eyes and let out a grunt. "I will obey," she managed to say as she began to pant. A wave of pain swept over her as she gritted and gnashed her teeth together. Her face became contorted as she let out a low moan of misery.

"It is time to bear down and push." Eden coaxed her into delivery as she waited between the woman's knees. She could feel the beads of sweat rolling down her body. She was certainly glowing now. Mazi returned with the water and bark cloth. He became unhinged as he watched his mate suffer in agony. "Go to Dahni and stay with him," Eden commanded.

She tied her hair back with a piece of twine and massaged Una's legs. Una let out a scream, and Eden remained steadfast and calm. Una's body heaved in agony as she shook her head from side to side. "It is no use. This baby will be born dead," she cried in a state of delirium. "Death surrounds me. It is in the air. I can sense it. All that I have come to love has been taken away from me. This child is another burden for me to bear."

Eden placed her hands on Una's face and looked straight into her eyes. "Listen to me, Una. This is not the time for such thoughts. You must pull yourself together and reach deep inside of you and find the strength to push out this baby. Be strong for Mazi...for Dahni. Be strong for this unborn child. I want you to push, Una. Push with everything you've got. The time has come for you and me to work together. Concentrate. Focus. Do this for Bale!"

Una's facial expression changed when she heard Bale's name. She closed her eyes and thrust her body down. She felt tired and weak. She bit the bottom of her lip and bore down again. She closed her eyes tightly and let out an afflictive mutter.

"Come, Una! Do this for Bale! Do this for Bale!" Eden cajoled her.

Una's breathing was rapid, and her chest heaved up and down until she was panting and gasping for air. "I cannot do this. I cannot do this anymore." Her head rolled to the side as the pain ceased for a moment. Another wave immediately came over her.

"Push, Una. I know you are tired. Please, push. You must try."

Una took one last deep breath and held her hand out to grab Eden's. With one final push, the head of the baby was visible. Eden moved in closer. "Come, Una! I can see the head of your child! Do it for Bale, Una. Please! Do it for Bale!" Eden begged. The shoulders of the child thrust forward, and within the next moment, the child slipped into Eden's hands. The baby's cry was that of the living.

"It is a girl!" The tiny infant was perfectly developed. Eden placed her on her mother's stomach. "You have a beautiful baby girl, Una!" Eden, Una, and the baby huddled together in tears of joy and adulation. Una held her daughter close to her face and kissed the baby on the top of her head.

"I am so grateful to you, Spirit Walker." Una's eyes were full of love. "I was afraid of you. You came to us with no warning. I was not prepared for such an arrival. Jita filled my head with lies…and I believed him, at first." Una hung her head. "I am so ashamed. Bale loved you. In my heart, I should have realized that he could never love someone evil. I beg you for your forgiveness."

"I was afraid of you too. I left my family with no warning. I was not prepared to come here to this place. I have babies too. I miss them more than words can say. I love them more than life itself." Eden's bright blue eyes looked up at Una. "I do not know if I will ever see them again. With every passing day, my desire for them grows. Yet my belief gets weaker and weaker. You, Una, have your family right here. For that you should count your blessings. I know you have seen a great deal of pain. I am truly sorry for your losses. I loved Bale as well.

"I, Eden Salina, have come to realize that I am the Spirit Walker. I believe in my heart that the Spirits will send me home someday. For the first time since I have arrived in your land, I feel ready to accept this destiny, this fate, which has been given to me for whatever reason."

"I shall call the child Wanyenya-Salina. She shall carry your name and the name of my young dead sister."

Eden smiled. "I am very touched. Welcome to the Clan Wanyenya-Salina. Such a big name for such a tiny baby."

By the time Mazi and Dahni returned, both mother and daughter were cleaned up and doing well. Yallowahii came with Sava's first mate, Tama. With them they brought a small tool of Sava's, which was used in childbirth to snip the cord.

"She is so small," Eden whispered to Yallowahii.

"Bale would be very proud of us." Una's face looked so much like her brother's at that moment. The two women had finally made their peace. And with that peace, they formed a bond, a bond as strong as the African sun.

If Eden Salina had ever wondered why she was sent to such a place, she felt as if she now held the answer. Such a tiny and fragile life. She watched as Wanyenya-Salina suckled her thumb, curled up in a ball, and slept. Big or little…from the innocence of a newborn baby to the gentle giant who lived before her. The lives she had touched and those who had touched hers filled her with a feeling of fragility. Life was tiny in comparison to the years. And each life, though precious, was like an aberration, a blip from life's viewing screen. For behold, we are Christmas Stars of Zanzibar.

THE DREAM

Christmas Stars of Zanzibar

Nine days had come to pass since Bursala went out to sea with his men. Eden was down in the plantain, gathering wildflowers for Yallowahii. Yallowahii's operation had been a success. The Village Elder did not have much say over the matter, as Sava and Eden badgered him endlessly. "You must have this surgery." Eden, vexed, pleaded with him. "You are all that I have left. Christmas Stars isn't that what you called us? You have a lot of life left inside of you, and I am not willing to let you give up hope." Yallowahii just had to look into those eyes of blue, and her wish was granted. Not since his own children had he felt a connection so strong, so powerful. He would stay alive not for himself but for the Spirit Walker. She needed him. Feeling needed meant feeling important again.

Sava performed the surgery with no kind of anesthesia. Sava explained to Eden that pain was a state of mind and that the mighty Chieftain would be able to stand such an ordeal. Eden held his hand throughout the entire operation. Her back was toward his leg, and her face never left his. She spoke to him in gentle tones and soothed his forehead with wet compresses. Sava used a red-hot spearhead to burn and sear the surface of the leg. The large end of a bullock horn was placed over the affected area. Sava placed beeswax and sealed the severed point of the spear. He then sharply inhaled the air within the horn to create a near-vacuum. The spear was placed at the center of Yallowahii's knee joint. Sava severed the leg from the knee down. The medicine man sealed the aperture with the beeswax using skillful movements of his tongue.

Yallowahii sweated copiously and wrestled in vain with agony, clinging to the faith of the healing power of his longtime friend. Rags that were dipped in the cooling sea were also dipped in strychnine, arsenic, and calomel, which immediately stimulated the Chieftain's nervous system. Sava's surgery had been successful. The ancient medicine man looked up and worshipped the moon to give thanks for the desirable outcome of his dearest friend's operation. Through it all, Yallowahii was hallucinating heavily. He told Eden he saw human shapes and faces in the bark of the trees. She pressed her face up against the old man's and listened as he babbled. His eyes were glazed, and his pupils were large. There was no pain…just a state of numbness as the poisons began to affect him. Deeper he fell into a dreamlike state of a strange euphoria.

Eden. She was with him. She looked like an angel under the glow of the moon. He was comforted by her company. She looked so young and small, like the little girl on the beach that day twenty-six years ago. He felt young and small and strong, too, like the boy he once had been in China. Yallowahii had two good legs, and he was running down an old dirt road. His bare feet barely touched the soft, packed earth. He stopped to get a closer look at a toad that hopped across his path. A boy of eight. So alive, so full of wonder and curiosity. He could hear his mother's voice off in the distance. She was calling out his name. It was probably time for him to sit with his family and have a meal. His small, dark fingers touched the frog's jagged back. Yallowahii smiled at it and tilted his head to one side. His mother's calls were echoing in his ears. "Yallowahii…come home…"

No. He didn't want to. He wanted to stay alone with his new little friend. The frog hopped away into the bushes, and little Yallowahii crawled to the spot. A man appeared from the bushes, and Yallowahii toppled onto his backside. The man was older than anyone his eyes had ever seen before. He wore a dark, shabby suit and a pelt of mink around his neck. An old, tattered fedora dipped over one eye. In the old man's hands, he held a cane and in the other a water globe. Little Yallowahii had never seen anyone or anything like him before.

The old man placed the water globe in the middle of the road. The child sat on one side of it, the old man on the other. Together they looked inside. The little boy peered through and saw the face of his elder looking back. No words were spoken.

The child saw visions. His mother waved her arms, beckoning for him to come home. A ship capsizing deep into the ocean. A little girl sitting on the beach. A man with blond hair going through a dark tunnel. A land so foreign with the sun burning high above tawny savannas. People whose skin was as black as the night. A King. A leopard. A woman crying for her homeland. The little boy looked up at the old man, who was now standing over him. His hand patted the child's shoulder, and he smiled. As quickly as he had appeared, he left just as mysteriously.

Yallowahii opened his eyes to Eden. She held his hands, and her eyes flashed like fireflies through the darkness. "You are fine. Sava has made you well again. You will not suffer anymore." Sava's face came into view alongside Eden's. Yallowahii focused his eyes on them. Their faces filled Yallowahii with solace. Sava held a rhinoceros horn filled with powder over his old companion and sprinkled it over his body to restore health and vitality to the aging man. Yallowahii's mind was aflutter. What was he dreaming about? He could not remember. A little toad hopping in the grass caught his eye. He reached out to touch it with his finger. A man of ninety. So alive, so full of wonder and curiosity. He could still hear his mother calling out his name...

Nine days later, Yallowahii was getting stronger and hobbled about with a walking stick that Mazi had made for him. It had been nine days since Eden had last seen Bursala. As she picked a purple flower, she held it to her nose and breathed in its sweet aroma. She remembered her last conversation with the King. There was a woman waiting for him on the island of Karagwe. Eden found herself wondering what the woman looked like. She was certain that this woman would take one look at Bursala, and her heart would beat as wildly as Eden's. She thought of his words: "My dear, I am ambitious as well as able. I shall return after the sun sets high on the tenth day of the noon sky." Tomorrow his canoes would bring him home.

Eden had to prepare herself mentally for his new Queen's arrival. This woman would take him to her bed, where she would lie naked with him. Eden felt a shiver run through her body. How silly to think such thoughts when she herself was married. Bursala was a loner. He was a King. Surely, he should live his life any way he felt fit. "And I shall be happy for him." Eden found herself talking aloud. "He deserves to be happy. He deserves to be peaceful." Yet deep in her heart, she knew they had both saved each other a little somehow.

There was sadness in Bursala's face. Even when he smiled. Oh, his smile was radiant. Eden was sure it could light up the darkest and coldest nights. It was as if she could look deeper into him. As if she could read between the royal lines. She missed him more than she wanted to admit.

She laid her basket of flowers down beside her and sprawled out on the soft grass. The tiny village by the sea in the distance was well illuminated. The stars and the moon twinkled above. At night, when it was quiet like this, she thought about the many things that filled her head during the heat of the day.

Wanyenya-Salina. So sweet and innocent. "She is tiny like you," Una would say as Eden came to call on both mother and child. Una wrapped a string of beads around the baby's waist and a string of wild plantain seeds around her neck. These were worn to give the child strength and to make her neck grow straight. A string was also tied around the baby's belly to prevent it from getting too fat. It was not tight, but it had medicine on it to protect Wanyenya-Salina from growing out of true proportions. Una carried the baby in a bark cloth sling on her back, which enabled her to continue her chores and still have the freedom of both hands.

Dahni. He loved his little sister, though she did not do very much. She would follow him with her eyes, and he tried hard to make her smile. Dahni learned how to bathe and feed her. "Someday, my son, you will make a very good father," Una would tell the boy.

Mazi. He adored his new family. He and Dahni were the men of the family. They would set out early to hunt and fish. Mazi crafted Dahni a small spear made of assegai wood, and he spent many hours teaching the boy the art of targeting. He was happy with Una. They were good friends, first and foremost. Mazi could not recall a time when he was happier.

Kimu and Zinga. They lived together down along the other side of the grove. Zinga came every day into the village to be near the new baby. "Soon it will be your time," the Clans people assured her. Zinga spent most of her afternoons with Eden. She loved hearing all about the progressive homeland from which she came. At the end of the day, she would travel across the plantain to prepare meals for her beloved Kimu. Together they sat, talked, laughed and carried on like newlyweds.

Sava. He was kept busy, as the medicine man was always caring for someone. He frequently traveled to other Clans in distant villages, as the word of his medical achievements had always spread throughout the land. When Sava was home, he was kept very busy with his five mates and twenty-one children.

Yallowahii. He was finally at peace, no longer dealing with the pain he had become so accustomed to. Small children, as well as adults, sat with their Chieftain as he told them ponderous stories of far and wide. He was the greatest storyteller Eden had ever heard. She looked forward to their times together. She continued to cater to his needs and helped him to the best of her ability.

Bale. He was missed every moment of every day among the village people. Eden sat at his thatched grave often to speak with him. His presence was strong and alive within her. Eden missed his kindred and quiet ways. Every day she would roll in the rushes of the sea where she and Bale had shared stolen moments. The absence of Bale left her heart empty yet stronger.

Jita. Peace had crept over the village now that Jita had been finally put to his death. No longer was he a threat to the people of the Clan. Now Eden could lie under the stars without any fears. With only her thoughts and the distant sounds of the splashing sea.

And with every passing day, although she did not talk about it, this was her time to remember her own family. Her children, how they must be growing. Her husband. Her love for him would never die, no matter how much time would pass. No matter how much Bursala's eyes continue to haunt her. As Eden's body fell heavily into the earth, she thought about and remembered her life back in New York. She fell into a deep sleep beneath the glow of the silvery moon, and she began to dream…

"Wake up, child. Wake from your sleep."

Eden rubbed her eyes with her hands and squinted through the darkness. Looming over her was a man. His hair was as blond as hers. His blue eyes bore into her own. "Daddy!" She got to her feet and blinked hard. "Daddy, it is really you!" She flung her arms around him and buried her face in his chest.

He held her close then took a step back. He held her hands in his and smiled. "Let me look at you, Eden. You are truly a vision to my eyes."

Eden began to cry.

"Shh, there, there. Daddy's here. Everything is going to be all right." His voice was as gentle as she had remembered it to be. "Come, Eden. I want to show you something." He led her to the ocean. As she held her hand in his, she felt like she was six years old again. "Look into the water, and tell me what you see." The splashing waves ceased, and her eyes were looking into still water that reflected like a mirror. She could see Bale's face come clearly into view.

"Edi, I am with your people now, my friend. Though I am tired, I am told that I must linger."

"She is alive. My wife is alive." She could see Frank sitting in a chair, holding his wedding ring in his hands.

There was Ben. He was in the snow looking at Bale. And Tara! Her face pressed up against a window. Oh, and her baby, Nicholas, standing right beside his big sister. They all looked so precious.

"I am with them." Bale's face radiated from beneath the water. "It is a strange place, this land that you come from. I am frightened. I know now how you must have felt when the Spirits brought you into my existence. Edi, I have journeyed through time. I, too, am a Spirit Walker. It is clear to me that our paths have crossed so that we may switch places." Bale's face started to disappear.

"No!" Eden cried and knelt down to touch the water. A thunderous wave hit her and knocked her over. She stood to her feet and was trampled by another wave. "Bale?" She screamed, looking all around her. She fell to her knees and held herself up by her hands. The waves kept rolling over her, one right after the other. "Bale, come back!" she pleaded. Eden dragged her soaked body up to the sand. "Daddy?" she called out in a low voice. "Daddy, where are you?" She turned her head from side to side. There was no one with her. She was all alone. Frank. Bale. Her father. Where did they go? Why were all the men in her life always abandoning her?

"I am right here, child. Daddy is right here."

"I am here, child. Open your eyes; you must have fallen asleep in the plantain grove."

Eden opened her eyes to bright sunshine. Yallowahii was standing over her, smiling. "When I did not find you in your hut, I decided to set out to look for you," he said.

Eden's heart pounded frantically as she stared into the face of the old man.

"Daddy?"

Yallowahii held her gaze. His dark, burnished eyes faceted a lustrous glimmer of blue. There was a twinkle in the old man's eyes. "I...do not understand. I had a dream. At least I think it was a dream. My father was with me. And Bale!" Eden sat up excitedly. "I saw Bale in the water. My husband and children...they were all there..." Her voice trailed off. "And when I opened my eyes, you were here telling me the same words that my father was saying. You are! Aren't you? You are my father!"

Yallowahii's eyes went dark again. "I have told you that if you believe in your heart, the truth shall be revealed."

"That is why I was sent to this place. You called me here to be with you. And Bale told me that he was where I should be! He was sent there to tell my family that I am alive. All of this time I have spent with you, I did not even know that I was your daughter. And I loved you from the moment I saw you. I understand. I finally understand. You wanted..."

"One last moment with you." Yallowahii finished her sentence. He sat down beside her and reached for her hand.

"My name is Yallowahii, and I am from China. When I went out on that ship twenty-six years ago, I met in my travels a young man, who was your father. He was already dead; I was dying. Together we traveled through the tunnel of brightness. He did not want to leave you. We became friends. We journeyed together to meet our Creator. When we arrived, it was suddenly decided that it was not my time. My family was already gone. There was nothing for me to go back for. I made a solemn promise with your father that I would watch over you. He is in me, Eden. He has been inside and a part of me for a very long time. Through me, he is alive."

Eden's mouth fell open. She squeezed Yallowahii's hand tightly.

"I can tell you anything about your life. It is as if I have lived the lives of two men. As Yallowahii and your father. We are here together as father and daughter. Do you understand?"

Eden nodded her head. Suddenly she felt as if she were truly home. "You are my family. So all this time, I was grieving for my family; ironically, my family has been right here with me."

Eden leaned forward, and Yallowahii cradled her in his arms. He held her the way her father had held her in her dream.

"I wanted to be with you again. You were so small when I left. The Spirits have allowed us to have this time. We are very blessed, you and I. I love you, Eden."

"I love you too, Daddy."

The Gazelle

Eden and Yallowahii sat in the plantain grove for most of the day. He told her stories about when she was little. Some of the things she remembered; most she did not. They laughed and reminisced, and they sat together like a long-lost, reunited family.

The remaining part of the day Eden spent doing her chores. She felt so complete knowing that through Yallowahii, her father was still alive. The sun was ardent upon her shoulder. All the while, she kept looking around, expecting to see Bursala riding toward her, perched majestically upon his horse. Every time she turned around, there was nobody there.

She decided to bathe down in the ocean. She tore off her tunic and dove deep into the waves. Her skin was browner than it had ever been before, and her hair was sun soaked, with bleached honey and wheat strands running through it. She scrubbed her skin with lilacs until she was satisfied with the fragrance and sheen her skin took on. She dunked her head under the water and rinsed it until her hair was clean. She was purified.

Eden came up from under the water feeling rejuvenated and smelling pretty. She threw on her tunic and sat on the rocks—the same rocks she sat with Bale when he had told her his lifelong secret. She wished he were here with her now so that she could tell him the news about Yallowahii. She still could not believe it. She played with the ends of her hair and began to braid strands of it, decorating each strand with tiny shells she picked up at her feet.

On the walk back to the village, she gathered some berries and flowers and made a necklace out of them. Zinga had shown her how. Once she got back to her hut, she changed into a fresh light-blue kaniki. It was trimmed with swatches of red and yellow and white around the neck, hemline, and sleeves.

This was one of Nalinya's most beautiful dresses, and Eden especially loved it. For the finishing touch, she fastened her amulet around her waist.

As the sun set over the African plains, the Clans people took their meals at their hearths. Eden sat with Yallowahii. He looked different to her now. She did not see an old Asian man; instead, she saw the man who had been in her dreams. He had not changed outwardly. No one else seemed to notice, at least. She realized then that when you love someone so profoundly, their face takes on a nuance, a glow all its own.

"Today is the day in which Bursala returns." Eden tried to sound nonchalant as she spoke in between bites.

"Ah, yes, Bursala. He has taken quite a fancy to you, Eden."

Eden sniffled and tried to hide her smile. "He is very charming. I do hope that his journey went well."

Yallowahii nodded. "He is a brave and smart man. You are not worried for his safety, are you?"

"No." Eden's response was too quick.

Yallowahii smiled. "I will clean up. Why don't you take a walk? You look very lovely tonight, Spirit Walker."

Eden could feel the heat rise to her cheeks. She bent over and planted a kiss on Yallowahii's face. "I will take a walk along the ocean. Would you care to join me?"

Yallowahii waved his arm. "No. I will stay here. I promised Dahni that I would help him make a rattle for Wanyenya-Salina. Go, child. Be safe and have fun."

Eden felt like a little girl going out on a first date. The whole thing was preposterous. She was a married woman. Bursala was the King of Uganda. The whole thing did not make any sense. Yet she just wanted to see him, to make sure he had returned safely. She splashed her feet at the cool water's edge. The ocean was her very favorite place in this land. Bursala would know where to look for her. She waited. And waited. And waited. Bursala never came.

On her way back to her hut, Eden hung her head low. "God, please let him be safe." If Bale were here, she would persuade him to hop on his camel, and together they could ride to the Royal Enclosure. Bale was far, far away. With a weighty soul and a heavy heart, she headed toward the village. As she neared her hut, she noticed a small fire smoldering in the dirt. She squinted her eyes. The only thing she could make out was a silhouette. "Who is there?" she asked.

"It is I. Come, child. Sit," Yallowahii responded. Eden sat across from him with only the fire between them. "You do look radiant, Spirit Walker."

Eden made circles in the dirt with her finger. "What does it matter?" She sighed.

The two were silent for a moment. Then Yallowahii spoke. "I want to tell you a story. Once there was a gazelle who had her heart set on becoming the fastest runner who ever lived. She wanted to make every movement a thing of grace and poise and beauty. She ran quickly and swiftly every single day beneath the hot desert sun. At night, when she laid her body down, she collapsed from pure fatigue and exhaustion. When the dawn broke over the horizon, she would wearily pick herself up and run again. Finally, the gazelle announced proudly that she would challenge all her animal friends to run against her. When the race was over, she waited for the others to congratulate her. A thick silence filled the air. One of the other gazelles moved forward and said, 'As the elected candidate of the group, I must say my piece on my behalf and those of the others. You are nothing special. Your gracefulness has a lot to be desired, and your form is less than adequate. Get it into your mind…you are simply a gazelle…just like me. You may have won the race, but you are far from the fastest creature that ever lived.' Laughing in mockery, the animals moved across the sand and into the sun.

"'How sadly mistaken they are,' said the gazelle out loud. 'I have worked hard each and every day until my feet blistered and my body ached. I have not seen dedication in any of them to be the best at something. There is no doubt in my mind that I am a terrific runner. I will continue to run, and I will continue to stay true to achieving my goal. I will continue to believe in myself. Not for them…for me. I will practice and continue to work long and hard. I will run…and run…just for myself.'

"That is what she did. It gave her a lifetime of pleasure." Yallowahii fell silent. Only the crackle of the fire could be heard. After a while, he spoke again. "Satisfaction comes to those who live to please themselves. If you depend on others to bring you happiness, you will always be disappointed."

Eden studied his face by the glow of the fire. "How did you know what I was feeling?"

"My dear child. We have traveled far and wide. You have come to understand, and I have come to understand. You believe in the words that people promise you. At times, that is good. At other times, people will let you down—only if you allow them to. It is important to remember that it is you who must never fail yourself."

Together they sat by the fire until the early traces of dawn crept over the horizon. Eden helped the Chieftain to his bed and then wearily fell into hers. When she closed her eyes, she dreamed of a gazelle with wings striding gracefully, taking off like a bird in flight.

Onward and Forward

Christmas Stars of Zanzibar

The sounds of a team of horses awoke her later the next day. She picked her head up and ran to the entrance of her hut. Was it Bursala? Had he returned? She cupped a hand to her eyes so that she could see through the comburent sun. There were ten or twelve Arabian horses charging across the countryside. Upon each horse sat a Kingsman. They came to a halt and lined up next to each other in a uniformed line.

She scanned every one of their faces. Bursala was not among them. Their faces were stern. Had something terrible happened to their King? Eden could feel her heart sink deep inside her chest. "Where is Bursala?" she demanded. She did not wait for an answer. She did not want to know. Let him stay alive inside of her heart. She fled across the dusty golden fields and ran to the refuge of Yallowahii. She could barely breathe as she ran into his hut. Yallowahii sat with another on the floor with their backs turned toward her. They turned their faces when they heard her coming.

Eden stood in the opening and almost collapsed at the sight. Sitting beside the Chieftain was a man wearing a long white chiffon veil tied with a braided silk rope around his forehead. It was the King himself! A full smile came across his face as he held a cup of ale to his lips.

"I thought you were..." Her words hung heavily in the air.

"Dead?" Bursala threw his head back and laughed. His expression turned to a serious one. "My dear, I would skin one hundred crocodiles alive with my bare hands to make my way back to you." Bursala stood to his feet. "The Island of Karagwe exudes extravagance, yet nothing can compare to the vision that stands before me now."

"Where is your new Queen?" Eden asked, trying to keep her voice from shaking.

Bursala raised an eyebrow. "Ah, yes, the Queen. I met with her over on her island. She was anxious for me to take her here to my land." Bursala shook his head. "Although she was lovely, it is not her that I desire."

Yallowahii held on to the side of the hut and slowly raised himself up. He grabbed ahold of his walking stick and tucked it under the nook of his arm. He hobbled past Eden and whispered in her ear. "And the gazelle ran and ran and ran." Yallowahii left the two alone.

Bursala moved toward her, unwrapped a sack, and pulled out garments made from the finest silk. "I have brought you dresses made from the most extraordinary materials. I do hope this pleases you." He placed them in her arms. "You were all I had thought about. I felt as if I was going mad upon the thunderous waves of the sea. I am elated to see your face again." He reached out his hand and touched her softly on her cheek. "Go. Put on one of those silken gowns. I have been riding upon the ocean with thirteen men. Such a ghastly sight. Go, my dear."

Like an angel on high, she glided into Yallowahii's sleeping quarters, which were separated only by a bamboo panel. "How is Junju?" Eden called from the other side of the divider as she slipped the soft material over her head.

"I do not know. My men and I have stopped here first. We shall see him soon."

Eden pulled the braids, beads, and shells out of her hair. The tight rows of braids had made her hair fanciful with ringlets as it flowed all around her. The gown fit her better than anything else she had ever worn in this land. She felt like a Princess as she emerged from the partition.

Bursala stood, mesmerized by her glorious wonderment. She took his breath away. "Spirit Walker, you do look glorious to these weary eyes. I had this wrap made especially for you by the women of the islands. It fits you exquisitely. You are an enchantment." His eyes fell upon her as he spoke.

She looked into his eyes. "When you did not return on the tenth day, I thought that perhaps you were lost at sea."

Bursala wanted to hold her. Touch her. Taste her. He had spoken the truth before. He would skin one hundred crocodiles alive with his bare hands for her. He would fight off any enemy, whether it be a man or a beast. Yet he could not battle his own burning desire for her, no matter how hard he tried. He reached out his hand and gently traced the delicate notes of her face. He throbbed for her with every drop of blood that flowed through his royal veins.

She allowed his hands upon her face. She looked up at him with wistful eyes, dreaming their fantasies. Bursala knelt on one knee and held her hands. He looked up into the loveliest of faces.

"There is nothing more that I would want than to carry you off and to keep you at my side until the end of time. However, I made a promise to Bale the night that he was murdered. I promised to help you so that you may return to your native homeland. I had a vision. I have prayed to Mungu at great lengths for a sign. Then, I looked all around me at the rolling rushes of the sea. The ocean rocked me upon her waves. It is the water, I believe, that will guide you to your home. Yallowahii found you at the ocean's edge. How else could you have arrived? I believe very strongly it is the passageway back to your land. I am not prepared to lose you. As you stand here before me, basked in luminescence, I know in my heart that you are the one true love of my life. Love is like sand held in clenched hands."

"You are sending me home?" Her eyes were wide, round, innocent pools of blue. "Bursala, how could it be so?"

"I believe, my lady, the answer has always been there, awaiting you. I treasure you so much that I would rather go on living without you than to see you stay here with such a sad, sad soul. You have turned around my heart's passion. All I ask of you is that we may share one last day together. And then..." He closed his eyes. "Then, I shall set you free."

Eden's eyes searched Bursala's face. She trusted him. She believed in his words. There was nothing more she wanted than to return to her family. "I will miss you. I will miss this grand place. It has all been like a dream to me. Some of it was terrible, but most of it was divine. I am ready, Bursala. I will never forget you and all the people I have come to know. Yes, I would like nothing more than to spend the day with you. You will live inside of my heart a lifetime. My only question to you is how? How do you say goodbye to the people who mean so much to you?"

Bursala shook his head. "You do not. You just move onward and forward, never looking back, yet always remembering the ones you left behind in your heart." Eden and Bursala knelt across from each other for a lengthy time. Very little was spoken as both were hypnotized by each other's brilliance.

Bursala knew how badly she wanted to go home. He would die without her. He could barely remember a time when he was not obsessed with her. The splendid Palace, his wealth and riches, and acclaim from the people of the land meant nothing to him without her. He would gladly trade them all in one instant if only he knew that she could love him. She could not. He envied her mate. What a lucky man he was, indeed. For this moment being, he was captivated by her, never wanting the moment to fade.

Eden wanted nothing more than to return to her life in New York. Her little house by the beach. Frank. The children. Annie and Dean. Her friends and family. Yet leaving now was going to be difficult. Bursala looked extraordinary in his formal Kingswear. His eyes, so dark and dreamlike, would always haunt her; she was sure of it.

Una, Mazi, Dahni, Wanyenya-Salina, Zinga, Kimu, Sava, and most of all, Yallowahii. She was going to miss them terribly. And this land, which breathed the very essence of dear, sweet Bale. Could she move onward and forward without looking back? She honestly did not know. All the people she had come to know and love in such a short period of time.

"What amazes me most about this place," she said to Bursala, "is how quickly people meet and care for one another. In my homeland it takes years to trust. Years to build a strong and meaningful relationship. Yet the days that I have been here have been immeasurable in the teachings of what caring for people is all about."

"'Tis true, my love. We trust and care and love very fast and unconditionally like animals do. If an animal is hungry and you feed it, it will depend on you. It will become your friend." Bursala tossed his head back and smiled. "Like Junju and Bale. It is quite simple, yet very complex. Bale accepted my poor one-armed brother, and Junju accepted Bale for his differences." Eden watched as he moved two fingers together. "Together, they connected and made a sacred bond, much like you and I. I am attached to you. Perhaps it was the abandonment I felt as a child when my mother was taken away from me. After all of this time, you have found your father. Yallowahii has told me all about your joining. That gives me the hope that I should continue to look over my shoulder for my mother. I shall never give up my search to find her."

Eden nodded. "Yes, Bursala. You must never give up."

He continued. "Perhaps it is because I never felt like I belonged to anyone anywhere before—until there was you." He took a step closer and held a strand of her hair between two fingers. "In you, Eden, I see a woman who has the ability to nurture the ones that you love. Like the way your eyes dance when you speak of your children...your mate. I can envision you holding your loved ones close to your breast."

Eden sat back on her heels as she felt her heartbeat pulsating inside her. "Bursala, you make me feel so weak."

"Ah, and you, my lady, make me feel strong." Their eyes locked together. Bursala placed his hand under her chin. "It is time for us to ride. Believe me when I tell you true. I would remain like this for a lifetime if I knew it could be so." He helped her to her feet, and together they walked out into the day.

They continued in silence to Eden's hut. "Bursala, if what you speak is true, then this is my last time in this little thatched hut that has become a home to me." She gazed around at the tiny quarters and remembered waking up on the first day to Una, who was terrified of her. She could still see Dahni bringing her water. All of the nights Yallowahii sat by her bedside and watched over her as she slept. She turned toward the opening, flooded with the memory of watching Bale and Mazi from inside. "Bale would bring me fruit...all kinds of fruit...and his smile would just light this whole place." She reached in between the sacks of grain and retrieved the knotted piece of plantain fiber. Twenty-eight knots for twenty-eight days. "This is all I have to give you to remember me by. With every knot tied into this rope, I have shed so many tears. Take it, Bursala, so that you will never forget my days here in your beautiful land of Zanzibar."

Bursala held the knotted piece of rope in his hands. He remembered finding her, left only to die. He thought of the way she threw it the night he had left for the island. He placed it in his pouch and patted it safely. "I shall never forget you, my love. I will keep it close to me always and forever."

Bursala sat down on her bed. "Go now to your people, and make your rounds. Do not say goodbye to them in words, only in thought. It is better that way. I shall wait here for you. And then...we shall spend our final hours together."

Eden nodded. She squared her shoulders and lifted her chin to the sun and stepped out into the colorful, busy little African village.

BUTTERFLY

M azi was the first person she saw. He sat outside his hut, hunched over a piece of wood. He was etching a spear for Dahni. His long parted hair fell over him as he worked. His clear gray eyes met hers as she neared.

"Another spear for Dahni, I see."

Mazi smiled up at her. "Oh yes. He is quite the hunter for a boy of eight. I am making this one a little larger. Dahni is growing. Someday, all too soon, he will be a man."

"And a fine man he will be. You are a wonderful father and teacher. A small boy needs positive guidance. I believe that Bale smiles down upon you every day. How proud he must be to know that his dearest friend is now married to his sister and the father to his nephew. Mazi, I do hope that all of your hunts are successful ones. And keep playing the *madinda*. Your musical talent far exceeds anything I have ever witnessed. Dahni, Wanyenya-Salina, and Una are very lucky to have you."

Mazi smiled up at her. "I remember a time—it does not seem like it was long ago—when Bale and I were little boys. Spirit Walker, I wish you could have grown up with us. Yet somehow, it feels like you have." He looked down and examined his spear. "Dahni is so much like Bale. Smart and quick and gentle." Mazi let out a sigh. "I miss him so very much. I still have trouble believing that he is gone. Bale has always been a part of me. I am at such a loss without him."

Eden took the spear from Mazi's hand and studied the fine workmanship. "We all miss him, Mazi. The night he was murdered, I mixed blood with him. He told me that he would always be with me, and I believe in his words. Not a day goes by when I am not reminded of his kind spirit. He talked of you often, calling you the brother he never had."

CHRISTMAS STARS OF ZANZIBAR

"His death was untimely," Mazi said dryly.

"You are right. He should still be with you and your people." Eden handed the spear back to Mazi. She leaned forward and touched his heart. "He is here, Mazi. Inside of you. Always and forever."

Mazi patted her hand and smiled. "Thank you for that." He leaned his head forward and continued his carvings. He cupped his hand over his eyes and looked up through the blinding sun. "Spirit Walker?" She was gone.

Una and her children were inside their hut. Dahni was whining because he was hungry. Eden watched him and sighed. Really, he was still such a small child. She would not be here to watch him grow. "My hands are full with two children!" Una smiled over at Eden. Una shot Dahni a look. "The big one is giving me so much grief today."

Eden placed her hands on the little boy's shoulders. "Where I come from, a child of eight is considered to be still very young. He would not be allowed to cross many streets or stay alone by himself. Yet here, there is so much expected from one so little. Let him be, Una. Embrace these years, for tomorrow they will flee, and he will be a man like his father, raising his own children." She shook her finger in front of Dahni's nose. "Only then will you know and understand how difficult it is to be a parent."

Eden picked up Wanyenya-Salina and kissed her. "Blessed baby who I helped bring into this world. Be safe...tiny one." She looked over at Una. "Tell her stories, Una. Stories of her uncle. Tell her about me and how much I loved her."

Una looked at Eden quizzically. Why was the Spirit Walker talking nonsense? As if she would not be here to watch her children grow. Eden gave the baby a final hug and handed her back to her mother. "Una, it gives me great pleasure to know that you and I have finally made our peace. Remember to count your blessings among the living. In my short stay here, if there is one thing that I have learned, it is how fast we are capable of love."

Una held Wanyenya-Salina close and draped an arm over Dahni's shoulder. In the busyness of the day, somehow, she had forgotten how rewarded she was. "Spirit Walker, it gives me joy to know that we are friends. I had never been a hateful woman, and I must admit, I did not like myself for the feelings I had toward you. Yallowahii told me that I would have to see things for what they are. I never dreamed that I would lose both a brother and a sister in such a short period of time. Through all the tragedies, I have made a friend. If I have not already done so, I take this opportunity to formally apologize to you for everything I have put you through. I am ashamed of my behavior, my sister, and I will always ask for your forgiveness."

"You and I are not as different as you may think, Una. We have both suffered losses, yet we have won. Sometimes the challenges in life are the ones worth living for. You and I are both mothers. We know and understand how easy it is to love a child and how difficult it is to raise one. In your land and in mine. In your time and mine. Love is love. That has never changed. I hold a deep respect for you, Una, more than you may or may not know. I am standing here before you now to tell you that I do. Wanyenya-Salina will grow up to be strong like you. Dahni will be three times the man of any other because he has had three fathers who loved and cared for him."

Una turned to place the baby on her bed. "Spirit Walker, why are you talking as if I will never see you again?" When she turned to face her, she was gone.

Eden proceeded over to Sava's hut. He was busy at work, extracting aloe from an aloe vera plant. Tama worked side by side with her mate. They both smiled as Eden neared them. She squatted beside the couple. Sava extended his hand and offered Eden a drop of the dewed substance. "It is good for your skin," he explained. Eden rubbed it into her hands, feeling the softness of the liquid. Her eyes met his, and she spoke.

"In all of my life, I have never seen anyone work with their hands the way that you do. Sava, you are a fine surgeon. Where I come from, they are called doctors...and you, Sava, are by far the most extraordinary of doctors I have ever had the pleasure of watching. You mended Yallowahii's leg, and for that I will always be grateful. You made me well when I thought I might die. I do not think that I have ever thanked you."

Tama spoke. "It is the Spirits who have blessed my mate with such high powers. There is no reason to thank him. It is his job," she explained. Tama then excused herself and went down to the plantain to retrieve more plants.

"My mate speaks the truth. Seeing you up and about is thanks enough. You have added mirth to our village. I was only too pleased to help you and make you well again."

"Sava, I have heard you secretly talk to Yallowahii about wanting to take me as your sixth mate." Eden bit her lip and looked at him demurely. "I am flattered that you cared so much for me." Sava smiled, displaying his usual broad smile of yellowed and decayed teeth. This time, Eden saw beauty in that smile. "You are a good man, Sava, and an old and dear friend to Yallowahii. He holds you in the highest esteem. Please continue to take care of him. Sometimes, I am afraid that he has lost his will to live. Promise me, Sava, that you will never let him give up."

Sava's face took on a pensive expression. "Spirit Walker, why? Why do you talk this way?" He studied the aloe vera plant he held in his hands. When he looked up, he was sitting alone.

*Eden watched from a distance as Kimu and Zinga ran through speckled fields of poppy plants. They were giddy and carefree like children at play. When they caught sight of her, they ran toward her. Zinga threw herself down and lay on her stomach while Kimu plopped beside her and tickled the side of his bride's face with a blade of grass. "It is a glorious day, Spirit Walker, and I have never been happier!" Zinga proclaimed.

Eden smiled. "I am glad for your happiness. Hold on to it. These are the days of your lives. You are young, and you are in love. Life could not be any grander. Never, never, never take each other for granted. Your love is vast out under these skies. I have told you stories of my homeland, and now you can picture things in your mind. I am very glad I was able to give that to you, Zinga."

Kimu picked a flower, reached over, and placed it in Eden's hair. Then he turned toward Zinga, tickled her, and wrestled her teasingly on the warm, soft earth. Eden's eyes glistened as she watched how merry they were together. "You are absolutely shining, Zinga. I can tell that Kimu brings you joy."

"Oh, Spirit Walker, he does." Zinga jabbed her mate playfully in the ribs. "You look blissful as well." Zinga leaned forward and whispered in Eden's ear, "It is Bursala, is it not? I saw him earlier in Yallowahii's hut. He is so very handsome, yes?"

Eden giggled with her young companion. "Yes, Zinga. Bursala is very handsome." She felt the need to share with Zinga the news of Bursala taking her to the gateway of her home. She could hear his words echo inside her: "Say goodbye to them in thought, not in words. It is better that way." He was right. She did not want to spoil such a cherished and peaceful moment for Zinga and Kimu.

Kimu bounced to his feet. "Come, Zinga! Catch me if you can," he called over his shoulder. Zinga laughed and stood. She began to chase Kimu through the fields. She turned toward Eden to beckon her to follow. Zinga stopped dead in her tracks and looked around. The Spirit Walker was gone, and she and Kimu were alone in nature's garden.

Eden trudged slowly to Yallowahii's hut. Her heart felt heavy as she entered. He was lying on his side, taking a nap. He opened his eyes the moment she walked in. "The heat of the day has gotten to me, I am afraid. Please, child. Come." He motioned. She sat on the edge of his bed and stared at him for a long time. She shook her head back and forth sadly, and tears were beginning to fill her eyes. Yallowahii touched her hand. "Where is Bursala?" he asked.

"He is waiting for me in my hut."

Yallowahii's thin and weathered face lifted into a smile. A very sad smile. "He is a fine man, so much like his father."

Eden nodded. "That story you told me last night about the gazelle was truly a wonderful tale. It is a story that will stay with me for a lifetime." Eden lowered her eyes and wiped the tears that were flowing heavily now. "I have learned so much from you."

Yallowahii shook his head. "It is you, Spirit Walker, who has taught me. I had almost forgotten how wonderful it is to love and care for a child of my own. The most difficult part about loving someone so much is the hurt that comes along with it. The suffering of letting go." Yallowahii tried to toughen his words, although he, too, could feel the tears brimming in his eyes. "Go to him. Do not keep the King waiting." Yallowahii turned his face away from hers. "You will not return to me. This I know."

"I do not know." Eden spoke quietly.

Yallowahii avoided making eye contact with her. "I promise you this. Someday, somewhere, in another dimension in time, we shall see each other again. Christmas Stars belong together in the heavens."

Eden's voice was small. "Am I going to die?"

"You will move onward and forward, butterfly. You will continue to walk with the Spirits. It is time for you to go."

Eden clutched the old man's hands. "This is one Christmas I shall never forget. The chance to be with you again has meant more to me than I could ever possibly put into words. I will always look back upon this time with great fondness. My father, my prolific father." Eden touched his face and turned it toward hers. "Will you always watch over me? Like the time I saw you at the ocean when I was six years old? And the time you were in the department store looking through the water globe? I need to know that I will see your face again."

Yallowahii looked into the blueness of her eyes. "I will always watch over you."

"Does Bursala speak the truth about the gateway to my home?"

Yallowahii smoothed her hair away from her face. "The answer lies within. It has always been. You came here to this land, and you felt death in your hands. With those same hands, you brought life into our Clan. You have come face to face with danger. You have looked into the eyes of love. You shall never be the person you were before. It is time for you to fly. Spread your wings, child. The time has come." Eden stood to her feet, and Yallowahii followed. They both fell into each other's arms, locked in an urgent embrace.

"I...I am not sure that I could walk away from you."

"Yes, you must. You are the Spirit Walker. The Spirits will walk you out and guide you. I told you before, the time will come for you to walk and never turn around. I warned you that you will know the time when it is upon you. Now you must leave. You must hold your head high and never turn around. Focus, Eden. Focus on looking straight ahead of you."

"But...all of a sudden, I feel as if I am not ready to leave."

"You are ready." Yallowahii's voice took on a stern tone, and he pushed her away from him. "Hold your head upward, and never turn around, from this moment forward," he repeated.

Eden's eyes drank him in for one last moment. To her, he was ethereal. She could still see the light around him. She turned her face toward the opening of the hut, and with tears streaming down her face, she walked out into the brightness of the day with every bit of courage she could muster. She never saw the tears that fell from Yallowahii's timeless face. And like a butterfly, she opened her arms and let the Spirits guide her home.

Goodbye, my little Spirit Walker. Goodbye...my Christmas Star of Zanzibar.

Bursala's Return

Eden held onto Bursala as they sailed across the East African coast. Acacia trees spread over the land like grand umbrellas sheltering the two from their stormy emotions. Eden watched as they sped past her. Bursala was riding at great speed, and his long ebony hair swept across her face. Bursala's entourage of Kingsmen rode behind him as if they could not keep up with the quick and powerful pace.

The lavish land unfolded all around them. In her heart, she knew that she would miss the once-so-foreign region that had become a home to her. She was leaving her father behind. Eden leaned her chin upon Bursala's shoulder and tightened her grasp around him. Her fingers could feel the muscles in his chest. His stomach was tight and rippled. His back was strong against her breasts. The sheen of his hair reflected the sun with dazzling strands of shimmering navy highlights. He smelled so good, like the wind and the sea. She could taste his adventurous spirit; she breathed in his dauntless freedom.

What if Bursala were wrong? She picked her head up suddenly. He was wise, and he was King, yet a passageway through the water sounded irrational. If he spoke the truth, the day Una tried to drown her in the ocean could have taken her home. Yallowahii had saved her. Had he not, she never would have found her father inside of him. And Jita! He had tried to kill her as well. He had kicked her beaten body down onto the water's edge. That time, Bursala had saved her. She thought about it. She could have journeyed home that time as well. And then...she would never have met him. This man of divinity whom she held so close to her heart. She decided she would not have traded her time in Zanzibar for anything. "It has all been like a dream to me," she said aloud with the wind in her face.

Bursala looked over his shoulder. "Did you say something, my love?"

Eden held him tighter. She could feel his chest tighten beneath her touch. "I am frightened, Bursala."

He came to an abrupt halt. As the entourage of men neared, he waved them on. "My dear, please do not be afraid. For it is I who will be left alone. Understand this if you can. Today you shall move forward to the place where you belong. With your family...with your..." Bursala squinted his eyes and looked out into the ocean. "With your mate. You are the Spirit Walker. You shall not die. Today, my lady, today is the day that I shall die."

Eden looked deep into the darkness of his eyes. How they would always haunt her. "You will not die, Bursala. You may feel sadness today. I know how that feels. It feels as if you are dead inside. Tomorrow will bring new and exciting things for you; I am sure of that."

Bursala jumped off his Arabian horse and held his hand out to guide her down. Together they walked along the shore and found a spot in the sand beneath a palm tree. He looked down at the sand and cupped his hands around it, allowing it to filter through his fingers slowly. "When I set you free, I shall die. I am not a Spirit Walker. I will not survive. I will not allow fear to enter into this heart of mine."

"Look at me, Bursala." He turned his ravishing face toward hers. No one ever had looked at her the way he did. "I do not understand what you are trying to say to me. You will not die physically."

Bursala nodded slowly. "The moment I set you free, I shall die. You are the true love of my life. Please, Eden, do not cry tears for me. Allow me to live inside of you for a lifetime. I am prepared to face my death. I am ready for it. I would rather end my life than to go on living without you." Bursala let out a small laugh. "I am not at all frightened."

Eden placed her hand on top of his. "I cannot let you do this."

"Oh, but you must. I will see to it that you return to your homeland. I gave my word to Bale. I am a man of my word."

"There is something I have been wanting to share with you. When my father died, I was just a little girl. I shared the same pain you did when your mother left you when you were just a baby. I, too, was abandoned by the one person who meant the world to me. Now, after all this time, I have found him again. You must never give up on the hope that you, too, will be reunited with your mother. I feel very strongly that you shall see her face again. Bursala, I believe profoundly that in each other, we have found what we are searching a lifetime for."

"That is why it is difficult for me to set you free. I feel the same way that you do." Bursala helped Eden to her feet. "Come. I am anxious to see my family."

They continued their ride to the Royal Enclosure at a much slower pace. The sun blazed feverishly above them out under the skies of Zanzibar. When they arrived at the walls of the Palace, Eden had to blink hard at the spectacular sight she beheld. There to greet them both was a herd of elephants—with Junju perched upon the grandest one.

"Brother! You have finally returned!" Junju's eyes danced, and his demeanor was advantageous. "Oh, and you have brought Edi with you! I am overjoyed to see you both again!"

Eden cupped her hand and looked up at Junju and waved to him. "I have never seen such magnificent animals!"

Junju nodded. "They are spectacular, I agree. Brother..." Junju's eyes widened. "Show me what have you brought me from the islands?" he asked excitedly. Bursala walked toward him and stroked the elephant's trunk. He handed his brother a sack filled with trinkets of gold and copper and silver.

"They are splendid indeed." Junju grinned. "These gifts are fine, and I thank you. However, nothing compares to the treasure you have brought for yourself, dear brother," he said, looking straight at Eden. Junju's face took on a serious expression. He placed his hand over his heart and made a circular motion upon his chest. "I miss him," he said sadly.

Eden knew he was referring to Bale. "Yes. I do too." She smiled up at him.

Bursala's sister Sanda came running along the hills of gold toward her brothers. "Bursala, I was scared half to my death when you did not return home to us on the tenth day. I do not know whether to hit you or hug you!" She chose the latter as she flung her arms around his neck. She then whispered in his ear, "I told you, dear brother, if it were meant to be, it would be." She was referring to the presence of the woman beside him.

Bursala wished that he could tell his sister everything, that within hours Eden would vanish, and he would die. He could not. He placed a hand upon her innocent face and touched her. Fondly, he would remember her as the free spirit she would always be to him. "For you, Sanda." He pulled out a string of pearls from his pouch and placed them around her neck.

She touched them with her hands and smiled up at him. "Bursala, they are very lovely. Thank you." Sanda walked over to Eden, and the two women admired the tiny, exotic white beads. He was home. His brother. His sister. The Royal Enclosure. The elephants and horses. This fair-haired lady by his side. If only it all could just remain...

Junju slid off the mammoth, as he, too, was interested in Sanda's necklace.

Eden turned to see a woman walking slowly toward them. The others turned to see who Eden was looking at. Bursala's face broke into a huge smile. "Dear Mother!" he cried. He ran toward her, filled with emotion. Bursala took his hands and pushed away the mourning veil that covered her face and kissed her. For that one moment, Eden noticed, he did not look like a gallant King. He did not look so noble. He looked like a young man in the arms of his oldest sister that he referred to as his mother. They shared the same shark like eyes. The same incredible face.

"Bursala." She spoke softly. "We are reunited once again. You are home with us now."

"Not for long, Mother!" he wanted to shout. "Your son is alive in flesh and blood only. Can you see? Inside I am dying...or I will be once I set the love of my life free."

"Sweet Mother, how your radiance fills me. Come. I would like you to make the acquaintance of someone very dear to me. They call her the Spirit Walker of our people."

Evanli slipped her arm through Bursala's and walked over to where Eden was standing. "So you are the one I have heard so much talk of. Junju speaks very highly of you, as does Bursala. I can see why." Evanli scrunched her nose and examined Eden's features. "You certainly are a sight of wonder to these eyes. How fair you are and lovely, like the morning sky. You are welcomed to our home and in our land."

"Thank you. Your kind words touch me."

Evanli turned toward Bursala. "Our father has come to me in visions. I hear his words clearly. It is your name he calls out. I am wise, Bursala. I am your sister, the only mother you have ever known. Do what it is that you believe you must. And if I should cry out to you, do not listen. Continue your journey, and follow your heart." Her eyes blazed into his as she placed her hand on his chin. "Do you understand me, Bursala?" Then she added, "Your sisters have prepared a feast in the honor of your return. Let us celebrate." Bursala watched his loved ones as they walked ahead of him. If everything went according to his plan, this would be his last walk through the gates of the Royal Enclosure.

In the splendor of the Palace, Sanda escorted Eden to her quarters. She drew a bath and filled it with sweet-smelling spices and herbs. The tub was surrounded by lit torches of fire. Eden sank deep into the water, breathing in the floral essence. Her skin felt soft and smooth as she bathed in a sea of rose petals.

Bursala sat with his mother in his own private quarters. He told her of his wild and great adventures while sailing over to the exotic islands of Karagwe. He brought her skins of alligators and the pelts of foxes and mink. "The greatest gift you could give me was the chance to see your face again," she told him. "It is not in accordance with tradition to marry someone who was not arranged by your mother or father. There are women, Bursala, whom, since the day they were born, were reared to act like a Queen. Sadly, this Spirit Walker is not among them. Yet here you sit before me. You are alive and well and happy—"

Bursala interrupted. "'Tis true. I am alive and well. But that is all."

"Bursala. If you love her, go after her. Do not let her slip away. If anyone could alter the tradition, surely it is you. Go where your heart may lead you."

"It is not that simple." Bursala sighed. "If only it were. She shall never belong to the likes of me. With all this wealth and power that surrounds me, I am left humbly alone. This woman loves another. She yearns for her loved ones back in her homeland. My vow to Bale was to help her find the gateway to her home."

A smile came to Evanli's lips. "Bursala. Bursala. You are a man full of passion. Full of dreams. So kind and good are you. Whatever you decide to do, please know that you are loved and adored by all whose lives you have touched. I know what you are planning. When Suna came to me in visions, he spoke about a waterway, which will lead to your death. You will save her life and risk your own. All in the name of love. Bursala, you have been, all of my life, like a son to me."

"And all of my life, Mother, I felt as if I did not truly belong to anyone anywhere. I knew I was different. Sometimes, Mother, I still feel that way. I want to run away from all of the pain. If I cannot have the one woman whom I have fallen helplessly in love with, then I feel like I do not have the will to go on living. I am afraid I am not talking much like a King."

"Bursala, you must not run away this time. You must learn to be still. You are headstrong, and you will do what you wish. This I know. Who, Bursala... who could ever replace you and take your reign as King?"

"It shall be revealed at the time of my death."

"Is there anything I can say that will keep you here with me?"

Bursala fell into his Evanli's arms. The mother who had brought him into this world would not see him out. His time had come. He longed to be with his real mother now.

"Just tell me...tell me where I belong in the great big world of sadness. For I truly do not know."

After Eden's bath, she changed into one of the robes that Bursala had given her. Sanda used artistic measures and outlined Eden's eyes with black charcoal. The gown that was given to her by Bursala was linen and dyed with crushed stones that featured rich deep-crimson hues. An exquisite braiding of gold was tied in an empire fashion. The bodice of the gown was low and plunging, and her breasts heaved with each and every breath she took. A cloak of gold was tied around her shoulders and cascaded and trailed behind her. The formal dress was created to represent the simplicity of an Egyptian Queen and the flamboyance of a Mesopotamian one. A coiled snake made of emeralds and rubies was fastened around her upper arm. Sanda twisted Eden's hair into a bun. She left long spiral tendrils to frame her face. She decorated her hair with jewels that glittered. "You look like a Queen above all Queens!" Together they joined the others in a feast of celebration.

When Eden stepped into the room, all eyes poured over her. Bursala was spellbound and immobilized by her majestic presence. He held out his hand and guided her to the Sacred Fire. There, he sat with Evanli on his right and Eden on his left.

There were Busoga bands and an abundance of the finest wines. And dancers! Eden had never seen so many exotic and extraordinary women with ornate headdresses made from long and colorful peacock feathers. Beads of copper and silver adorned their necks and arms and shimmered against their native dark skin. Ear ornaments constructed of gold and bedazzled with jewels dangled gracefully to their bare shoulders. They danced in front of and only for Bursala, yet he seemed never to notice them. It was as if he and Eden were all alone. Eden watched as the colorful array of women thrust their bodies in front of their King to the beat of the music. She was drawn in by their sexual spell.

Eden could feel her heart flutter as her eyes met his. Then he winked at her. *So handsome is he*, she thought. How she would miss those eyes...those sexy Arabian dark eyes that clicked the trigger to her heart with no warning at all.

There were drums and fifes and laughter. There were priests of high mediums who had traveled far and wide for the gala affair of Bursala's return. They ate pheasant, sweet potatoes, horse mackerel, and sole. There were baskets filled with fresh-picked fruit and loaves of sweet-smelling bread. Eden watched as Bursala held a carafe of wine to his moist, dark lips. He leaned close to her and whispered in her ear. "Eat. Drink. Enjoy."

She obeyed and sipped the wine that was poured for her. It was stronger than any wine she had ever tasted before. She felt bemused as the potent drink made her drunk. The dancers encircled them, moving so fast they became a display of colors orbiting around her. They were sensually riveting, and Eden could feel the heat of desire filling her with every sip of the wine she consumed.

Bursala raised his jeweled chalice to his mouth. He, too, was feeling the powerful effect of the dancers. Yet it was not a dancer he craved. Beads of perspiration formed on his forehead beneath the silken rope that was fastened over his brow. She looked captivating tonight. Lovelier than he ever dreamed any woman could ever be. He wanted to taste her, to kiss her, to feel her body next to his. The intoxicating night was full of pure magic.

Eden watched as Bursala remained sure footed and confident throughout the affair. Women batted their eyelashes at him and giggled and laughed as they spoke to him. Men were in awe of him. They spoke to him in revered tones and admirable gestures. All through the night, no matter whom he talked to, Bursala's eyes bore into hers. He laughed and took turns dancing with each of his sisters. Eden watched as he trumped through the crowds with an aire of finesse.

Junju stood before her. "Dance with me, Edi." His eyes pleaded with her. "Tonight is a celebration, for my brother has returned." Eden held onto Junju's hand and immediately felt the effects of the wine as she stood to her feet. "Bursala is happy. Happier than I have ever seen him. Edi, I do believe it has all to do with you." Eden realized that Junju was the only one besides Bale to call her Edi. She liked that. "Look at him." Junju nodded in his brother's direction. "He dances, and he laughs, yet he never takes his eyes off of you."

Eden swayed to the music. She did not know how to move to the tribal sounds of the dance. She looked over at Bursala, and he smiled at her. His movements were strikingly exciting and mysteriously different. Through the sea of people and the loud, heady music, Eden felt as if his every movement were designed especially for her.

After the dance, Bursala clapped his hands together twice, and silence fell upon the room. He looked around at the many faces and cleared his throat to speak. He spoke first to his men. "Prepare my finest canoe, and leave it for me at the ocean's edge." Quickly and without question, the Kingsmen dispersed and obeyed his command.

"Brother, are you going somewhere?" Junju spoke out from the crowd. "You have returned for only a short spell."

Bursala looked over at Junju. Poor, poor one-armed Junju. His eyes then fell upon Sanda and the rest of his sisters. Evanli. His family. His friends. His servants. His guests. The dancers. Then his eyes found Eden. "Yes, Junju. My duties take me away once again. I made a vow to a friend."

Bale, Junju thought. *He made the promise to Bale, and he remembered.*

Eden walked across the room to where Bursala stood. "The time has come, my love. For if I should wait a moment longer, I may become selfish and keep you here all to myself," he whispered into her ear.

"Bursala, you mustn't. I am afraid for you and for me. Let me stay here with you. Please, I beseech you. Do not risk your life for me. I could not bear the thought of any harm coming to you." Her full lips sparkled like the wine.

Bursala turned toward her. Eden had never seen so much love in anyone's eyes before. "My dear, your words do so tempt me. There is nothing more that I would rather have than you." His hand reached out and touched her face. "Yet I know that your words are spoken in fear. For if you should stay here with me tomorrow, you shall come to resent me. No, I would rather live on fondly in your dreams. The time has come for you to be strong. Be strong for the both of us, Eden, for I do so love you." Bursala and Eden were whispering to each other. His voice was like poetry in her ear.

"Where will you go?" Sanda asked, standing close to Junju. "And when, dear brother, shall we expect your return?"

Bursala could feel his throat tighten. He folded Eden's hand in his. "I will never be far, for I shall live in all of your hearts as you shall all continue to live in mine."

Evanli placed her hands over her face and began to cry into them. Junju and Sanda embraced their oldest sister. Bursala kissed Eden's hand and then let it go. He walked over to his mother. "Sweet, sweet Evanli. Do not cry for me." He looked up at her and held her hands. Evanli dropped to her knees and held him. "Our mother is calling me. Be happy for me." He locked his eyes with hers. "I deserve to see her face again." Evanli ran her fingers through the wealth of his shiny black hair. She stroked the long strands that hung past his shoulders.

"You, Bursala, deserve everything that is good and pure. I will miss you."

Bursala's eyes were alive and bright. The tiny creases around them danced. "Oh, and I shall miss you."

Sanda placed her cheek upon the top of his head. "My brother," she said, "for all of my life, you have been so dear and close to me." She did not cry. Bursala admired her bravery. One by one, each sister came over and added to the huddle. Finally, Junju walked over, and Bursala stood to meet his brother. They wrapped their arms around each other. He held Junju's face in his hands and looked at him for a long and lengthy time. "You are the man of the family now. I leave to you my Kingdom and my throne."

"Bursala, I am not a King. My deformity…I am a disgrace. People will mock me. They will laugh at me."

Bursala shook his head slowly. "No, Junju. When I look at you, I see an intact man. Our brother Kiro was the deformity, for he was born without a heart. You are strong, Junju. I have always admired you…and…I always will."

Eden watched. She decided at that moment that she would not let Bursala die. "Come." He held her hand. "Let us move into the night. Our time has come for us to move onward and forward."

Evanli's cries went into loud hysterics. "No! Bursala, no!" She wailed as she stretched out her arms.

"Sister," Junju said bravely, "let him go. His destiny awaits him."

Oh, and if I die before my time

Oh, sweet sister of mine

Please do not regret me

If I die

The Forbidden Fruit

CHRISTMAS STARS OF ZANZIBAR

Outside the Palace the cries from Evanli, joined by the others, echoed through the night. Junju's cries were loud, and Bursala could feel them penetrating through his heart. The sky was dark as if the heavens were cursing him. Without words, Bursala held Eden's hand and guided her over the wooden bridge that led to the sandy shores of the Indian Ocean. They were alone beneath the starry skies of Zanzibar. With the glow of the albescent moon on his skin, Bursala looked entrancing. "It is only you and I. I have dreamed of this moment for a lifetime. You are like the dawn of a new day to me. Full of light...full of life's promises." He spoke gallantly to her.

"Bursala, I—"

"Shh." He placed his finger upon her lips and traced them lightly. "Before I enter into the next state, I long to feel your lips upon mine. I know that your heart belongs to another, and believe me when I tell you I would never step in his way. This love is a forbidden one. We shall keep this secret in the dark and carry it to our graves. What I need to know from you, Eden, is this: Do you wish to kiss me?"

"Yes." Eden breathed into his ear.

Bursala placed both hands upon her radiant moonlit face. His eyes drank in each of her delicate features. He placed his mouth over hers and kissed her passionately...emotionally. The fire rose inside him as her lips parted and his tongue found hers.

And she let him kiss her. Feeling weak and powerless to his touch. She could feel his heart beating against hers. She felt as if the entire heavens were spinning and spinning. It was difficult to hold her ground. Impossible to hold on. Bursala moved his body closer to her, his hands never leaving her face. He pulled his face away and stared into the bluest eyes he had ever seen. They were sweet and brilliant and so full of life. He smiled and brushed her hair away from her face. He pulled her close again, and she rested her chin upon his strong shoulder.

"It is most unfair that soon I shall release you, for I have only just found you." He breathed into her. His hands moved slowly from her face to her shoulders. "I want to look at you. I want to see you and capture your memory inside of my heart forever," he whispered.

She untied the cloak and allowed it to fall to the ground. She slipped off the ornate gown and stood unveiled before him and positioned the jewel-encrusted snake on his toned arm. Bursala's mouth caressed her neck, and slowly his tongue fluttered against her ample breasts. She tossed her head back and touched his long silky hair with her fingertips. Her body burned for him. He set her on fire like no one had ever done before. Not even Frank.

"You are bewitching." He sighed and tasted her. "I want to lay naked with you. For one sweet moment in time, I want to feel the warmth of your skin so close to mine. Do you want me, my love?"

"Yes. Yes, Bursala. I want you. Take me over the edge. Take me..." She pulled off his silky robe, and together they fell to the ground with urgency. Her hands stroked him. "Bursala," she confided. "Oh, Bursala, you are every inch a King."

He rolled her down to the sand and licked and kissed every square inch of her body. He used his tongue erotically and sensually, and she felt the roughness of his shadowed beard rubbing against her silken thighs. He opened her up like the petals of a flower and experienced the nectar of her forbidden fruit. He was starving for her with an insatiable appetite. He tasted her slowly, breathing fire deep into her. Taking full possession of her region, his mouth explored and absorbed her completely.

She felt her senses escalating as the lower portion of her body rose in pure, shameless pleasure. Relishing his amorous sensitivity and losing all reasoning of her sensibility, she became empowered by his heat. Allowing him to dangerously devour her while she ran her fingers wildly through his hair. He stopped for a moment, looked up at her, and with a frenzied desire, he began again. This time vigorously, humming noises that reverberated into the depths of her being.

"Oh, Bursala. You make me feel so..." she crooned in delight and ecstasy. He traced his lips over her thighs and made his way to the softness of her belly.

Eden sat and drew him close. She ran her fingers across his chest and began kissing him there. Running her tongue across his nipples and up to his shoulders, which glistened golden beneath the moon. He clasped his hands together behind his head, kneeling before her naked and beautiful like a god. He turned his head to the side, and with his teeth, he began to bite his shoulder. So sensual was he to her eyes; it made her shudder.

She removed his mouth and replaced it with hers. Running her tongue over his muscular arms, tracing the skin of his sturdy torso and taking great pleasure in doing so. She could hear his breathing become more rapid, and he allowed his body to fall back onto the sand. Her hair fell over him as she continued to brush her soft, wet lips against his skin. Never before did she desire to kiss a man the way she was kissing Bursala now. With every touch of her hands and with every movement of her mouth, she delivered to him rich and deep feelings of love.

Bursala took her in his arms and kissed her. He then sat up on his knees and placed her in front of him. From behind, he wrapped himself around her and touched and fingered her firm, full breasts. She tilted her head back toward the moon. His hands worked magic over her as she closed her eyes to the night. On the roundness of her derriere, she could feel the warmth of his manhood. It excited her, took hold of her, as she dug her hands into the sand.

"I love you, Eden," he whispered in her ear with lusty wetness. "I always will."

She turned to face him. "Bursala." Her voice was low and sultry. "I will always love you too." She draped her strong and slender legs around him, and with a burning desire, she received him. A tantalizing vibrational wave began at her toes, arched into her back, and flowed out of her eyes. Her entire being was alive and awakened by him, and every molecule of her body felt as if it were levitating closer to God.

Being inside her consumed him. He was tuned in to every one of his cells. There was no division between him and her. A pure, unfiltered fervor ran feverishly through every vein in his body. He was fully surrendering to her.

They exploded together in the throes of passion as he continued to hold her hands in his. With gentle touches, he brushed her hair away from her face. "You are glowing, my darling," he crooned. The tiny creases around his eyes seemed to dance, and his thumbs remained incompressible against her cheekbones.

Her eyes searched his, and she replied, "Tonight, you made me feel like a Queen. For as long as I live, I know I will never forget this moment." Together they stayed locked in an embrace as Bursala continued to stroke her hair. Eden comfortably nuzzled close to him and rested her chin upon his chest. "Tell me all about yourself." Her eyes pleaded with his. "Tell me everything so that when I am far, I can feel the closeness of you."

"I am King Bursala of Uganda."

"What is your favorite color?" Eden asked, wide eyed like a child. She stretched her naked body out over his and rested her face upon his beating heart.

"Colors? The sky, the ocean, the grass, the trees." Bursala touched a strand of her hair. "The color of your hair...I do fancy the color of your hair. They say that from birth, I was destined to become King. My brothers and I were given land to each of us in different districts. As you know, by the time I was two, my mother had died. At the age of four or five, my father, Suna, commanded me to leave my family. Evanli is the only mother I can remember. It broke my heart to leave Junju and my sisters.

"A man was appointed to me to become my guardian. This land, which was given to me, was used for my guardian and I to dwell upon. A Mujtaba tree was planted to show my possession of the land. The estate was later known as the Mujtaba because of that tree.

"My father would come as often as his duties allowed. I was being reared every day of my young life to someday become the King of the land. I never truly felt like I belonged to anyone anywhere. I always felt as if I were all alone. My oldest brother, Kiro, also had his own land in his own district. There he lived with his guardian. My father did not have great faith in him for his own obvious reasons. Only on very special occasions was I allowed to visit the Capitol, or the Palace, as you know it. It would make my heart so sad to see Junju and my sisters riding horses, playing in the fields, and playing games like Weso. The thought of never truly knowing my mother always filled me with sadness. There was very little time for me to be a child."

Bursala took on a faraway look in his eyes and shifted his jaw to one side. He sat in the sand, naked and exposed, with one knee bent. His mane was tousled and hung down past his nipples. The snake wrapped around his arm captured the moonlight. "Ah, yet there were times when I would come home for a visit, and Junju and Sanda would say to our father that I was thinking in the fields." His eyes began to dance as he spoke. "They would hide me in the stables, and there we would play throughout the day. Junju would make me laugh so. Sanda gave me no special attention, which I adored. Understand, I am accustomed to people bowing at my feet. Serving me. Catering to my every wish and whim. You, my lady, are much like Sanda. Perhaps that is why my heart cried out for you." Bursala leaned forward and kissed Eden on her nose. "Tell me about you."

"Your Majesty," she said through long, dark lashes. The charcoal liner around her eyes added even more dramatic glamour to her lovely face. "My name is Eden Salina." She placed a finger upon her lips and thought. "My favorite color is purple. Like the color of your robe and the sky right before it turns to black. I grew up in a place called Queens." Eden saw Bursala's expression, and she giggled. "It is not what you think. Believe me, Bursala, in your wildest dreams, you could never picture such a place. Buildings in the city that reach up to the sky. And rows and rows of them! People everywhere. Technology...I would not know how to explain it all to you.

"I went to school; that is a place where children learn to read and write. I had friends. There were parties and dances and football games and boyfriends. You would be truly dazzled by my world. And my whole world would be dazzled by you. My family was simple, not rich and elaborate like yours. We lived in a small house, and we loved each other and had a lot of fun growing up. In comparison to you, Bursala, my story is quite ordinary.

"I lived with my family until I was twenty-one. Then I got married to a man." She hesitated for a moment and then continued. "To a man I love very much. We have three beautiful children—Benjamin, Tara, and Nicholas—and a little house with a garden. Now I am here with you.

"Yallowahii told me that I had traveled with the Spirits. I do not know how such a thing could be possible, but I believe him. After all these years, just like you, I was always searching for my father. In Yallowahii, I have found him. And I am going to miss him." Her eyes looked over to the dark, foamy waves. "I shall miss Bale. Fuck it...I am going to miss you so much."

"Fuck it!" Bursala repeated, and they both laughed. They laughed and rolled around in the sand, naked and frolicsome.

"Bursala, it has been magical lying here with you in your arms. I almost do not want to leave. The thought of that ocean tonight terrifies me. Help me to understand what is about to take place. You will not really die tonight, will you?"

"I shall, my love."

"I cannot let you do this. What kind of person would I be if I did? I will stay here with you and Yallowahii and all the people who have been so kind to me. Bursala." She looked deep into his eyes. "I cannot let you die for me."

"I am touched by your concerns. However, I am a man of my word. Do not be afraid for me. I am not afraid to die. I would be more afraid of living each and every day without you." Eden laid her head back down upon his bare chest. They lay like that for a long time without another word spoken. They left their clothes and jewels in the sand for vagabonds to find. He picked her up in his captive embrace and walked over to his canoe. He gently set her inside, stood in the sand, and pushed the canoe into the rocky waters. He hopped over the side and let the waves carry them out. They sat opposite each other, consumed with enchantment. Then he leaned in close to her. "Do you believe in me?" he asked.

"Yes, Bursala. I do. With all of my heart."

"After this moment forward, we shall no longer be together. You must believe in my words when I tell you true that you have made my life complete. You are the *Love of My Life*. We will always be connected. We shall always share a secret bond. How would I be able to go on from sunset to sunset without you, dear one? If I did not drown tonight in this ocean, I would surely die of a broken heart. It is better this way. All I ask of you is this. Remember me forever...until...the end of time."

Eden bit her lip and looked up at the twinkling heavens. She had witnessed the historic North Star. The majesty and the glory of the first Christmas. She had made love to a King, a Wise Man who followed that Star. She had been the chosen one. The stars glistened luminously, casting ribbons of silver upon the waves. She could imagine Yallowahii brought down so low and so sad over her departure. "I will always remember you, Bursala. That is my promise to you. In my dreams at night, you will always haunt me. I feel connected to you now. I will always be connected with you."

"Your amulet! It is still on the sand! I will fetch it and come back to you."

"Bursala, please do not leave me alone."

Bursala dove into the water and swam through the waves. "I will only be a moment," he called out to her. True to his words, he returned and climbed back into the canoe. He tied his silken rope onto her wet amulet and handed it to her. "This amulet will keep you safe. You must travel with it. When you touch the rope, I will always stay alive inside of your heart." He fastened it around her waist and showed her his own pouch. Inside was the knotted piece of plantain fiber with the twenty-eight knots tied into it. He patted it and fastened it to his waist.

"When you close your eyes to dream at night...dream of me and our time together. I am happy that you have found your father after such a long time. My own mother awaits me. Soon, very soon, I will be in her arms, and you will be in the arms of your loved ones. We are both going home to the places in which we belong. Now take my hand. Together we shall jump into the sea. She is calling out our names. Listen, Eden. Listen to the ocean." Eden listened to the splashing sea and held his hand tightly in hers.

"Farewell, my dear. My love, my sweet, sweet girl."

"Goodbye, Bursala. Goodbye."

They stood on the edge of the canoe and looked at each other for one last time. A long and lasting stare. Hand in hand, they jumped into the blackness of the Indian Ocean.

The Passageway

Their bodies descended into the deep. They could still see each other. Eden's hair flowed all around her like a mermaid of the islands. Bursala's locks moved all around him. Hand in hand, they journeyed farther and farther down toward the ocean's floor. Bursala's hand escaped from hers. Frantically, Eden tried with all of her might to grab ahold of him. She was frightened and frenzied, and through her panic, she lost sight of him. "Bursala! Bursala! Where are you?" She tried to swim in the direction she had last seen him, but the current was too great. For that split second, Eden wanted nothing more than to stay with the mighty and powerful King of Uganda. Under the stars and beneath the water, she felt a love so strong for him.

Now she was on her own.

New York (Present Day)

Dr. Mutebi covered Bale's face with a sheet. "I am so sorry, Mr. Salina. I am afraid we've lost him. We did everything we could."

Frank cried into his hands. "Oh God." He sobbed. "Oh God."

Annie put her arms around him. "We came so close, Frank. It just isn't fair. There was nothing any of us could do to save him. You have to believe in his words and know that Eden is out there somewhere. And that she is alive and safe."

Frank rubbed his hands over his face. "The moment we lost Bale, we lost Eden. Don't you understand that?" Frank's shoulders heaved as he cried. "We lost her, Annie. We've lost her forever."

"Frank, I'll never give up on Eden. She's a fighter. As long as she is alive, I believe in my heart that she will return to us. Don't give up on her, Frankie. You are stronger than that. Pull yourself together and be strong. I know you can do it." Her eyes bore into his, and she shook him. "Keep the faith alive, Frank. You've got to keep your love alive."

"I can't, Annie. I just can't anymore." He sobbed more heavily. "I just can't."

Dr. Mutebi placed a hand on Frank's shoulder. "Come, Mr. Salina." Both Annie and the doctor helped escort Frank to the door. Frank turned to take one last look over at Bale's covered body. "Wait!" He broke free from their hold and ran over toward the bed. Annie and the doctor exchanged glances. "Something is moving under the sheet. He's still breathing. He's still alive!" Frank shouted. Annie and Dr. Mutebi turned to see a still sheet lying upon a dead man.

"Mr. Salina! No!" the doctor warned.

Frank tore the sheet from across the bed. Lying beneath it was Eden! She was gasping and panting for air. Naked, wet, and shivering, her hair tangled with seaweed.

"Dear God in heaven!" Annie placed a hand to her forehead and felt her knees go weak.

Dr. Mutebi shone a small surgical light into her eyes, and Frank pushed him aside.

"Eden, honey. It's me! Frank! You've come home, sweetheart. Can you hear me? It's me, Frank!" he repeated. Frank stroked his wife's forehead. Eden's eyes fluttered for an instant, and then they opened. Frank's face slowly came into focus. She looked straight into the face of her husband.

A staff of doctors and nurses flooded into the room. Frank took a step back and watched as the medical team examined her. He held Annie's hand tightly in his. "She's come back, Annie. Eden has come home!"

She was wrapped in warm blankets by the medical team.

"Frank...Frank..." Eden called out his name.

"I'm right here, babe. I'm right here." He fled to her bedside and reached for her hand.

"The children. Where are the children?" she asked groggily.

With shaking hands, Annie called Dean and told him to bring the kids to the hospital immediately.

Ben, Tara, Nicholas, and Dean exploded into the room. "Mommy! Mommy!" the children chimed.

Tears streamed down her face as she held each child in her arms. Frank joined his reunited family.

Annie came forward and threw her arms around her best friend. "Oh, Eden! I've missed you. We've all missed you." Her voice quivered.

Eden reached under the pile of blankets and felt the amulet that was still fastened around her waist. Yallowahii. Bale. Bursala. Three different men who represented three very critical roles to her. She untied the braided silk rope and held it to her face. She thought about Bursala. She thought about Bale. She thought about Yallowahii. Three Wise Men who would forever remain in her heart as *THE CHRISTMAS STARS OF ZANZIBAR.*

Then, her eyes glanced over to the nightstand next to her bed. Nestled on top sat a water globe. The tiny white flakes were scattered upon the Holy Family. The words *Peace on Earth* were inscribed into the wooden base. Eden lifted her head to get a better look. "Where did this come from?" she asked.

A voice sounded from the back of the room. "It is a gift. A Christmas gift for you." No one else heard him.

Standing by the door was an Asian man wearing a shabby dark suit, a tattered fedora, and a pelt of mink around his neck. He leaned upon a cane. Eden could see this light all around him.

"Christmas Stars belong together," he said.

"And she ran and ran, and she ran!" Eden announced triumphantly.

Basque, Spain— The Crusade Years

CHRISTMAS STARS OF ZANZIBAR

Bursala pulled himself up on the shore and lay on the sand. He rolled over onto his back and held his hands above his face. He studied them beneath the rays of the sun. He was alive. As he looked around, he knew he was sitting upon the shores of a distant land. He glanced up at the sun...the very sun that had shone down on Eden and Bale and his people in Zanzibar.

Off in the distance, he saw a hamlet. Clutching the knotted piece of plantain rope, he began his journey...walking side by side with the Spirits who would lead him to his life's destiny. Olive and sycamore trees towered above him. Fruit seemed to be plentiful here. Along the shore there were covered huts and tents. Dried-up grape vines settled in mud.

Bursala walked as fast as his legs would take him. He could not believe his eyes when they fell upon a city made of stone up over a hill. The city was hidden behind a wall, and as far as he could see, everything about that city was made of stone and marble. There was a bridge gate in the foreground and mountains behind the city with a stone wall that spiraled its way to the top, where it led to a castle. Inside the stone wall were hundreds and hundreds of stone dwellings, which looked to Bursala as if they were in no particular order. Trees dotted and grew in between the cracks of stone. The mountains were green against the city of white.

Bursala had landed on a new stone quay. In the water, Vikings manned their vessels. The ships moved in toward the massive gray walls pitted by the sea wash and coated with tar. Pilgrims were leaving the hot decks of the galleys, their bodies feeble and tired, lifting their packs upon their stiff backs as they anxiously looked about. Merchants in tattered coats, ladies in cloaks made from bright silk with trains so long they trailed behind them forever. These ladies were of wealthy stature. They waited for their servants to carry them through the dust and over the mud. Monks clad in black hoods. Brazen-faced minstrels with gitterns slung across their shoulders, jesting children in short cloaks and long striped tights. Simple folk kneeling in front of shrines gave thanks that they were alive after long weeks upon the thunderous sea.

Grouping together like cattle, the people moved up toward the hill. Most of the men had their hair and beards clipped short. There were knights who dressed in plain black robes with heavy silver crosses, which hung from around their necks. People sat on rugs near the wells. Sallow-faced Hispanic merchants set up stalls, and children played among the herds of sheep near the gates of the city. Bells chimed from the steeples of thirty towers. Bearded patriarchs pulled horses through the twisting, winding cobblestone streets.

On the top of the hill sat a castle triple the size of the Royal Enclosure. The castle was surrounded by mighty double walls, and perched upon the top was an astonishing bronze dragon, the size of one hundred men put together.

This place was one of wonders. Bursala leaned against a tree and tried to figure out what he was doing there. Would he, the King of Uganda, ever see the love of his life again?

"Spirit Walkers never die," he said aloud. "We move onward and forward." And with every ounce of courage he could muster, he walked toward the foreign city made of stone.

ZANZIBAR (PAST)

Bale continued to swim toward the water's surface. Finally, he dragged his body onto the dank banking. He looked around and noticed the familiar acacia trees outlined by the light of the moon. He knew he was home. Torches of fire were heading toward him. Quickly, he pulled his body up and hid behind a tree.

"Search the waters until we find him!" Junju gave the command. Junju watched as his entourage plunged into the ocean in the hopes of finding their King. "We will not stop until my brother has been found...alive or dead."

"He has followed his destiny." Bale spoke from behind the tree.

Junju held the torch close to his face and squinted through the darkness. "Who goes there?" he demanded.

Bale came out from behind the tree. Bale reached for Junju's torch and held it to his face. "Do not be afraid," he warned.

"Bale! You are alive! How can this be?" Junju ran over to him and held his friend in an embrace. Bale and Junju stayed in a clasp for a long moment.

Then Bale spoke loud for all of the men to hear. "The Spirit Walker has journeyed back to her homeland. It would not have been if not for Bursala's bravery. Our paths crossed for one last moment in time. Bursala is alive and well, and we will make it our lifelong quest to find him and bring him back so that he may continue to rule us as our King. His courage and love should be a lesson to us all. If you listen long enough, you will hear that the wind will forever call out his name.

"I have journeyed as only Spirit Walkers can. To a time and a place of the future. I was sent to Eden's people to tell them of her well-being. She was sent here to teach us that nations of people may look different on the outside; however, we are all the same inside. For it is not the color of our skin that should matter; it is the colors in our hearts that does. Someday, I pray that all of the people will live together in peace and harmony."

Junju beckoned his Kingsman to bow down low with their faces to the ground. "It gives me great joy to know that Edi is home with her family. Knowing that Bursala is alive gives me the hope that he shall come back to us one day and take his reign as King. You, Bale, have traveled with the *Spirits*. Your eyes have seen the future. I believe that you can lead the people of Zanzibar to a new beginning. The blood royal runs through your veins because of the night we became blood brothers. I speak the truth when I tell all of you people that until Bursala returns to us, I know he would want you, Bale, to take the reign for his people.

"Hail to the King!" Junju shouted up at the full moon.

"Hail to the King!" The voices of the men echoed through the night.

EPILOGUE

Bale began to sweat profusely. His fever had gone back up, and his body felt as if it were on fire, yet he shivered from a chill deep inside of him. He could hear Frank's pleas over and over in his mind. "You must hang on. You are my one and only hope that will lead me to my wife." Bale shook his head from side to side. He could not tolerate the agonizing pain swelling up inside of his brain. The rest of his body already felt dead. "I...I cannot hold on any longer," he said contritely. "It is my time. I can see this...this..." Bale's words hung heavily in the air as his neck fell to one side, and his eyes rolled up into his head.

"No!" Frank cried. "You can't die. No, damn it. No!"

Bale's massive body felt weightless as he plunged deeper and deeper into a pool of luminous light. He used the resistance in his body to swim against the strong force that pulled him farther down to an immeasurable depth. Bale sank to the bottomless pit of the ocean. He felt peaceful. There was no more pain. No more confusion. He let the water guide him without so much as an effort.

"Bale, dear friend. Bale, it is you!"

Bale saw a figure, hazy at first, and then she came clearly into view. "Edi!" He felt the powerful force of life seep back into him as he grabbed ahold of her hand and pulled her close. "Edi," he cried. "I never thought I would see you again!"

"Bale. You are alive!" She held onto him and hugged him and kissed his face. "Oh, Bale, we are going home. We are really going home! Bursala is here with us. I cannot find him. Please help me, Bale. You must help me find him and save him."

"Hold on to me, Edi. Do not let go. I see him! Bursala! Bursala! Do not give up!" Bale called out to him.

"Hurry, Bale. I am afraid he will die. We must not let him die!"

With Eden holding on to him, clinging to him for dear life, Bale thrust through the water until he was only inches from the King. He reached out his hand. "Bursala, try to grab hold of me." Bursala's hand grabbed onto Bale's, and the three were huddled in an embrace.

"I am not dead!" Bursala announced disbelievingly.

"Spirit Walkers never die. We move onward and forward," Bale replied.

"Our destinies are waiting for us. I love you both so much," Eden added.

Their bodies began to detangle themselves from one another, although they desperately tried to hold onto one another. Under the ocean appeared three of the most illuminating lights. Eden's, Bursala's, and Bale's bodies drifted separately into their light. They called out to one another until dark, foreboding silence fell over the entire ocean. Their final destinations took them far away from one another.

This is not the end, for Spirit Walkers move Onward and Forward

To Be Continued....

The Characters

Eden Salina	The Spirit Walker
Frank Salina	Eden's husband
Benjamin, Tara, Nicholas	Eden and Frank's children
Annie Jurgens	Eden's best friend
Dean Jurgens	Husband of Annie
Una	Dahni's mother, Bale's sister, Mazi's wife
Yallowahii	Chieftain of the Heart Clan/Spirit Walker
Dahni	Una's eight-year-old son
Bale	Una's brother, Uncle of Dahni
Wanyenya	Una's dead sister
Jita	The leopard ghost
Mazi	The music man/Bale's best friend/Una's husband
Keswa	Una's dead husband/Dahni's father
Sava	The medicine man
Tama	Sava's wife

Zinga	The fantasy child / daughter of Sava and Tama
Kimu	Zinga's love
Bukiwa	Zinga's young sister
Nalinya	Sava's beautiful fifth wife
Mungu	God
Bursala	King of Uganda
Ali of Timbatu	Bursala's medicine man
King Suna	Bursala's father
Junju	Bursala's one-armed brother
Sanda	Bursala's sister
Kiro	Bursala's evil brother
Evanli	Bursala's mother/sister
Wanyenya-Salina	Una's baby girl
Dr. Mutebi	Doctor from Zimbabwe

Christmas Stars of Zanzibar

Eden

Judy Bond

Una & Dahni

Christmas Stars of Zanzibar

Yallowahii

Judy Bond

Bale

Christmas Stars of Zanzibar

Wanyenya

Judy Bond

Jita

CHRISTMAS STARS OF ZANZIBAR

MAZI

SAVA

Christmas Stars of Zanzibar

Zinga & Kimu

Judy Bond

Bursala

CHRISTMAS STARS OF ZANZIBAR

JUNJU

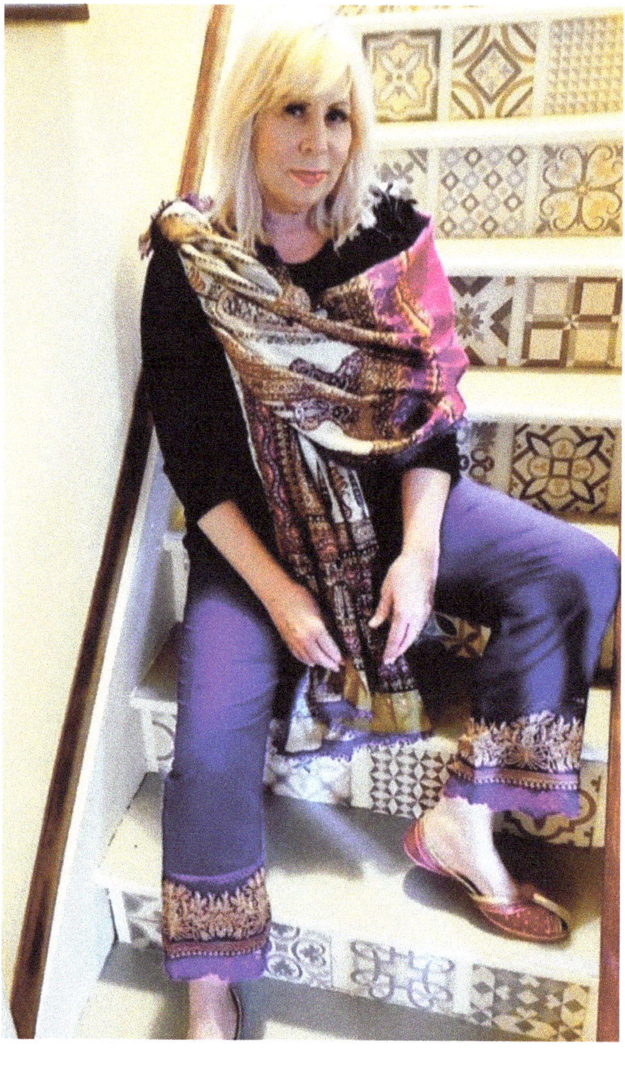

About The Author

Judy Bond is my pen name, a.k.a. Judy Pomposellli, Locke, Hofman Bond (Po Lo Ho Bo if you take the first two letters from each name). Kinda cheeky!

Native New Yorker, born, bred, raised, and awoken here. A city kid, Long Islander, Queens girl, Bronx brat: that's me. Proud of it too!

Travels have taken me to Italy, Switzerland, Germany, France, the Netherlands, Jamaica, and Bermuda (and all over the nifty US of A). I dream of writing under a tree in Ireland and spending a night in a lighthouse in Scotland.

Ruled by the tides, I am over the moon for the moon. I sleep in the stars and am crazy in the sunlight (yes, indeed).

My four children, Chase Locke, Alana Locke, Jen Hofmann, and Will Hofmann, along with their significant others, Lisa Locke, Rob Bush, and Jim Frasca are my "everything bagels." My husband, Michael Hofmann (affectionately known as "Hof" to all who love him), is the cherry on top of the crème brûlée of our blessed lives. And my mom, Fran Bruno, who is the most amazing role model to all of us! At the time of this book release, I have a grandbaby (who is about the size of a blueberry in its mommy's belly). I cannot wait to meet, love, and spoil you, Baby Vegas! xx

I love music. Zeppelin, Heart, the Grateful Dead, Queen, Dolly Parton, Dave Matthews Band, Bruce Springsteen, Sting, U2, the Eagles, The Band, and Willie Nelson are among my favorites. I enjoy everything from rock to Bach and all that is sandwiched in between. Music is our medicine. It heals us and helps our lives to make sense.

Castles enchant me, fashion delights me, and I am obsessed with make-up (as our faces are like canvases). There is a passion inside me to create in a notebook, in a garden, on a piece of paper, or by beating on a drum. I love to embroider, write, dream, fantasize, and imagine. I have always been told that I was a dreamer.

The moment that I heard that Freddie Mercury died was the precise moment this book was born. It began with this simple sentence: "And they spoke in the Swahili tongue." (Weird, I thought.) That one sentence morphed into a paragraph that dominoed into a chapter that avalanched into this book.

I REALLY hope you like it.

I welcome you here...to the phantasm that lived inside my heart. Feel free to fall deeply in love with the characters that were designed to whisk you away from your personal struggles as well as from the conundrums of the real world.

Thank you, JoAnn Baty Russo, for all of your enthusiasm and help! Couldn't have done this without you. Thank you Gregory Smith for all of the hours we poured over my manuscript!! Thank you to The Real Bursala....this one is for you xx

*Songs mentioned in this book:

Sting, "Gabriel's Message"

Sixteenth century / author unknown, "God Rest Ye Merry, Gentlemen"

Band Aid, "Do They Know It's Christmas?"

Franz Xaver Gruber, "Silent Night"

John Lennon, "Beautiful Boy"

Led Zeppelin, "Stairway to Heaven"

Dave Matthews Band, "Bartender"

*There are many references to Heart and Queen lyrics throughout this story.

* "The Gazelle": I am not taking full credit for this tale, as I heard it once before. I tried to research its author to no avail. I do not want to take credit for an idea that was not mine.

Please stay tuned for the sequel: Bursala's Rhapsody, written and illustrated by Judy Bond

JuBo

CPSIA information can be obtained
at www.ICGtesting.com
Printed in the USA
BVHW090602161121
621687BV00019B/979